Miss Savannah

Druecella McNair

Druecella McNair (signature)

❀
BLENDD Publishing

Published by BLENDD Publishing
4280 Richmond Drive
Ethel, LA 70730

Manufactured in the United States of America

ISBN-13:9781492338291
ISBN-10:149233829X

Acknowledgments

I owe special thanks to my daughter, Jenenna (Nena) Elise Yochum for spending hours doing research, reading, editing and listening to me talk on for hours and hours. And when it came to the music, well she's a music lover like her mother and together we were able to weave those special songs into the story. Without her input and the joy she has added, Miss Savannah would not be the pleasure to read that it is.

Robert Courtney has patiently put up with "Miss Savannah" beckoning to me at all hours of the day and night. He and I sat up until the wee hours of the morning reading through the proofs, editing and getting them ready for print. I sincerely thank you!

Disclaimer

Other Books by Drucella McNair

Miranda

Giggles, Grins & Things to Ponder

Genevieve

My Mother's Apron
(Soon to be Released)

Dedication

This book is dedicated to my daughter, Jenenna Elise Yochum. Why God chose me and graced me with this wonderful daughter I'll never know but I am now and always have been thankful. I am truly blessed. She has laughed, cried and rejoiced along with me in the writing of this novel.

Embracing Memories

Sometimes you don't know the true value of a moment until it becomes a memory. Sometimes your greatest moments are those created by reading a book. Removing yourself from the moment, immersing yourself into another time, another place. Knowing that this time is just for you and you alone. Sometimes a memory can transport us to a moment. The moment you realized you had spent all day on your grandmother's quilt under the mimosa tree reading your first hundred page book, the first romance you read that made you cry, the first book you read to a grandchild cuddled on your lap. We learn to treasure the moments as they happen, but embrace the memories for a lifetime.

Jenenna (Nena) Elise Yochum

Chapter 1

Miss Savannah just couldn't understand how a person could read a book and not hear the characters actually speaking. When she read a book about Ireland she read it hearing the characters speaking in the strong brogue known only to that region. The same thing applied to novels about Italy, France, the strong accent of Cajuns or the northern pattern of speaking eliminating r's from some words and putting them in other words where there was none.

On entering her home or apartment the first thing you noticed was the multitude of books that lived in her home. Yes, lived. They were a part of her life as she was theirs. She took it upon herself to be their caretakers. Books stacked on tables, under tables, almost every surface laden with volumes of books. The accumulation was stacked, piled and otherwise strewn over everything. Most times in order to sit you had to relocate a pile of books to another surface which was a difficult task. So, a place on the floor space had to suffice in most cases.

Having the means to do so, every so often relocation to a larger residence became necessary. The day she entered her present place of residence and saw that there was just a path to walk through and every available surface was piled high she knew it was time to start searching for a larger and roomier home for herself and her beloved books. Never did it occur to her to give away or sell any of them. It would have been like getting rid of family because that's how she thought of them, family.

She made her way through the jumble of stacks and located her phone and directory and turning to the real estate section, closed her eyes and ran her finger down the page. She dialed the number and made an appointment to see an agent. She didn't know at the time that the person answering her call was the sole proprietor of the agency. Explaining that she needed to locate a larger residence so the agent could do some research and have a few properties ready for her to visit, she hung up the phone and wrote down the time of the appointment on her calendar.

Making her way through to the kitchen she brewed a cup of coffee and sliced a piece of banana bread she had baked last night when she couldn't sleep. When insomnia overtook her the way she controlled it was to bake. That was her first love, baking. Her kitchen was about the only room that didn't have books littering everywhere. All her recipe books lived in a floor to ceiling bookcase placed against the wall behind her tiny table. Actually it was an antique ice cream parlor table and had only two matching chairs but since she rarely had any guests it was perfect for her lifestyle. Her kitchen was spotless with shining food preparation surface, sparkling serving pieces peeking through glass front cabinet doors, spices in alphabetical order, ingredients lined up in the pantry and her huge assortment of baking pans stacked and organized ready for the next time her nemesis, insomnia, visited.

Chapter 2

Miss Savannah entered the modern office building and located the name she had written down in the little notebook she always had tucked in her tote. She located the suite number on the directory and proceeded. Stepping into the office she was surprised that it wasn't a suite of offices but a medium size single office with one desk and a seating area.

Seated behind the desk was a young woman probably in her mid-thirties, very blonde hair with even blonder highlights and hazel eyes that were drop dead gorgeous. She had perfectly applied make-up, flawless skin and when she smiled Miss Savannah saw a ten thousand dollar smile. The young woman stood and couldn't have been larger than a size six and she appeared to be quite tall until she stepped from behind the desk and Miss Savannah noticed the five-inch heels she was wearing.

"Can I help you?" She said in a professionally trained and well-modulated voice. Standing before her was a lady a couple inches over five feet tall, dressed in well-worn jeans, tee shirt with a zip up hoodie over the tee and open toed earth sandals.

"I have an appointment with a Miss Melody. I'm sorry I didn't get her last name."

"That's me and I have no last name. It's just Melody. I had it legally changed a couple of years ago. You must be Miss Savannah? And I'm sorry. I didn't get your last name either."

Miss Savannah smiled and held out her hand. Nice to meet you Miss Melody."

"Oh the Miss isn't necessary. Just Melody is fine." Motioning towards the chair opposite her desk she said, "Have a seat and we'll see what we can do to find you the perfect piece of property. After our conversation, I pulled a few listings and I thought we might go over them before leaving the office."

Miss Savannah looked around the office. "We?"

Taken off guard Melody replied, "We what?"

"You said *we'll* see what *we* can do. Does someone else work here with you?"

Melody flashed the ten thousand dollar smile. "That's just a business term."

Miss Savannah didn't say anything but just looked at her.

Melody tried to explain. "We … business terminology … It's just me here. I own this business and am the broker."

Miss Savannah continued to look at her. "So did you find anything that's like what I'm looking for?"

"Well now. Let's just see what we have here!"

"Once again Miss Savannah's eyes looked around the office.

Realizing she had said it again Melody corrected herself. "I have pulled these files and thought these may be a good start. You know get a feel for exactly what you're looking for?"

Miss Savannah looked at each folder with a full narrative from Melody with perfectly manicured fingertips pointing out the finer points of each listing. Shaking her head after each folder was closed after an hour she was no closer to finding a home for herself and her books.

"Maybe if you see the properties in person, we can get a better idea." Once again, a correction. "*I* can get a better idea."

"That's fine with me."

Melody picked up her cell phone and touched quick dial for her answering service. "I'll be out of the office a couple of hours. Catch my calls, please." She touched the screen again and ended the call. "Ready?"

"As ready as I'm going to ever be."

"Exactly what price range are we looking at?" … "Dang" again flashed through her mind. "Sorry. Are you looking at?"

"I haven't looked at anything yet, but when I see it I'll know." Noticing that Melody was getting ready to lock the office door she replied. "It's a bit chilly out today so you may want to grab your coat."

"I'll be okay. My car has a very good heating system in it." Frustration had set in for Melody and the thought crossed her mind. "I need to view some of the properties again so take advantage of the afternoon out of the office and appease this old woman."

Entering the parking garage Melody pulled her remote from her Gucchi bag and the silver BMW in front of them chirped recognition. "Where did you park? I can get your ticket validated if you parked in the garage."

"That's mine over there." She pointed to a 1960's era Volkswagon bus with more Bond-O patches and colors than a tie dye tee shirt. On the very front a peace sign had been painted no telling how many years ago.

Melody rolled her eyes. "How long have you had *that*? The bus?"

"I bought it brand new back in 1964. Drove it off the show room floor myself. That's my "Baby" and it's been good to me."

"I just bet it has." Melody always judged the financial status of her clients by the vehicles they drove, the clothes they wore, their jewelry, their current addresses, anything that would denote how much they could afford to spend. And, by what she had seen this woman couldn't afford a new refrigerator box. She sighed and "what a waste of time" went through her mind.

The afternoon was spent with Melody opening homes and checking them out and Miss Savannah shaking her head that this still wasn't the right one. Half way through the afternoon Melody wished she had taken Miss Savannah's advice and grabbed her coat. She had to keep reminding herself that even though they were having a few days that it

5

felt like spring, in fact it was still in the dead of winter. Heading back to the office, Melody pulled into a fast food restaurant drive through to pick up something to take back to the office. "Want anything?" She asked Miss Savannah.

"This food is going to kill you if you keep it eating it. I'll just take a bottle of spring water please."

This didn't surprise Melody. She had already figured out that Miss Savannah was some old hippie chick mentally stuck back in the sixties and was a health food nut and had burned one too many joints in her lifetime. In spite of her frustration she smiled.

Chapter 3

When parking her "Baby" in the parking garage at Melody's office doubts began gathering in Miss Savannah's mind again. She realized that Melody must be getting tired of showing properties and at times they never made it inside the house for her to look at. Some of them just didn't have the right feel, right aura, too much upkeep required, too small, a poor lay out in the kitchen, no shower, a myriad of things that she had in her mind that needed to be just perfect. Frustration on the part of Melody and herself grew each day, and those days grew into weeks but Miss Savannah was determined to not just settle for something she couldn't live with or did not want. She knew the right piece of property was out there, she was just going to have to bide her time.

She grabbed her tote and headed to Melody's office for yet another afternoon of, what had become to her as sightseeing trips. She knew Tulsa like the back of her wrinkled hand and also knew the right piece of property was just waiting for her. She had a good feeling about today for some reason.

Later that afternoon after another flurry of viewing properties and nothing, *nothing* had been what Miss Savannah was looking for. Melody was driving through the Maple Ridge District to avoid heavy traffic. They were headed back to the office and Miss Savannah was looking out the passenger window of the car when there it was! *The* house! She could feel it. A shiver had run down her back when Melody had turned onto the street. She already knew what the interior was like and knew it was perfect. It was a pitiful looking piece of property. It had been neglected terribly with broken windows, chipped paint, what looked like a leaky roof and one of the columns on the front porch was atilt looking like it was ready to come crashing down at any minute. But, that front porch wrapped around and she could see doors leading out to it from other parts of the house. In an instant she saw it as it must have been at one time. It called to her. She knew that must sound strange to anyone but she couldn't help almost yelling at Melody to stop.

Waving her arms and pointing, the words gushed from her lips. "That's it! Back there. That's the house I've been looking for! Circle the block so I can see it again!"

Melody stomped on the brakes and almost put her through the windshield and would have had her seat belt had not been fastened.

"What?"

"There's a house back there. My house! The one I've been looking for."

"But there's nothing listed in this area for sale. I've researched everything."

"I don't care. Circle the block and I'll show you."

Doing as she was told she circled the block and slowly retraced the route they had just taken. Before they got to the house, Miss Savannah started pointing out the window. "Right there. That one. Pull in the drive. I've got to see it up close."

Color drained from the Melody's face. She couldn't believe that this decrepit old house that was falling to pieces was the dream house of the eccentric old lady sitting beside her. At one time it had been one of the grand mansions well known in this area. Dollar signs flashed through her mind and thoughts were spinning like crazy. "How could something like that be in this neighborhood? It needs to be razed to the ground and something befitting this neighborhood built in its place, something new and contemporary. She couldn't understand how this piece of property had been ignored and not be listed or torn down piece by ugly piece and the prime building lot sold. It was clearly unoccupied and looked like it had been for years." She quickly jotted down the address.

"Before we go any further, do you realize how much work it's going to take to even make this house livable? Just look at it! And you said you didn't want a house with stairs. It's got to be a two story at least, maybe three."

Her last words were spoken to an empty car because her passenger was already out of the car and making her way up the front porch steps.

"Wait a minute she called out as she was exiting the car. We're trespassing. We can't just go on someone's property without making certain its ok!"

Miss Savannah had cupped her hands around her face to cut the glare and was peeking in the windows. There it was, just what she had been searching for! "Oh my! This is it!"

Repeating what she had said to an empty car just minutes before she said, "But, you said *no* stairs. And, I don't even know who owns it or if it's for sale!"

"Well, find out," Miss Savannah said while taking the door knob in her hand and giving it a healthy turn. To Melody's surprise, the door opened and she followed through into a house with wall paper hanging in strips from the walls, carpeting that could hardly be called carpet anymore, light fixtures hanging by wires from the ceiling, and she could swear she heard something skittering around somewhere. She looked around and Miss Savannah was nowhere in sight but Melody heard movement from the back of the house. Following the sound she discovered Miss Savannah standing in the middle of the enormous kitchen, her hands on her hips and nodding.

"It's what I've always wanted. Just look at the cabinetry and the windows across the back … and the door leading out to the garden."

"Garden? All I see is a backyard overgrown with weeds!"

"I can see it, can't you?" Walking across the kitchen she ran her hands over a vintage range that stood stately on porcelain legs. "Oh my goodness! This is beautiful!" Her eyes had taken on a warm glow that showed nothing but admiration for the poor old kitchen. "When do you think I can start the refurbishing?"

"What?"

"Yes. Refurbishing. It needs to be done before I can move in and I want to start right away."

All that had transpired in the last few minutes had Melody's brain in overload mode. She reached out to support herself against the door frame and immediately removed her hand and started digging through her purse for a moist towelette to remove the sticky residue from her hand. In all her years of being in business, this was a first and hopefully her last. She made up her mind right there and then to dump this eccentric woman as soon as possible so she could get back to the world of the normal.

Miss Savannah was digging through her tote she carried with her everywhere and pulled out two small boxes and was frantically trying to open them. At last she pulled out a tiny black cone and lit it with a wooden match which she had removed from the other little cardboard box.

"What are you doing? You're going to catch the place on fire! You can't do that!"

Miss Savannah ignored her and set the little incense cone in the bottom of the stained white sink and stood back watching the minuscule tendril of smoke waft and disperse into the air. Her only response was, "I'm cleansing."

Trying to pull herself together she almost spat out the words. "You're what?"

Miss Savannah calmly and serenely repeated herself. "I'm cleansing."

"Well. You just can't do that!"

Just as calmly as before Miss Savannah said, "Why not? It needs it."

Melody tried to pry her five-inch heel from the old linoleum flooring, sputtered and said, "Now I've heard everything! Just come on out of this … this … this pile of … of rubble. This is the most insane thing I've ever experienced."

Miss Savannah smiled at her. "Now just stay tranquil and let the incense do its job. It won't take long." She was moving her hands through the smoke and dispersing it through the room. "There now. Don't you feel the cleansing effect already?"

"I don't feel anything but… but … I don't know what I feel but it's certainly not clean! This is just crazy! Trespassing, getting filthy, and watching you try to set fire to a kitchen that at its best should have been gutted or torn down decades ago!" She waved her hands in front of her face and coughed. "And all that damned smoke! What are you a crazy old woman that was specifically put on this earth to drive me insane?"

Miss Savannah turned and looked at the woman with sympathy and shook her head. "You young people just don't understand. It's not insanity. It's quite the opposite. You think just because something's not pretty any more or sanitary or updated that's its worthless. Let me tell you something and I want you to listen carefully because I'm not going to repeat myself. I don't believe in repetition." She straightened up and took a few paces so she was within a couple of steps from Melody. "Some of the most valuable things on this earth have age. Have you not traveled to other parts of the world, seen and witnessed the wonders there? Have you not set down and had a conversation with an old person? Have you not taken the time out of your busy schedule to reflect on how things may have been years, decades or centuries ago?"

Melody was dazed at the words that were being spoken to her. They were not spewed, spat out or said in anger. They had a sorrowful connotation to them, a sorrow that she couldn't comprehend at this moment. It was like the old woman felt sorry for her. They were spoken slowly and clearly. "How dare she?" flashed through her mind. She turned and left the house. After getting to the car she realized she couldn't just leave Miss Savannah. She had to wait on her.

After a while Miss Savannah exited the house, carefully pulled the front door closed and made her way down the steps. She got in the car, fastened her seat belt and folded her hands in her lap. "There now.

We've found the house. When can I start the renovation? I can have money transferred any time you say."

"You mean you still want to work with me after what I said in there?"

"Of course. Why wouldn't I? If not for you I'd have never found that wonderful house I've dreamed of."

Melody started the car and reversed out of the drive thinking to herself, "Where do I start?"

By the close of the next business day the owner of the property had been located. Actually it was owners. The house was part of an estate that had been tied up in court because of legalities for years. When informed of this all Miss Savannah said was "Well, contact them right away. The house has been calling out to me and I need to start on it right away."

"Just promise me that you're not going to go over there and try to do that cleansing thing anymore."

"Well, I did drive by there today."

"Promise me?"

There was a hesitation.

"Promise me!"

"Oh. All right but…"

Melody interrupted. "No buts! You've got to wait even if it's weeks or months. These things take time."

"No it won't."

"And just how do you know that?"

"Believe me." Miss Savannah hung up the phone with a smile.

Melody heard the click on her cell phone and knew the conversation was ended. She ran her hands through the two hundred dollar hair cut she had just had done. She put her elbows on her desk and rested her head on her hands. "Why me?"

True to Miss Savannah's words after contacting the owners and discussing the situation a final deal had been struck and papers were in the process of being drawn up for the sale of the property. It all had taken place within ten days. They estate was anxious to sell to a buyer that wasn't going to demolish the old house and build a modern monstrosity in its place. They had refused all the former offers because that's exactly what prospective buyers wanted to do. They just wanted the building lot not the home. Now there was someone that loved the house not the pricy piece of land.

This all took place after Miss Savannah made a call to the owners and spoke to them personally. Melody held her breath when Miss Savannah had suggested allowing her to talk to them but after the conversation was closed Miss Savannah looked at her with that gleam in her eyes and gave her a thumbs up, a gesture that Melody had not expected at all.

The closing went smoothly and quickly and having paid cash for the piece of property there were no financing worries. Everything happened so quickly it had Melody's head spinning but not so much that she forgot to collect her sizable fee and deposit it into her account. Dressed in her designer suit and five-inch heels she let out a sigh of relief thinking it was all done and over with.

The next morning after the closing Melody's phone rang. "Melody. This is Miss Savannah and I need a bit of assistance. I need a list of reliable and dependable contractors in this area. I thought if anyone knew of any it would be you."

Taken by surprise Melody stalled and said she would have to do some research, that she was in real estate not home repairs. But, a few phone calls later she had compiled a list and called the information to Miss Savannah. "I don't know how soon any of them can start but these are the most reliable ones I can come up with for you in such a short time."

"Thanks a lot. I'm going to start calling right away and see when they can start."

Melody shook her head after the call. She knew that good contractors were in demand and Miss Savannah just might have to wait her turn.

The following afternoon Melody had a showing near Miss Savannah's house and decided to just drive by and take a look. To her surprise there were trucks in the driveway being loaded with debris from the interior of the house. There were workers in the process of repairing the leaning post on the porch and there was a new red Jaguar sedan parked on the street. Her curiosity got the better of her and she parked behind the Jag and walked up to the porch. Maneuvering and stepping over the debris strewn everywhere was a challenge in her heels. She no more got to the steps when Miss Savannah stuck her head out the front door and motioned to her.

"Come on inside and see what's happening. I don't know how to thank you for all the information you gave me yesterday. I called the information to my financial advisor and his staff started making calls." She waved her arms around the rooms. "Just look what is happening!"

"I don't know what to say. I thought surely you wouldn't be able to get anyone here to do anything for at least a couple of months." Then Miss Savannah's words struck home. "Your financial advisor? Did you just say that?"

"Well that's what he does for me but I don't call him my financial advisor. He's my nephew. I call him Quinn. His name is Quinton and he hates it when I call him Quinn but with what he makes off my money, I feel I can call him anything I want." She laughed. "Come on in to the kitchen. I gotta show you something." There were sawhorses set up with a sheet of plywood resting on them and on that plywood table was a set of plans.

Melody shook her head. "Now you're not going to tell me that someone already drafted plans for you?"

"Didn't have to. When those young men were tearing out some of the old built-ins that must have been added twenty or thirty years ago they found these. Look! They're the original plans for the house."

"I don't believe it."

"Well, you might as well because that's what they are. Lucky. Huh?"

"I have a question. How in the world did Quinn ... Quinton get a crew together so quickly? This is just unreal!"

"Well, another thing is that one of my other nephews, James is a home builder and he takes care of that kind of family business. He made a few calls after Quinn called him and" ...she clapped her hands together like a magician ... "Presto! Just look! It helps that winter is the slow time for construction too. James was more than glad to take this on. You know. It keeps his crew together so he doesn't have to start all over each spring trying to put a new one together. Construction can be a mighty mean mistress at times."

Melody did look. She peeked out the back kitchen windows and what looked like a full landscaping crew was making progress on the still half frozen, weed infested back yard. Cabinet doors were being removed. Linoleum was being ripped up in spots and the flooring was being examined to make sure the wood was what it appeared to be. What appeared to be a repairman was disconnecting the range and preparing to remove it. It was a bee hive of activity and Melody was trying to avoid getting any dust, dirt or anything else on her attire. She looked around and tried to spot the owner of the Jag that was parked out front. Whoever owned that lovely car had to be loaded and she was always looking for people with money. That was her business. "Does that new Jag out front belong to your nephew? I'd love to meet him."

Miss Savannah glanced over at Melody. "Neither of my nephews is here today. They're busy with other things. They just do this kind of thing to keep me off their backs. They know I won't give up until I have my way, so …"

"So who owns that Jaguar?"

"Oh that's what you want to know. That's mine."

"But I thought you drove the Volkswagon bus."

"I do but it was time for its servicing so I had to have the Jag brought over so I would have transportation. I'm surprised you didn't see my baby leaving when you were driving up. They just left with it."

Now Melody's head was spinning. She had been surprised when Miss Savannah had funds transferred to pay cash for the house at the closing but now it seemed like Miss Savannah's source of funds were … well were much healthier that she ever imagined.

Miss Savannah looked out back and evidently saw something that required her attention. "Melody, just make yourself at home if you can for a few minutes. I see something that I need to take charge of. I'll be right back."

"That's okay. I just stopped by. I need to get back to the office. I'll drop by again sometime and see what kind of progress you're making." With that said, she carefully made her way back through the house, across the porch and down the steps. It wasn't until she was sitting in her car that she dared to not look down to see where she was stepping. She made a mental note. "Next time I decide to drop by I've got to dress more sensible. Designer suits and heels just don't cut it."

Chapter 5

That evening after Savannah had bathed and changed into her night shirt she lit a stick of Nag Champa incense and picked up a book to pass the hours until bed time. The book didn't speak to her so she laid it aside, selected a smooth jazz CD and loaded it into her sound system. Of course, moving a few stacks of books was involved but this evening she just wanted to listen to a bit of jazz and perhaps travel down memory lane. The music started soft and sexy just as she remembered. There was nothing like a sax. She had always loved blues and smooth jazz. As a matter of fact she loved almost all music except the new stuff she couldn't understand. If she didn't like it she didn't buy it but held nothing against the young people that did. She had lived through many music transitions.

Her mother and father had been there through the Big Band era but when she was a child she remembered them listening to country music. Her father even had a French harp and would play it every now and again. But her mother always loved to do the jitterbug when no one was around. Savannah could remember her mother putting one of the big LP's on the turntable and doing the jitterbug in the living room when she thought no one was watching.

Savannah's mind went back in time to the men in her life and there had been quite a few. She had loved them all but only married two.

The first ended in divorce and the last time she had been married her husband had died and when that happened it broke her heart. She had never remarried but had a number of men friends and an occasional companionship that always lasted until either she or her companion decided that things just weren't right and moved on. She couldn't truly say she loved one more than the other but loved them at different times and in different ways. She had been lucky in love and unlucky in love depending on what was happening in her life at the moment.

She got up and made her way to her desk that was as organized as her kitchen. She pulled open a drawer and flipped through the files until she came across what she was looking for. She pulled the paper from the folder and began to read words that she had written years before.

My Loves

Perhaps you think this is about my love of chocolate, lobster, traveling, decorating and redecorating my house, writing or the myriad of things I say I love. Well, I do love those things but this is about the men that have been in my life. My loves!

It seems there comes a time in one's life when it becomes necessary to sit back and reflect on our lives; our youth, our careers, the good things we did as well as the things we wished had not done, forgive ourselves, quit carrying that burden and get on with our lives. One of the most important things I've been reflecting upon is the loves I have been fortunate enough to have in my life. I find I cannot lump all of those loves in one category and leave it at that. None of them was the same kind of love so there cannot be a comparison between them. One is no less important or felt more deeply than the other. They were all special to me and each love became more valuable and meaningful as I grew older. I suppose it's because I have fewer years left on this earth and I cherish and endear my loved ones more deeply than before.

What brought two lovers together in my youth was infatuation, the breeding instinct to procreate and pass along our lineage, whether I recognized it at that time or not. Looking back I see only a surface, superficial love that was more lust than anything else. Perhaps that's the way God intended it to be to keep his earth populated. However, at that time in my life, I thought my love to be the greatest thing of all time. It didn't last because we simply grew apart over the years for reason left unspoken.

Then there were the adventurous years of my life, loving the new explorations of places, things and people. My loves during these years were lovers. I did love them at the time though, or at least I thought I did.

Then there was my first mature love, one that lasted until, as our vows said "Until death do you part." Every time I saw him he made my heart flutter to the point that it tried to leap through my chest. Things seem brighter when he was around, more vivid, more meaningful and I loved him with my mind and soul. It's sad that such a love had to be taken away. They say the good die young and I think that way about this love. That it died way too young even though it was in my later years. It was a lasting love.

My love now is so very comfortable. It's like no other and I don't expect it to be. We take care of each other, share our lives and wait to see what tomorrow brings. He spoons his body against mine when we fall asleep each night. I relax against him and I thank God that He put another good man in my life for me to love.

The one thing I do know is that I have truly loved them all! They were and are my loves.

It was not signed as she had a habit of doing, nor was it dated but she remembered the exact evening she was written it. She supposed that's all that mattered, that she knew. Smiling she placed the paper back in the file and slipped it back in the drawer. She sighed, thinking, those words were so true when I wrote them and I suppose they still are. It was never planned but it had seemed like each time a relationship ended within a few weeks another was sprouting and waiting to grow.

People questioned her at times about her relationships and the source of her wealth but as far as she was concerned, it was none of their business. She had worked hard and invested in petroleum and let it ride for most of her working years. So when it was retirement time, she was financially secure. But it had been a large insurance policy that she had known nothing about until after her beloved husband's death that had put her in a financial situation where she needed someone else to handle her investments. She lived off the dividends and interest and lived quite comfortably. If she needed a large amount of money all she had to do was give Quinn a call and he'd take care of it for her. Actually, the interest accrued so quickly that any significant amount withdrawn was built back up in a couple of years. No, money was one thing she didn't have to worry about. Not for anytime soon, anyway.

She had never been blessed with any more children after she had given up a baby girl for adoption when she was still in her late teens. She had never been able to conceive again. So she had doted on her nephews. She had no nieces. Seemed like the male gene was dominate in her family but that was ok. Her nephews had married wonderful young women and supplied the family with a new generation. Often she had wondered if … well she had wondered about the child she had only got to hold close to her for five minutes before she was taken away. Her Higher Power had not seen to give her any more children and she very seldom questioned that fact. We each have our crosses to bear and she believed that to be hers.

When younger, traveling to wonderful places and meeting friendly people was her love. She still corresponded with some of them, even after all these years. But her main love through her entire life from as far back as she could remember was reading and her books. At one time she had thought about becoming a literature teacher but the thought of *having* to read and having to teach would have taken all the pleasure out of it for her.

She chose to live frugally. It was her choice. She had rather jump in her bus and hit the garage sales on weekends than go to the mall. She chose to see if something could be repaired before tossing it away and buying another. And when she did buy another, most times it came from one of the garage sales. There was one exception: her kitchen. She loved a fully stocked pantry and nice dishes to eat from. Paper plates, in her opinion, were not every day dishes. Almost every kitchen she had been in for the past forty plus years had a dishwasher so why not use it? She knew this was just one of her idiosyncrasies and didn't bother to deny it.

Speaking of kitchens, she crossed over to her tote and pulled out brochures that had been given to her earlier in the day. They were about her new appliances. She had put up a good fight about salvaging the stove already there. She wanted it repaired and in working order but she also wanted a double built-in oven and a surface unit with at least four burners. A large freezer and two refrigerators had to be ordered and a powerful dishwasher. There. She had come full circle back to that important appliance.

She reached over and dug through the tote trying to find her notebook. She wanted to see if the cabinet man or finish carpenter could repair the old Hoosier cabinet that had been left behind. She thought it would be a perfect place for her kitchen computer. She was going to see if he could open the lower front for knee room and make doors that concealed the opening when not in use. The roll top could easily be pulled down to keep the computer out of sight. She loved computers but also loved them out of sight. Notes made she tossed the notebook back into the bottomless pit of a tote.

Looking around she noticed her electronics and she knew she could not survive without her music. She dove back into the tote. Thank goodness the notebook was still right on top. She made another page of notes about building them into the cabinetry in the front area somewhere.

Realizing that her relaxing evening was turning into a working evening, she went to the kitchen, made a cup of caramel mocha coffee, decaf, of course and headed to bed. It was still early but she loved to prop herself up in bed with mountains of pillows and read. She flipped the ceiling fan on and climbed into bed. With the cup of delicious coffee on the night stand and a good book what more could an old woman wish for? She opened the cover and caught her fingertip where the bookmark was waiting and began to read. Read and sip. Read and sip. Before long it was just read because she had been totally pulled/absorbed/transported, however you want to describe it, into the story. The old mantel clock chimed midnight and she had fallen asleep with the open book resting on her chest. She roused enough to mark her place, scoot the coffee cup over so she wouldn't knock it over during the night and turned off the lamp. She scooted down in bed and pulled the quilt and comforter up to her chin and slept through until morning.

Chapter 6

The next few weeks pretty much followed the same routine. Wake and have coffee. Grab a loaf of some kind of home baked bread or muffins or cinnamon rolls, fill a thermos and head to the house. She was spoiling the laborers but that was okay. Someone had brought a coffeepot and set it up on one end of the old cabinet that hadn't been stripped yet. Water was kept in a five gallon plastic water container so there could be a constant supply of freshly brewed coffee. Every morning it was magically replenished with fresh water.

Finally things began to take shape. All the plumbing had been completed and there was actually water in the house. Electrical wiring was done. She had allowed the bathrooms to be updated. The one off the bedroom she was going to use had a shower for her, a shower with a seat! When the old carpeting had been removed, strong hard wood floors had been hiding underneath. With the sanding done and the refinishing completed Miss Savannah was delighted, "I know carpeting makes the house warmer but with the new in-floor heating system I don't think I'm going to have to worry about these old feet getting cold.

One thing that took so much time was the bookcases. Miss Savannah wanted them built all along all the exterior walls except for where there were windows. Every room on the lower floor, with the exception of the kitchen had to have these built in. They went from floor to ceiling with a ladder slide installed at the base.

The largest improvement that took some doing was the small elevator so she could go to the upper levels. Those were to be her work rooms and she had to have access to them. This had not been an afterthought but had been being worked on all the time during the construction. It had just taken a long time because of the mechanics involved and lots and lots of planning and reinforcing. It didn't have to be very large. Just large enough for two people and a book cart. Furniture that was needed on the upper levels was going to have to be carried up the stairs not taken up in the elevator. When the construction manager had paid Quinn a visit and explained what was going on, Quinn had just looked at him and said, "Do it! If she wants it done and it's possible, just do it! Understand?"

Chapter 7

Miss Savannah realized time was growing near for the move she had been anticipating for months and it was time to call in her reinforcement; the one person she had relied on for years to stage her homes. They had spoken recently and kept in touch but had not had the one-on-one visit they cherished in a few years now. She picked up her address book and flipped to "G" and ran her finger down the page to "Gypsy". Readjusting her glasses she punched in the number.

She still had not adapted to the cell phone because she hated to be electronically linked to anyone or anything. For years while working she'd had to be on call to pagers, beepers and anything else the corporations she had worked for decided to track her with.

The phone rang a couple of times and she heard the so familiar, "Hey Girlfriend!"

"Hi there. Where are you?"

"I'm in Florida right now. Planning on returning home in a few days. Why?"

"Well I thought I'd try to track you down and see if you wanted to play?"

Gypsy's voice took on that excitement Miss Savannah knew so well. They had been through a lot together over the years and their fondest times had been late night bonding, whether is was rearranging an entire houseful of furniture until six o'clock in the morning or sharing a bottle of wine and just talking the night away. "Oh Girlfriend! You know I'm always ready to play! What's on your mind this time?"

Miss Savannah started to explain her situation. "Well, I've bought this house in one of the historic districts in Tulsa, Oklahoma and it's almost refurbished and I was just wondering if you'd like to decorate it for me. There's plenty of room so you don't have to worry about a place to stay, well, once we get some bedroom furniture and linens."

"Girlfriend! What have you gone and done now?"

"Nothing I haven't done before but kinda on a grander scale this time."

"You said Tulsa? What part?"

"Well, do you remember when we went to the Rose Garden and then over to the Philbrook Museum … the old Maple Ridge District?"

"How can I forget! Don't tell me got one of those historic homes!"

"Yep. Sure did!"

"But, Girlfriend, those are half million to a million dollar plus homes."

"I know but I didn't have to pay near that much. Not even half the lowest amount you just said, including all the closing costs. Anyway, we'll talk about it when you get here. That is if you want to tackle it."

"You've got to be kidding!"

"Nope. I wouldn't kid about something like that."

"How big is it?

Picking up the closing papers she rifled through the pages. Here it is. She adjusted her glasses again. Let's see. "For a quick rundown … There's eighteen plus rooms in the house and its three stories. The bathrooms are not included in that count. Plus there's a partial basement and furnace room. The footage is somewhere between six and seven thousand square feet, more or less, of actual living area. Then. Get this! There's over 4,000 square feet of porches and verandas. Then there's a three-car garage that has a four-room servants' quarters apartment over it. I thought I'd make that into a rental if it's permitted in this area. Haven't checked into that issue yet. At first I thought I'd use it for an office but I don't have to worry about that with all the footage in the house."

There was silence on the phone. "Gypsy! Are you there?"

"Damn, Girlfriend! Yes, I'm here. I'm just shocked! I don't know what to say."

"Well if you don't want the job, I'm just going to have to hire someone else to do it."

"Oh, it's not that I don't want to do it. It's just so much to think about. You don't believe in giving a girl any warning, do you? There's the porches ... the apartment ... the house itself and what about the grounds?"

"Oh the grounds are already being taken care of. And you won't have to worry about any paintings or pictures on the walls downstairs."

"What in the hell are you talking about. No pictures?"

"I had bookshelves built on all the exterior walls. Everywhere there's not a window there's book cases."

"You what?"

"Gypsy, listen to me. Let me explain. OK?"

"Go ahead and try to explain this one. I remember that gold velvet sofa and chair you bought that time that matched absolutely nothing else in your home and we had to pull it all together. At least with the rug and paintings and pictures and pillows, it looked beautiful when we were finished but no walls to hang anything on?"

"Gypsy. I said all the exterior walls have book cases. *The exterior.* The interior walls are still bare and nothing's on them."

"Oh good! At least you left some space for me to work with."

"So you're going to do it?"

"Girlfriend, I could never say no to you."

"When can you be here?"

"When are you planning on moving in? I'd like to get some of it done before everything gets delivered."

"Well, that's another thing. I don't have that many pieces of furniture, even with the few nice pieces I have in storage there's not enough to fill that house so shopping was going to be part of the job. Oh,

28

I have enough of the bare essentials for a couple of bedrooms until new furniture is purchased and I can fully stock the kitchen but I was thinking you might like to take charge of everything else... you know coordinating everything so everything flows."

"Okay. I'm already getting excited about it and I haven't even seen it yet! Can you send me some pictures so I can start getting a few things in mind?"

"I'll do it right now. Are you near your computer?"

"Sitting right in front of it. I was looking at some tea sets I'm thinking about ordering in."

"Still dreaming of putting in that tea room, are you?"

"That dream has never left my mind. It'll always be my dream. Maybe one of these days when I retire. We'll see."

Savannah pulled up the pictures and attached them to an email. "I just sent the pictures to you. They should be there any time now." Savannah could hear Gypsy clicking keys on her computer.

"Holy shit, Girlfriend! That is a mansion!"

"Yes, I'm afraid it is. You see why I need you?"

"Are there interior pictures?"

"Not yet. I've been trying to stay out of everyone's way. The guys have really done a great job and a fast one. I really didn't expect to be living in it for about a year and it's only been a few months. You can do a walk through when you get here. When will you be flying in? I'll be there to pick you up."

"No need. I'm driving this time. Give me a few days to finish up here and I'll head that way. That's if I don't have any more problems. This has been a nightmare. Anyway, I'll give you a call when I get near. You do still have your cell don't you?"

"Still have it but it lives in the desk drawer. The best way to reach me is at night here at this number."

"Girlfriend! When are you going to start carrying a cell? What if "Baby" breaks down one of these days?"

"That's no problem. I've made another little purchase since I last saw you."

"You got rid of "Baby"?

"Oh don't even think that! That's never going to happen. I bought a new car."

"Good for you! What kind?"

"A nice little red Jag. You know I always wanted one but felt it was like being unfaithful to "Baby".

Not knowing what to say, Gypsy said nothing.

Hearing silence on the line again Savannah repeated what she had said earlier in the conversation, "Are you still there?"

"I'm here but my mind is in overload at the moment."

Savannah laughed. "That's not a bad thing, now is it? Listen I need to ring off and get some of the things done around here, like packing boxes of books."

"Ring off? You've been reading one of those English novels again, haven't you?" Gypsy was laughing this time. "I can always tell what kind of reading material you have by the way you talk."

"I suppose that's true but you seem to be the only one that can tell. I'll be waiting for you call in a few days. Love you!"

"Love you too. Goodnight."

"Caio Bella. Goodnight."

Chapter 8

A week had passed since her conversation with Gypsy and moving time was quickly approaching. Finishing touches were being done on the house and the maid's quarters were almost completed. The driveway was being resurfaced and patterned and the roofers had finally completed the repairs to the fired clay roof. Guttering had been installed and the herb garden she had always wanted was just about finished. She had requested raised beds in that area so she didn't have to bend over so much to harvest the fragrant herbs she loved to cook with. Lower back problems had plagued her for some time.

Miss Savannah was outside surveying the efforts of the gardeners when she heard a car door slam out on the street. Turning around she saw Melody making her way across the front lawn in her heels. She smiled. Well, maybe she would aerate the grass while she was walking across it.

"Good morning Miss Savannah. Thought I'd stop by and see how things have been coming along."

"Glad to see you. You know you're welcome anytime. Sorry you had to hike across the lawn because the driveway is blocked off. It's not quite ready for cars yet. I think tomorrow they're going to be here to take down the barricades. The new surfacing should be dry and cured by then."

"So, is it finished inside?"

"I think so. Wanna have a look?"

"I sure do. I can tell you right now that I never thought it would look like this!"

"See. What did I tell you about old things when we first looked at it?"

They walked up to the back steps and Miss Savannah reached out and opened the kitchen door. When they stepped inside Melody's eyes just about popped out of her head.

"Wow!" She paused to try to think of something else to say but "Wow" was all that seemed to come out of her mouth. She was standing on hard wood floors that shone like a new penny. The cabinets had been refinished and the glass front doors were sparkling. The old stove had been repaired and cleaned and put back where it had been but there was an island now that had a surface range and small prep sinks. Double ovens had been installed and what appeared to be cabinetry with wooden fronts were actually the freezer and refrigerators. They were concealed. And of course the new dishwashers. Yes. Two of them. One in the prep area and the other by the deep double country sinks. Of course there was a place for the small table and chairs in the large in-kitchen eating area. Miss Savannah walked over and opened what appeared to be a panel in the wall and there was a bookcase that had been built in... double wide of course. Now her jumble of different shaped, different bound recipe books she had collected from her travels had a place to live and were out of sight

"Now that's for all my recipe books."

"I love it! It's absolutely the most beautiful kitchen I've seen in any of the homes in this area."

"Well, I don't care about the other homes in this area. I just knew what I wanted and this is it."

Melody spotted the Hoosier cabinet. "Is that the old piece of junk that was here that first day?"

"Sure is and look." She slid up the roll top and opened the doors beneath the food prep surface and there was her computer system for the kitchen and a place to keep a stool to sit on.

"Come on through. There's more for you to see."

"I never realized the rooms were so large. And I love that you've had all that old tacky carpet removed. The floors are beautiful. They look like liquid honey. Are they like that throughout the house?"

"Pretty much. I chose to have carpeting in the bedrooms just because I like it. I also chose to keep that old vintage bathtub on legs in the main bath. When it was refinished … well, I love it. In my master bath I needed a shower so that's what's in there. The other baths needed hardly anything except a good cleaning, plumbing and electrical updates. I've not done much interior decorating as you can see because I'm waiting for my friend to get here."

"Mind if I look on through?"

"Not at all. Take your time and enjoy."

"Wait! I can't believe this! You actually had an elevator installed?"

"Had to. I can't handle stairs. I thought I told you that the first day in your office. And, since there's a basement, there was no problem having one installed. It goes all the way to the attic so I can access all the floors if I want to."

"I'm not even going to ask how much it cost."

Miss Savannah knew Melody was fishing and refused to play her game. All she said was, "Good." Turning towards the back door she said, "I'll be out back when you're finished looking around. I can't seem to stay away from the herb garden. I may just be spending all my time back there. Well, have fun. Find me when you're through."

"I will. That is if I don't get lost."

Watching Melody teeter on her choice of footwear, Miss Savannah turned back and said, "You know dear, you really need to start rethinking you're footwear. I used to wear shoes like that all the time. Oh the heels weren't that high but they really took their toll on my back as I've gotten older. Just think about it."

Melody flipped back her hair before she glanced down at her shoes and started to say something.

Miss Savannah replied, "You don't have to say anything. I was just commenting on my observation of how you have to concentrate on your balance all the time and 'Oh my Lord', how your feet must hurt at night."

Chapter 9

The start of moving had become a logistic nightmare for the movers. It wasn't bothering Miss Savannah at all because she knew exactly what she wanted done and when. Gypsy had called and said she was going to be a few more days because she was wrapping everything up so she could devote all the time she needed, without interruption when she got there.

Miss Savannah had arrived at the house early and the first thing she did was light incense to insure her day was going to be a calm one. She wanted the house and everyone and everything in it to remain calm and serene.

She had packed her beloved Keurig coffee maker and a couple boxes of pods that morning before she left the apartment. She was waiting for it to brew a cup of Fog Lifter coffee when the doorbell rang.

Two huge men stood at the door. They were dressed in the company uniform of khakis and button up shirts with the logo of their company on the pockets. And, around their middles were black back support vests of some kind. Mentally she thought, "They're certainly going to need those!"

She motioned them through to the kitchen where she had all her papers lined up and in order. "Now. I want the contents of my apartment moved first. This is the address and the owner is aware you'll be there this morning. She just lives next door but she'll be expecting you. She'll open it up and stand by while you're there to make certain you remove everything."

She looked up at the man that seemed to be the boss. ""Okay?"

He nodded.

Then she handed the movers a sheet of paper with a list of storage units. "These all need to be moved too. I've already made arrangements with the managers to be expecting you." Jingling a set of keys, she handed them over. "You'll need these to get access." There were at least a dozen keys. "Now on that list I have numbered them in the order I want them moved. The cartons are all marked and labeled with the contents too. And! This is *very* important! If a box says *Fragile*, that's exactly how I want it handled! Some of those things are older than you are and I don't want them damaged after all these years. They're not replaceable! Anyway, when you get them here I'll direct you where they go. Understand?"

The driver just stared at the paper.

"Do you need further instruction? I thought I explained things quite clearly."

"No ma'am. But, you do realize this is going to take days."

She looked up at the big man and smiled. "Of course. Now just handle it. By the way, is that the only truck you have?"

"Yes ma'am."

Miss Savannah just shook her head and looked back down at her notebook and checked off another thing on her list. Still looking down at the notebook she noticed the man's feet. He was still standing there.

"Yes? Is there anything else?"

"No ma'am. Just."

"Yes?"

"Just… how much stuff do you have?"

She smiled at him again. "A lifetime's full."

Within hours the house started filling with moving cartons and boxes and furniture. True to her word, the cartons had been labeled as to which room the cartons were to be placed so distribution of the items went fairly smoothly.

She noticed that a second truck and a couple more men had been called in to assist. She thought, "Now the man's using his head. They would still be moving things this time next week with just the two of them. And when they get to that Rosewood dining set, it's going to take all four of them and they're still going to need more help."

She had called the unemployment office and ordered four people to assist her through the duration of the move. She had specifically told the lady exactly the kind of people she was looking for and to make certain they knew how to alphabetize. She thought the first thing that should be done was to get the bedrooms in order so she could sleep there that night. She hadn't bothered purchasing bedroom furniture except for a king size mattress and frame and a make do chest when she was in the apartment. After all, the bed took up most of the space so there wasn't anything else for her to do. That seemed like a good thing now. So she sent the temps upstairs to hang clothing in the closets and put fresh linens on the bed. She could organize her clothes later.

She oversaw the unpacking of her kitchen items and directed where each thing should be stored. There were empty cupboards everywhere but she knew as soon as the movers got to the unit with her collection of dishes and glassware that would be taken care of. Oh how she loved her dishes she had collected from her travels.

One of the temps was solely responsible for keeping the boxes of books in alphabetical stacks. When the time came to unpack them she didn't want to have to handle them any more than absolutely possible.

When the items from her apartment arrived the first thing she did was spot the cartons that held her electronics and put one of the young men to unpacking and setting it up. Within a short while there was music wafting through the rooms spreading a tranquil atmosphere over a chaotic situation. Miss Savannah believed in the old adage that music calmed the beast and adhered to that belief. She had grabbed a handful of carefully selected CD's and stuck them in her tote before packing the others the night before.

Load after load of her belongings kept arriving and she directed each load of cartons and furniture to where it should be placed. She realized the men's legs and backs must be killing them after what seemed like a million trips up and down the stairs but she did not want to relinquish the use of the elevator to them. There was a weight limit and she discerned it would be pushed to its capacity if she allowed its use. So, she comforted herself in the fact that with what they were charging, there was no way she was going to make their job easier for them. She also knew that when they saw the area where the house was located the price of the moving automatically doubled anyway.

By mid-afternoon after her bedroom was in order and the baths were stocked with towels, bathroom tissue and soap plus her kitchen put in order she dismissed two of the temps but asked them to return the following day after everything had been delivered. It seemed like she had been over enthusiastic in what she expected to get accomplished with all the moving going on.

She fixed herself an iced coffee and took a break, retiring to her herb garden to relax a few minutes before the moving trucks once again arrived. She knew the next load would be her dining room furniture and she would scalp any one of them if they dare to damage it. She had babied it too long to tolerate any scuff, scrape or even put a nick in it. Solid rosewood, it was ... the kind that could no longer be purchased in the United States anymore because it was an endangered species now. She leaned her head back against the bench and thought back to the many dinner party guests that had been seated around that table. Oh, there had been so many wonderful conversations that had taken place and special occasions celebrated. She shook her head and told herself. "That's in the past. Let it be. You can't go trying to relive them. They're nice memories but that's what they are. Memories."

After resting a few minutes she heard men's voices coming from inside. She knew it had arrived at last. The final storage unit had been emptied. Stepping into the kitchen she heard the young lady she had left in charge directing the movers to the dining room. "This is exactly where Miss Savannah wants it put. She said to measure because it's to be precisely centered on that wall. Precisely!" In a few more minutes she heard the young woman again. "Don't slide it on the floor! Put a pad under it! And, don't put it all the way against the wall because you're going to have to plug in the lighting first. Then you can scoot it back." Miss Savannah liked this young woman. She liked her spunk ... her kind of lady. She decided not to even enter the room until everything was in place. It had been a few years since she had seen it and she wanted to see it the same way it was the first time she had set eyes on it. She sat down at the kitchen table and continued to listen. "Where's the Oriental rug? Miss Savannah said there was a rug to be put down first then the table." Miss Savannah smiled. "It's too heavy for that old woman to try to move by herself so I want to make sure it's right where she said it should be. Hear?" She could hear the movers groaning from the weight of the furniture. "That table's not straight on the rug. Look it needs to come this way about three or four more inches. There now. I think that's just fine. Miss Savannah said there's supposed to be some little tables with inlay that go in here too. They go right over there." To Miss Savannah it sounded like this young woman knew exactly what she was doing and could take direction as well as carry those directions through. "Don't leave just yet. I need to look this over and make sure it's not damaged anywhere before you take those papers to Miss Savannah. I'd hate for her to find something I missed. Just wait one minute." Miss Savannah could hear the young woman moving about. "All right. I don't see any scratches or anything. You can go find Miss Savannah now. I think she's either in the herb garden or in the kitchen."

The man in charge came through to the kitchen with a handful of paperwork. "I need to get you to sign off on these if you will Ma'am." He was mopping the sweat from his face with a bandana. "That is one more heavy piece of furniture in there. Don't think I've ever seen another one like it."

She nodded. "Yes. They're rare now days."

"I just need for you to sign off on these and I think we're finished."

Miss Sàvannah looked each paper over and noticed that all the items had been checked off. She signed them. "I'll be by the office tomorrow and settle up paying the balance. The lady I spoke to said it was okay."

"Yes Ma'am. If you need us again be sure and call."

"Oh, I think this is the last time this old woman is going to be moving, but I do appreciate it. I have no problems recommending you to friends if they should need movers. You seem to have done an excellent job. Thank you for being so careful with my belongings."

He had never had anyone say that to him and he didn't know how to reply. "My pleasure Ma'am."

His crew had folded all the moving pads and removed all the moving equipment that had been required and were waiting in the trucks for him. She could tell by the way he crawled into the truck that he was tired, probably more tired than he had been in a long time.

She closed the door and leaned against it looking at the stacks and stacks and stacks of boxes lined up in the rooms. Speaking to herself she said, "Okay, Savannah. One box at a time. One box at a time."

The young woman was waiting for her to return to the kitchen. "Miss Savannah, do you want me to polish the dining room suit? It looks like it needs it after being stored."

"Let me show you what I want done." She grabbed a couple of soft dish towels and held one of them under warm water then wrung it almost dry. "Follow me. I need to explain something. This wood is finished with natural resins. It's never had furniture polish on it. Watch me." She took the wet cloth and wiped it across one end of the table. Then she took the dry one and began to rub in fast circles over the damp spot. "Here. Feel. Feel the warmth?"

The young woman nodded.

"What's happening is the warmth of rubbing kind of activates, for the lack of a better word, the natural resins. When they're warm they kind of melt back together and smooth out and shine. Never, never put any kind of polish on this table or any of the Rosewood furniture or you'll ruin it."

The young woman reached over and took the towels from Miss Savannah. "You go rest. I'll take over here. You look tired."

When the young woman had finished and ran a dry mop over the wood floors she put everything away then went looking for Miss Savannah in the herb garden but she wasn't there. Looking around she spotted her sitting in the porch swing. She had dozed off. She gently touched the old woman on her arm. "Miss Savannah? It's time for David and me to go. Are you going to need us again tomorrow?"

Sitting up straight Miss Savannah looked at her and asked. "What's your name? I don't think I ever asked. I apologize. Sometimes I just get so caught up in what's going on around me I forget my manners."

"My name is Tawnie."

"Tawnie. I like that." She repeated it again. "Tawnie. That's a real pretty name."

Tawny blushed and said, "It's actually Tawnie Marie because Mother liked Donnie and Marie." She laughed. "She made it up but everyone has always liked it."

Well, Tawnie, yes. I do indeed need you for tomorrow and maybe a few days after that too and I'm sure David, that was what you said his name is isn't it? Well, I'm sure there's more than enough to keep him busy too."

"What time do you want us here?"

"Let's get an early start. Maybe around eight. I'll have coffee ready when you get here."

Chapter 10

Miss Savannah pulled herself up from the porch swing after Tawnie and David left and made her way to the kitchen. She hadn't eaten very much that day and was feeling it. She browsed through her fridge and even though there was food in it, nothing looked good to her. For the first time since like forever, she picked up the phone book and ordered pizza to be delivered. And it was there within thirty minutes so she didn't get it free. She couldn't believe how good it tasted. She hadn't realized how hungry she was.

With her kitchen in order and coffee set up for in the morning she turned out the light to head upstairs. Then it dawned on her. She had never been shown how to use the elevator. She remembered the serviceman being there and speaking with her but she was just too busy to take the time for him to show her everything about it. She walked to the bottom of the stairs and took hold of the banister. Looking up she knew she'd never make it as tired as she was. Her hips had already started complaining earlier and being stubborn she hadn't taken her medication for the pain.

She walked to the front of the small elevator and stood there staring at it with great apprehension. She spoke to herself. "Savannah, don't be silly. It can't be any different than a regular elevator. Just push the button. The door opens. You get in and push another button. That's all there is to it." She reached out but she could not make herself push the open button. She mumbled, "What if I get stranded in it? There's no one in this house to help me and I don't have a cell phone to call for help."

She walked to the staircase again and looked up. Shaking her head she knew she was going to have to use the elevator. She took a deep breath and went back to face her obstacle. Sternly she scolded herself. "This is just crazy. You've conquered worse things than this in your lifetime and not a blasted thing happened to you. Now put your big girl panties on and push that button." And she did. The door quietly slid open and waited for her to enter. Cautiously she stepped into the elevator and looked at the panel of buttons. She positioned her finger over the button for the second floor, closed her eyes and pushed. She heard the door slide to and felt the elevator start to rise. In a few seconds it stopped and the door slid open again. She opened her eyes and looked around then stepped out into the hallway. One more button was pushed to close the door and it was done! She had accomplished one more feat on her own. A small feat it was but she had tackled it and for a seventy year plus old woman she was proud of herself.

Entering her bedroom she found her bed perfectly turned back and a fresh nightshirt had been laid out for her. A book was on the nightstand and a carafe of water was there in case she needed it. She was impressed at what Tawnie had accomplished. She opened her closet and everything was in order the way she liked it, her shirts and blouses were together, sorted by color and all facing the same direction. Her jeans were on the lower rack and her dress clothes were hung on the opposite rack. Now she was even more impressed.

She went in the bathroom and everything was in order there too, even to the point that towels and wash cloth were next to the shower for her nightly bath. She found nothing that she was unhappy with. Maybe someone with a more temperamental personality would have found something to complain about but she found it thoughtful and caring that Tawnie had taken the extra time to make certain she was going to be comfortable.

After her shower and nightly routine she settled into bed with her mountain of pillows propping her up. Lord, how she loved this luxury. All her life she had adored pillows. It didn't matter what shape or size. She just loved them all.

Opening her book to settle in and read, she thought she heard music coming from downstairs. She was certain she had remembered to turn everything off. She threw back the quilt and comforter and was scooting her feet into her slippers when it stopped. She thought to herself, "Must have been someone driving down the street with their radio turned up loud because I hear nothing now. Whatever. I'll have to get used to this new neighborhood. Once I do I won't even pay attention to things like that." She stepped to her window and looked out over the street below but saw nothing. Whatever it had been would already be way on down the street by now anyway.

Crawling back into bed she pulled the covers up under her chin, picked up her book and in less than a chapter she had fallen asleep woven into the romance novel that now rested on her chest. Later she would rouse enough to put the book aside and turn off the lamp.

In her dreams she once again heard the music and voices of people seemingly having a dinner party because she could distinguish the clinking of glasses and dishes.

Chapter 11

The next morning dawned way too early for Miss Savannah. She grabbed her robe and went downstairs, via the elevator, and made certain coffee was brewing. She glanced in the freezer and pulled out a package of her favorite breakfast muffins and set them out to defrost.

When the coffee was ready, she poured a cup and added some flavored coffee creamer. Glancing at the clock she realized Tawnie and David would be there any minute. She took her cup and headed out to the herb garden to take a look. She thought, "If the neighbors don't like my robe they can just kiss my …" Before she could finish the thought she heard car doors close. David and Tawnie were parked in the driveway. "Good morning." She said. "How long have you been out here. I didn't even hear you drive in. I was going to wait for you out here but we can go on inside." She pulled at her robe with her free hand to make certain it wasn't flapping open.

Tawnie quickly said, "You don't have to go in. I know you love it out here. Just tell us what to do and we'll start."

Miss Savannah seated herself on the garden bench and told them her thoughts. They headed inside. "Oh, there's fresh coffee made and when I go back inside I'll have some of my favorite muffins for you. You'll be needing a coffee break about then."

They nodded and went about the duties they had been assigned. Miss Savannah relaxed and enjoyed her coffee. When she was ready for her second cup she felt the muffins to make sure they were defrosted and popped them in the microwave for just a few seconds. She arranged them on a pretty plate and picked up her cup of coffee. As she headed upstairs to get dressed for the day, she let them know it was break time and things were laid out for them.

She punched the button, the elevator door slid open and she stepped inside. She was going to really like this!

After getting dressed she decided to wander through the house and try to get set in her mind exactly what she wanted to do with all the rooms. The second floor was pretty much designated to bedrooms and baths. No many decisions to make about that. The house already had that decision made for her.

She used the elevator and went up one more floor and stepped out into a huge open room that had doors leading from it. Opening them she found a maze of smaller rooms, each with windows looking out over the property. "What a wonderful view," she thought to herself. Right then and there she decided that this was to be her workshop area. The clutter of books, computers, sewing items and even her craft items would never again clutter her living space. She had always wanted a room just for her sewing machine and all the boxes of fabric. She checked one of the rooms again that was on the north side and found it large enough to set up her mother's quilting frame. The lighting was perfect. She designated this as her sewing room. She opened a door leading from that room and it was a walk-in closet. "Perfect! Just perfect!" Now she had storage room for all the boxes of fabric that set in the center of the outer room.

Hearing the doorbell chime, she headed back to the elevator to return downstairs. When the door slid open, there stood Gypsy looking around in awe. She and Gypsy started towards each other at the same time. "Girlfriend! Oh my God! You've really done it this time!" Their arms were already wrapped around each other in a hug.

"I've got coffee made. Come on through to the kitchen" They made their way with Gypsy taking in everything as they went. Noticing the low level in the coffee pot Miss Savannah started to make another pot. "Wait. Girlfriend, I'd just soon have… let me see .. she was turning the little coffee pod carousel around seeing what kind was available. "I think I'll just have this one." She picked up a coffee mug set it under the spout, popped the pod in and pushed the button. "I still love these machines!"

"You don't know how glad I am that you turned me on to them. Just stand still for a moment."

"Okay. Why?"

"I just want to look at you. That's why! Gypsy, you look wonderful. Looks like life's treating you good."

"It is. I always wanted to actually own my own business and I've haven't regretted it one minute. Not one hard working minute!"

"Got anyone special in your life?"

"Nope! I'm through with that … forever! Girlfriend, I can do what I want, when I want, go where I want and take care of my business the way I want."

Miss Savannah had led them out to the back yard so they could set out there and have their coffee. A saucer with a couple of muffins was in one hand and her cup in the other.

Gypsy surveyed the back of the property with a professional eye. "Hmm. I see that the garage area and the servant's quarters are over there. Kitchen herb garden … Porch … Veranda … What's that back there? It looks like a barbeque pit. Brick to match the house too. What are you going to use that for?"

"Well, since it seems not to be in working order I told them to just clean it up and leave it. I don't know what I'm going to do with it yet."

"Oh Girlfriend, when I was at market I saw the most wonderful stones that glow and they had been fashioned into everything from pool surrounds to fountains." Looking around she asked, "You don't have a pool do you?"

"Not this time."

"Thank God."

"Spa?"

"Just a hot tub over there by the veranda. It's a pretty good size one and I did remember to have them to build new decking, steps and rails so I can get in and out of it. It's even got a music system and LED lighting. Quite the set-up."

Looking the spar area over Gypsy made some mental notes of what was needed to complete the area.

Miss Savannah noticed she was still holding the saucer of muffins. "Will you just look at me. I've been walking around carrying these." She set them down on a nearby table and she reached over and gave her dear friend another hug. "Gypsy, welcome to my domain! What you see is what you get. I think this house is ready for you to make it into my home. When we finish our coffee and you're ready we'll take the 'grand tour' of the house."

"I can't wait!"

"Still want to take the job? I've already told Quinn that you'll be submitting invoices to him and he's to take care of them right away."

"I have no problem with that." She laughed. "I know you're good for it."

There was a few moments of silence between the two friends. Then Gypsy replied, "You don't have any surprises for me like that tepee you bought in Portland when we were at Saturday Market, do you?" She laughed.

"Well," Miss Savannah pointed to the upper story. "It's up there somewhere stored with the Indian doll collection."

"You still have it!"

"After carrying that tepee all the way from downtown Portland, and on the transit system, do you think I'd get rid of it?"

"That was so funny! I'll never forget it."

"Oh, Gypsy, we do have some good memories don't we?"

Miss Savannah took a close look at her friend. She still had those beautiful dark eyes and dark, dark Italian hair, a mane so thick and luxurious, and naturally curly too, hair that she had always envied. Touching her own hair which was soft as a babies and that she could never get it to do what she wanted, she smiled. Of course Gypsy was a picture of Victorian elegance, the way she dressed, the way she held herself, the way she moved her hands. She was a vision from another era.

Gypsy had always dressed like that and the way I dress ... I'd always looked like I had crawled out of a ... a ... well jeans, bibs and tailored suits could never compare with lace, velvet, girlie clothes that Gypsy was known to wear. Diamonds and leather never could compare with diamonds and lace.

Miss Savannah let out a deep sigh. "You ready for this? You may as well see what you've gotten yourself in to."

They picked up their cups and the saucer and went back into the house. Miss Savannah stopped by the sink to rinse the dishes and put them in the dishwasher. Tawnie touched her arm and motioned that she'd do it. "That's what I'm here for. Now you and your friend go on with our business."

Gypsy raised one eyebrow. "And who might this be?"

"Oh where are my manners. Gypsy. This is Tawnie and the young man over there hefting those heavy boxes of books is her husband, David. Tawnie, this is my very best friend in the world, Miss Gypsy."

Tawnie flashed her bright smile. "Nice to meet you."

"Is this one of your nieces?"

"Oh no. She and her husband were sent out from the employment agency. Why?"

"She has those same beautiful eyes like you. Hadn't you noticed?"

"Hadn't paid any attention. Anyway, at my age I don't stand in front of a mirror any longer than I have to. Haven't you noticed all these wrinkles that have cropped up since we saw each other last time? When you get my age, you'll understand."

"Well, Girlfriend, I'm not far behind you."

Not liking the turn of the conversation Miss Savannah said, "Shall we?" and motioned for them to take a look at the house.

Gypsy picked up a small Victorian bag which held her tapestry covered notebook, a laser measuring tape and a camera and replied, "Okay, let's see what we have here."

After going through the downstairs, taking measurements and pictures of every angle of every room, Gypsy looked up the stairs. Miss Savannah just motioned for her to follow her. She pushed the button and the elevator door slid open. She motioned for Gypsy to step inside. "Girlfriend, this is wonderful!" They proceeded through the entire house, Gypsy stepping back and surveying spaces she knew might become a challenge and sometimes walking from one room to another, repeating the same thing then making notes in her book. Miss Savannah had seen her doing the same thing before. She was mentally decorating before she purchased one piece of furniture.

Miss Savannah glanced down at her watch. "It getting close to lunch time and I need to run by the movers and drop off a check. How about I take you to lunch?"

"That sounds so good. I am starting to get a bit hungry. Why don't we just grab a salad or something and we'll go out to dinner tonight?"

"I usually don't go out late, especially after dark. These old eyes just won't let me drive after dark. I'm afraid I've become a strictly day time person."

"Hey, that's no problem. I'll drive."

"Then it's a deal."

When the garage doors opened Gypsy saw "Baby". "She still looks just like she did when I first saw her!" Then she spotted the Jag. "Wow! It's even prettier than I thought. Can I drive?"

Miss Savannah tossed the keys to Gypsy. "There's one condition."

"What's that?"

"Just don't drive her like you use to drive my little Honda on the turnpike. You remember that?"

Gypsy laughed. "Were in a hurry and I didn't want to get us there late."

"Well, all I can say is that my butt was hanging on the seat when I looked over and you were well past a hundred miles an hour."

Gypsy was still laughing. "When I looked over and saw the look on your face I knew I had to slow down. I promise to drive carefully."

"You should have been a NASCAR driver the way you like to drive fast."

Gypsy thought a moment and said, "Maybe you're right. Where do we have to go to drop off that check?"

"It's not too far. I've only been there one time myself so I'll have to tell you as we go."

"You still drive by stores as markers don't you?"

"Can't help it."

Gypsy shifted the Jag into reverse and they were on their way.

"You know I can't wait to get all those pictures downloaded and see what ideas I come up with."

They made their way across town. Miss Savannah said, "I supposed you noticed that sleeping arrangements are kind of sparse right now. Turn right at the next light. But, I thought I'd wait about getting anything more until you got here. Up there at that pool supply place make a left. I saw a bedroom suit in a furniture store window the other day that I liked. We'll have to run over there and take a look. Slow down because you have to make a right turn right up here back into this industrial area. I have to look for the street. There it is. The one where that sandwich shop is. Anyway, I don't really know what style I want to do the house in yet. That's why I called you." Pointing she said, "There's the place I need to drop this check off."

Gypsy whipped into a parking place close to the door.

"Be right back. This shouldn't take too long."

A few minutes later she emerged from the office holding papers in her hand. She got in the car and sighed. "Now what are you hungry for?"

"Let's find an Applebee's and have one of those Oriental chicken salads. I haven't had one of those in a long time. You?"

"Not since the last time we were there together."

It didn't take long for them to spot what they were looking for and a few minutes later were enjoying a nice cold Bloody Mary while waiting for their salads. An hour later they were on their way back to the house.

Tawnie and David were sitting on the porch swing eating a sack lunch they had brought. Miss Savannah had noticed that Tawnie had set a couple of cans of soda in the refrigerator when they got there that morning.

"Everything been going okay?" She asked.

Tawnie smiled. "I've got about half the dishes put up in butler's pantry. I don't think I ever saw so many before. Well, outside of a store that is."

"I do love them." Miss Savannah replied with a softness in her voice.

"You wouldn't believe how much fun we used to have setting the table for every holiday or just when the craving to redo it overtook us." Gypsy joined in. "One time we cut a lace tablecloth apart and lined the shelves of the china closet and decorated it with all those lovely amber depression dishes. We even strung lights inside to back light them. It was beautiful when we got done."

"It should have been. We worked on that for hours and hours."

Miss Savannah realized they had cut Tawnie and David out of the conversation. "So David how are you coming along with organizing the boxes of books?"

He almost looked startled when spoken to. "If I don't discover any more boxes, I think I just about have them in order like you want."

As an afterthought Miss Savannah asked, "Do either one of you know much about computers? I mean like data entry?"

Tawnie shook her head. "I took some computer classes in school but I'm just not too good at it, I'm afraid."

David just shook his head.

"Why do you need a data entry person?" Gypsy asked.

"Well, I've kind of gotten behind entering all the books plus I need to update all the prices for insurance purposes. There's some valuable books in there. You know there's several complete collections of first editions, some are so old they need special care and well, I just need to take the old computer files and update everything. I just thought if Tawnie knew how to do it …"

Tawnie spoke up. "I don't know how, but my mother is a computer genius. She can make them do anything." She hesitated for a few seconds. "She is kind of proud and I hate to say anything but she sure could use a job right now to see her through. She's been trying to find a job but either she's overqualified or they're looking for someone that's just starting out in their career. She's not that old but the corporations just don't want to hire a person her age."

Miss Savannah and Gypsy glanced at each other. They knew exactly what she was saying. Those years just before retirement are tough.

"Tell you what. Why don't you have her give me a call and I'll talk to her. We might just be able to work something out."

"Thank you, Miss Savannah. I'll have her call you tonight."

When they got inside Gypsy said, "Before long you're going to have that whole family working for you."

Miss Savannah just looked at her and said nothing.

"I'm sorry. I didn't mean for it to come out like that. It wasn't meant in a bad way."

Miss Savannah put her arm around her dear friend's shoulder and gave her a squeeze. "I know. Sometimes things just come out before we think. I still do the same thing at times."

The afternoon sped by in a flurry of activity and when it was time for Tawnie and David to leave, Gypsy and Miss Savannah were ready to kick back and put their feet up.

"Gypsy, do you still want to go out to dinner tonight? I've been sitting here thinking I have a wonderful casserole in the freezer I can pop in the oven and it'll be ready in no time. That and some warm buttered rolls will make a good dinner."

"I am kind of tired. That sounds great to me. I just don't want you spending all evening in the kitchen."

"Give me ten minutes and I'll be right back her with my feet up."

"Where's the liquor cabinet? I think I'd like to fix something cold and refreshing before dinner."

"The liquor cabinet is right over there by the sound system but I'm afraid it's still empty. I don't think it's been unpacked yet but I do have a few bottles of that nice wine you introduced me too in the wine cooler. It's just to the left of the cabinet. There should be glasses in the upper."

"Got it. And where the opener?"

Miss Savannah stuck her head around the door. "Just keep pulling out drawers until you locate it then you can tell me where everything is."

They both started laughing.

"Seems like we've been through this together a time or two before," Gypsy said.

"That's exactly what I was thinking. Want to put on some music while you're there?"

"Sure. No problem."

Miss Savannah heard doors opening and closing and soon heard the wonderfully haunting, soft melodies of Steven Halpern's "Sound Healing".

"Perfect!" Miss Savannah called from the kitchen.

"You want your wine in there?

"Nope. Just finished up. In about thirty minutes our food will be ready." She collapsed into the chair where she had been sitting before. "Getting old's a bitch, you know. I just can't do what I use to."

"Tell me about it! I keep wondering how much longer I'm going to be able to keep the company going. It's not the business end of it. It's the physical end of it that gets to me."

"Well, I've always told you, you have a place to live wherever I happen to be and it looks like it's going to be right here in Tulsa, Oklahoma of all places."

"Yeah, we've both traveled half-way round the world and back again and end up here. At least I'm here for the moment." Gypsy picked up the bottle of wine. "More?"

"Sure. Why not?" She held her glass out for a refill and took a sip. "You know at times I wonder where in life I'd be now, had I never left this area in the first place." She motioned with her arms. "Not this neighborhood right here but Oklahoma."

"I know. I suppose we let destiny guide us and this is where we are supposed to be."

"I guess."

"Girlfriend, do you have any regrets?"

She thought a moment. "Well, I guess we all do … all the what if I had done this or maybe done it a different way. Sometimes I wonder about it but there's not a darn thing I can do about it now so why dwell on regrets."

"I kind of thought that's what you'd say."

The buzzer went off on the oven and the phone rang at the same time. "Sounds like its dinner time to me. Okay if we eat in the kitchen? I'll grab the phone and we'll eat in just a few minutes."

"That's the best place to enjoy a meal. There's just something about the feel of it. Nice and cozy."

Miss Savannah nodded and said, "Good because I've already got the little table set."

After Miss Savannah hung up the phone they ate dinner in a constant chatter of catching up on what had been happening since they had spent time together. Clearing the table and sticking their plates in the dishwasher they sat back down at the table and finished off the bottle of wine.

The mantle clock chimed and they were both surprised at how late it had gotten.

"I guess I need to head to bed. That was Tawnie's mother on the phone just before we ate and she's going to come over with them in the morning."

"Think she's going to be up to all this?" She motioned to the stacks of boxes. "I know how you are about your books."

"You know what? Have you ever picked up the phone or walked into a room or just been around someone that's pure sunshine?"

"Yep, but not very often."

"Well, that's exactly what it was like talking to her. I think it's going to work out just fine."

They turned out the lights and made their way to their bedrooms. "Good night, Gypsy." Miss Savannah called down the hall.

"Good night, Girlfriend."

All of a sudden Miss Savannah said, "Good night, John boy," and they both burst in to laughter. They use to giggle like that all the time. Miss Savannah realized how much she had missed it. She made her nest in the pile of pillows and picked up her book. She thought, "Good night John Boy! Where the hell did that come from?"

After she had turned her lamp off and was on the fringes of sleep she could have sworn she heard children's giggles coming from downstairs. "It's just the wine talking. Go to sleep old girl."

Chapter 12

It seemed like morning arrived much earlier than usual that day. The wine she had drank the night before was letting her know she had over indulged just a tad. She slipped on her robe and said to herself. "Coffee! I need coffee!"

She remembered she had forgotten to set up coffee the night before so she punched the button on the Keurig so she could have a cup "right now". While it was filling her cup, she made a fresh pot of coffee so it would be brewed and ready when Gypsy came downstairs. Just as it had sputtered out its last stream Gypsy entered the kitchen. She was dressed, hair in place, make-up applied and looked like she was ready for another day at the office. She was all chipper and chatty.

Gypsy hugged her friend and reached for a cup. "So what's on your agenda for today?" She picked up a slice of raisin bread and spread butter on it.

"How in the hell can you be so perky in the morning? And look at you. You're already dressed for the day. And, to answer your question. I'm going to talk with Tawnie's mother when they get here and see if she can do what I want done. But first I need to head upstairs and get some clothes on and do something with my hair."

Gypsy sat down at the little table and said, "I'll be right here."

She grabbed her coffee cup and headed out of the kitchen. It took Miss Savannah a bit longer than usual to get herself together, lining out in her mind just what she wanted to get accomplished today. She thought to herself, "Dang that wine! Kicks my butt every time." When she got back to the kitchen Gypsy was offering coffee to Tawnie, David and a mature duplicate of Tawnie.

Tawnie spoke up. "Miss Savannah. This is my mother, Jenny. Mother this is Miss Savannah."

Jenny smiled and the room lit up. "Nice to meet you, Miss Savannah. Tawnie has been telling me about you and how kind you've been to her and David. I appreciate it."

Miss Savannah had trouble concentrating on what Jenny was saying because her voice was like bubbles. She bubbled when she spoke. Immediately Miss Savannah felt better and peppy. Jenny was like a shot of happiness! "Just give me a few minutes and we'll talk about what I was asking Tawnie about yesterday."

Miss Savannah handed a list to Tawnie with the day's instructions on it. "When you finish your coffee … I remembered this morning that my mother's quilts still haven't been unpacked. I had one of the upstairs walk in closets lined with cedar to store them in. I'm sure the boxes are already in there so you shouldn't have to lift them or anything, just fold them to fit the shelves so they look nice."

"Yes Ma'am. I know the closet you're talking about. I'll get right to it."

"No rush. Go ahead and finish your coffee and there's raisin bread over there too if you want some."

"I think I'll pass but I appreciate the offer."

David had taken his coffee outside and was concentrating on the herb garden.

During the introductions and Miss Savannah giving instructions for the day, Gypsy's phone rang and she stepped out of the kitchen to take the call.

Tawnie rinsed out her cup and put it in the dishwasher and headed up the stairs with her list in her hip pocket.

Miss Savannah refilled her cup adding a generous splash of flavored creamer and turned to Jenny. "Sorry about that. I just needed to get things to going."

"No problem." She bubbled. "Having raised a houseful of kids, I know some things take priority over others."

"I swear when you talk you're like a bubble machine spouting bubbles of cheer and then they pop filling the room with happiness and sunshine!"

Jenny actually blushed. "Thank you. I believe in the power of positivity."

"Well, it certainly shows. Now. Did Tawnie explain to you what I need?"

"She tried but when she started I knew I'd have to talk with you about it in person. Computers were never her strong point." She laughed.

Miss Savannah found herself laughing too. "Well, bring your coffee and I'll show you. It'll be easier than trying to explain." They went through to the rooms filled with boxes. Miss Savannah turned the computer on and while it was booting opened the flap of the box on top. Noticing the computer was ready she pulled up a spreadsheet with all the data on it.

Jenny's eyes immediately scanned the screen and nodded. "I see what you're doing." She pointed to the information and began analyzing.

Miss Savannah took one of the books on top and opened it. "Now I have everything in here alphabetically by author, then title,..."

"Yes. I see two columns for price... current and original ..., publisher, edition information and just about everything pertinent to the edition."

"It's taken me a long time to get it this far and I know it's not near complete, plus I haven't updated current prices in forever. As a matter of fact most of them are still the original entry I made ... no telling when. So it's going to take some time and research to get the current values of the books. Just type in the new prices over the ones there. The cells aren't protected."

"I don't know if I'd do that or not. You know, type over them."

"Why not?"

"Because you'd be losing valuable data for comparative purposes. I think you'll need to keep that information for insurance purposes and pull a percentage when it's time to renew your policy. You know to see if you need to increase your coverage on them. See, you could just insert a column next to the current price listed, change the heading to reflect the year of the update. I'll need to protect that column so nothing can be typed over it and destroy valuable information. Then, when everything is entered and totaled at the bottom, you can pull your percentage of profit or loss for that year."

"Well, I had never thought of it that way."

"I really like the way its set up. Did you do this?"

Miss Savannah nodded. "At one time when I was working everything had to be prioritized, organized, and alphabetized. This spreadsheet is just one of many I created and kept up for years."

Jenny took her eyes from the computer monitor and asked, glanced at her "You do have them insured don't you?"

"Just along with my household contents."

"Oh, Miss Savannah, I think you need to rethink your coverage." Jenny paused. "I'm sorry. I may have let my mouth overstep my bounds again. I have a habit of doing that."

"No. No problem at all. What you said makes perfect sense. I don't mind someone speaking their mind if what they have is worth saying. And, what you said is logical and has merit." She was still holding the book in her hand. She laid the book on the computer desk and moved aside so Jenny could take a seat.

Jenny looked at the binding, spotted the author and typed in a search. "Hmmm. This one's not in here." She quickly inserted a row where it should be listed and began typing in the data. "Where do you get your current value from?"

"Oh there's a couple of sites I go to and take their market value. I put the list over there so you'd know which ones I use."

Jenny nodded. She glanced around and saw that she was connected to the web. A few quick keystrokes and she was at the first site. "Do you take the highest price or lowest? I've found this one, the edition, publisher and everything but there's more than one price."

"Well, it depends on the condition of the book. I've also printed out a copy of that for you."

Jenny looked around, spotted it and began reading. "Oh my. I never realized there was so much to it. This may take a while until I get used to it."

"Well, just do the best you can and if you have any questions, I'm not planning on going anywhere today. I think I just might bake something. I really haven't taken a day to just kick back in quite a while now. I'll be in the kitchen. Need a refill on your coffee?"

Jenny picked up her cup and finished it off. "I'm fine for now." She laughed and those invisible bubbles rose and began filling the area with happiness. "I love my coffee but if I overdo it, I'll be spending my time in the nearest bathroom." She laughed again.

"Well, why don't I just take your cup back with me? I'm headed that way anyway."

Jenny started to get up. "I can do it. Don't want to be any bother."

"No bother. Just see what you can do with all this mess of boxes. I can't wait to get all of those books on the shelves so we can appreciate them."

Jenny looked around and sighed. "Miss Savannah. This could take a long time."

"We've got time." She turned and disappeared into the kitchen.

Gypsy was sitting at the table with a worried look on her face.

"Something wrong?"

"I'm afraid so. It seems like a client isn't happy with some of the choices *she* made, mind you against my advice, and now wants them changed back to what I had planned. And, to top it off, she won't work with anyone but me so I can't send someone else to do it. And, to top *that* off she's refusing to make final payment until everything's to her liking."

"Oh no."

"I'm afraid so. I have so carefully planned everything so when I got here I could be here as long as it takes. Girlfriend, I've just finished making my flight reservation for this afternoon. If you don't mind, can I just leave my car here so I don't have to leave it at the airport?"

"Of course you can. Just park next to "Baby". I'll run you to the airport. What time is your flight?"

"I've already arranged that too. I have a couple of errands to run before leaving but I'll be back in a couple of hours and my ride should be here in plenty of time to get me to the airport."

"Need me to go with you? It's been awhile since you've been here in Tulsa. You still remember your way around?"

"Got it under control, Girlfriend. I've got the latest electronics in my car. Have to have as much as I'm on the road. Don't worry. I can find my way around. Besides that, don't you think you need to stick around until Jenny gets the hang of your system down?"

"Oh she's got everything under control too. Have you heard her laugh? It's the most wonderful sound I've heard in a long time. Pure happiness."

"Yes I did and I agree. I couldn't keep from smiling and I didn't even know what was going on."

"Yep."

Gypsy looked down at her watch. "I need to get going if I'm going to get everything done before my ride gets here. She picked up her purse and grabbed her keys. I'll be back in a little while."

Miss Savannah stood at the kitchen windows and watched Gypsy leave. "Wonder what business she already has in Tulsa?" she wondered to herself.

The morning passed quickly and by the time Gypsy returned the house was filled with the aroma of freshly baked apple pie and yeast rolls were rising on the counter. Rosemary rolls to be specific. She had experimented with the recipe until she had it perfected. The first time she had them was in a little restaurant in Portland, Oregon. Her favorite waitress would always put two or three of them in a to-go bag for her every time she ate there. The recipe was a secret but time and perseverance had finally won out. Now her rolls turned out exactly as she remembered.

Miss Savannah followed Gypsy to her room and sat on the side of the bed while she packed.

"Sure wish you didn't have to go."

"I know but I do. That's the price I pay for being in business for myself."

"I know."

"I'll be back in a few days, a week at the most. It shouldn't take more time than that." She picked up her Daytimer and glanced at her schedule for the next few weeks. "Damn!"

"What's wrong?"

"Market! Dallas furniture market is coming up and I really need to be there for at least a few days to see what's new. Tell you what. If you want to, I'll fly you down and we can do it together. You might see something you like and I can get it at a great price."

"Gypsy. Look at me! Do I look like I belong at a furniture market? You're the one that fits in. I'd stick out like a sore thumb."

"Don't talk like that, Girlfriend. You're as beautiful as ever and I know for a fact you've got a closet full of business suits that you never wear."

"You're right about the clothes, but I guess I've become ... well, I'm just more comfortable at home now."

Gypsy zipped her luggage shut just as they heard a horn honk in the driveway.

"Sounds like my ride is here."

They went downstairs and gave each other a quick hug. David appeared from nowhere and took her luggage. Another quick hug and Gypsy was on her way calling out "Caio Bella." Miss Savannah waved bye to her from the front portico. She thought, "Her name suits her, Gypsy."

Chapter 13

Making her way back through to the kitchen she paused to see what kind of progress Jenny was making. She noticed that there were books on the shelves. "On Jenny I don't want the books put on the shelves until they're entered and alphabetized."

Jenny looked up from the monitor she was concentrating on. "Those already are. I couldn't see any reason to put them back in boxes again, so I've been lining them up as I go. See. They're in order. When I get the A's finished I'll get David to come and put them on the top shelf for me. You do want to start on the top and work your way down, don't you?"

"Excellent idea! You've already got all these done?"

"Yes Ma'am. Most of them were already entered so all I had to do was update the pricing. It appears to be a significant increase in what I've done so far. Do you realize how much your collection could be worth?"

"You know, I've never thought of them as assets. They've just always been my friends and I feel like I've been entrusted to take care of them." She looked at Jenny and saw something in her eyes.

"I understand," was all Jenny replied. "I really do. You know a lot of these books I've read before. Oh, one more question. As I complete the A's and get David to put them on the shelves, don't you think I need to have him leave some extra space just in case something else shows up later that needs to be incorporated? And I know we need to leave a little wiggle room. It's not good to try to get them so tightly squeezed into a space. It can ruin the binding. What do you think? "

"I think you're absolutely right." She selected a book from the shelf and the minute she opened it the story started flashing through her mind like a movie. *"I just don't have time to spend with you right now. But soon!"* She replaced it. "It looks like you're coming along just fine in here. I've got rolls in the oven and it's just about time for them to come out."

"And they smell wonderful!"

"They do, don't they. Somehow bread baking in the oven always makes a house seem like a home no matter where you are." The phone rang and Miss Savannah went to the kitchen to answer it. She tucked it under her chin and grabbed a couple of oven mitts. "Hello."

"Girlfriend. It's me. Listen I forgot to leave the keys to my car. I'll have them over nighted to you when I get there."

"You don't have to do that. I've got "Baby" and my car if I need to go anywhere. Where are you anyway?" She was juggling the phone and trying to remove the hot baking pans from the oven at the same time.

"I'm at the airport and getting ready to board. I'd feel better if you had the keys, just in case."

She set the pans on a cooling rack. "Okay but ..."

"Gotta go! I'll see you in a few days. Caio Bella."

She placed the phone back on its base. She loved her "walk-about" phones as she called them. She had always detested the long cords that coiled and tangled and pretty much kept you anchored to one area when talking.

She made a pitcher of raspberry iced tea and was filling glasses with ice when Tawnie stepped into the kitchen.

"Miss Savannah, I found these in the bottom of one of the boxes when I was unpacking the quilts this morning." She carefully laid a stack of hand stitching on the table. "Did your mother do these too? If so, maybe you might think about having them framed. It's a shame to leave them stored away." She ran her fingers over the fine stitching. She laid one aside. "I think this sampler is my favorite."

Miss Savannah picked one up and looked at it closely. "My dear, I did these. There's a bunch of them already framed around here somewhere."

"You did these?"

"Sure did. That's when these old eyes would allow me to. I quit stitching years ago." She was picking each one up, examining it for a missed stitch and then laying it aside. "I sure enjoyed doing these. Stitching was my quiet time from my busy career. I didn't have to think about anything but the next stitch, then the next one. I could fill hours doing these."

"Everything's so perfect."

"Counted cross stitch is what it is … no pattern stamped on the fabric or anything… just a coded chart to follow. I guess it satisfied my perfectionist nature at the time yet allowed me my unwinding time." She restacked them carefully.

"So you want me to leave them out or repack them?"

"Just put them on one of the shelves in the quilt closet and I'll think about it. I don't know if they're worthy of framing or not. I didn't do them to display or anything. I did them because I enjoyed it."

Tawnie picked them up. "You know a thought just crossed my mind. I know you've set aside one of the rooms on the upper level for your sewing room so why not frame these and hang them in there?"

"I'll think about it. When you get those put away, I have raspberry iced tea ready. I think it's time for a break."

While she was pouring the iced tea her mind was working overtime trying to uncover her feeling of a kind of resentment. Then it registered. Unpacking her books was a pleasure she had wanted to do by herself at her own pace because no one else understood the value she placed on the written words of others. Books had been her friends since she was a child and would remain so until she could no longer hold a precious book in her hands and leaf through the pages and get lost in another world; a world someone else had imagined and carved out a time, a place, a story that lived in their mind for others to enjoy and in turn record in their own mind. But she had broken her rule this time. She was allowing Jenny to do what she had always done. Her only comfort was that Jenny seemed to love the books as much as she did. She could tell by the way she ran her hands over the covers and the way handled them. It was something you just couldn't fake.

When iced tea had been served and everyone was taking a break, Tawnie spoke up. "Miss Savannah, David got a call this afternoon from the employment agency. It seems they have a job for him that has possibilities of turning into full-time employment. They also said there would be insurance benefits too and we really need that with the kids."

"Children?" Miss Savannah's face illuminated. "You never told me you had children."

"Oh, yes Ma'am. We have four little boys. Three are in school now and doing so good."

"And the baby?"

"Oh he's not old enough so he goes to daycare at our church. I used to work there myself. It's right near the house within walking distance and the older boys ride the school bus."

"Oh my! You've got your hands full!"

"Anyway, Miss Savannah. I'm afraid this will be the last day David will be here so if you have anything special you need for him to do, just tell him and he'll take care of it. And there's another thing. We only have the one car. I think David can drop us off here before he goes to work but right now we don't know how late he's going to have to work."

Miss Savannah waited for her to continue.

"We can try that a few days and see if it's going to work out. I know for certain Mother and I will be here the rest of the week."

"Hmmm. Let me think about this. I don't want to lose any of you but I understand what David has to do. He has a wonderful family to take care of and the insurance is so important these days."

Miss Savannah glanced over to Jenny and there was almost a look of panic in her eyes. She knew Jenny couldn't afford to lose this bit of income nor did she want to lose Jenny. The one day she had been here had already brought so much joy into this house.

"Let me see what I can do."

Tawnie and Jenny nodded their heads. David ducked his like he was ashamed.

"David. Don't do that!" Miss Savannah said. "I understand. You've got to do what you can to support your family."

David spoke up, which was unusual. "I've been thinking that if there's things that you still need done, I can do them on weekends when I'm not working the other job."

Miss Savannah thought for a minute. "You're going to need your rest but I can use you on Saturday's and that'll leave Sunday so you can spend time with your family. That sound okay?"

He nodded and mumbled, "Thank you!"

The remainder of the afternoon passed in a strange silence as everyone was in deep thought about the new dilemma. When their day was finished Miss Savannah handed them a bag of rosemary rolls to have with their dinner. She had two different bags.

"You don't have to do that. And, you can put them all in the same bag. Mother's staying with us for a while."

Miss Savannah didn't know why this kind of shocked her but again, being around this little family she could tell they took care of each other. She admired them.

That night she had problems falling asleep. Even in her nest of pillows and a copy of one of Savannah Addison Allen's books "The Bungalow" in her hands, the book failed to bring forth the vivid description of Bora Bora. When she had read it before she could hear the waves splashing on the shore, see the tropical forest and the vibrant colors of hibiscus, and feel what the young heroine was going through. Tonight it was pages and pages of words. Words that wouldn't come to life for her. She finally dozed off but within hours was wide awake again. She looked at her clock. 3:00 am.

She had *that* feeling! Miss Savannah's insomnia was a bane. She'd wake up in the middle of the night knowing something was wrong but not know what. That's what she was experiencing again tonight. There was a horrible feeling deep inside that something bad had happened to someone or something in her life. It was a restlessness that sat in the pit of her stomach and brewed.

When insomnia gripped her like this it was usually foreshadowing something she really didn't want to face, that was going to hurt. She got up and checked everything in the house to make sure everything was alright She knew there were no problems inside her home. This night's episode would just not go away. She went downstairs and decided to do something constructive like polish furniture. How much noise can a can of Pledge make? She stood there with the can of Pledge in her hand. Deciding against cleaning, she put the Pledge back in the cleaning closet and started to catalogue the stack of books piled beside the computer but that didn't hold her attention. She knew if she kept busy, the sinking feeling should go away.

The next question that entered her mind was if she should go ahead and make coffee at 3:19 in the morning? A nice hot cup would taste so good but she would never be able to go back to sleep. Oh, to heck with it, she decided to do it anyway. Digging through her supply of little pods for the Keurig, she found some decaf and punched the button. Done! Now all she had to do was wait until she heard that unmistakable gurgling the coffee pot made when it ushered out the last bit of steaming brew.

She could tell right then that the upcoming day was not going to be one of her better days. First she'd make a call to her nephews and make sure everyone was okay then start checking with friends. She wouldn't rest until she found someone that was having a worse day than hers and that was responsible for this horrible feeling she had. She laughed at herself for this train of thought. *"Why does someone else have to be having a worse day than you for your feelings to be justified? Crazy old woman!"*

This had happened to her all her life though. Even as a child she'd wake up and know something was wrong (well, as wrong as a child's world could be.) Now at the age of seventy and counting there were so many people she loved dearly and didn't want anything to happen to them.

She heard the gurgling swoosh that indicated the coffee was ready so she headed back to the kitchen for a hot cup of "Joe". She had heard that in an old war movie the other day. "Cup of Joe"…

Leaning against the counter she wrapped her arthritic fingers around the coffee cup and taking the first sip of coffee she thought, *"Okay … I've killed twenty minutes so far. I don't have any idea how I can kill the remainder of the night?"* She headed back to her computer to see how much of a dent she could make on getting everything entered and organized. Setting her cup down on the desk she pulled up the spreadsheet and just sat there looking at it, with the cursor blinking at her. *"This is insane. Jenny is doing a perfect job so there's no need for me to touch anything."*

She put on some smooth jazz and lay down on the sofa just to relax for a few minutes. The next thing she was aware of was knocking on the back door.

Startled at her surroundings when she first opened her eyes, it took a few seconds before she was oriented. She knew she had overslept and Tawnie and Jenny were already there.

When Jenny saw Miss Savannah she put her hand on her shoulder. "Oh my goodness! Looks like you had a terrible night last night." Tiny sparks jumped and danced in the air from the touch. Jenny's words were barely heard because at her touch a surge of power flooded through Miss Savannah's body. It was like an electrical shock but instead of the pain associated with shock it was warmth and a healing energy had shot through her.

"What in the world was that?" Miss Savannah said rubbing her shoulder where Jenny had touched her.

Tawnie whispered quickly, "Mother, I told you to be careful. Not everyone understands."

Jenny's face glowed. "I'm sorry. I shouldn't have done that. It's just …"

"It's just that you have that healing power!" Miss Savannah was in awe. "I knew someone a long time ago that was blessed with that gift too. I saw her giving a massage one time and sparks flew into the air every time she touched the person. She used to have a portable massage chair and she'd visit people in their homes and "treat" them. She was such a special person. But it's sad that she couldn't heal herself."

Tawnie visibly relaxed when she realized Miss Savannah understood what had just happened.

Miss Savannah started a pot of coffee while talking. "I actually went to healing seminars in Alaska and was certified in healing practices but I don't think I've met anyone else besides Mary, that had the power you do. Mary was my friend's name. About the only thing I could do was work on joints. You know knees, elbows, ankles and shoulders. I could bring some relief to them but nothing like you just did. Guess I just wasn't ready for it at that time in my life. Wish I had been because I saw Mary do so many wonderful things for people."

"It seems like I always had it so some extent. It works better for someone that has an open mind and unquestionably accepts the healing power." Jenny paused gathering her thoughts. "You know …for someone that doesn't question it."

"I know. I also realize that a power like that has to flow from a pure soul and mind."

Jenny said, "Yesterday while we were here and I noticed you lit sticks of incense and placed them by all the entries to the house. I knew you were cleansing and protecting."

"Well, I can't remember a time I didn't. It's just something I believe in." Miss Savannah was feeling energy. "I need to shower and get dressed for the day. When the coffee's made help yourself. I'll be back in a few minutes." She paused in the doorway and said, "Tawnie, I made your list early this morning and it's over there on the table."

When she came back down, Jenny was already busy at the computer and Tawnie had disappeared from the kitchen which meant she had already started her work for the day.

Miss Savannah opened the little cabinet inside the butler's pantry and retrieved a set of keys. She walked across the driveway and slowly climbed the steps to the little apartment over the garage. Opening the door she stepped through into a perfectly appointed small living space. The pieces of furniture worthy of saving that had been found in the attic of the big house, she had sent out to have cleaned, shampooed and reupholstered and stored here, thinking it may come in handy someday. She walked around surveying what was there. Of course it needed to be stocked with kitchen and bathroom items but for the most part everything was there except for a bed. Sparsely as it was furnished, it would do for what was forming in her mind. She left, locking the door behind her. Holding tightly onto the rail she made her way back down the stairs. She breathed out a sigh of relief and subconsciously rubbed her right hip that always acted up when she attempted to climb a full flight of stairs.

When she got back to the house she located the anti-inflammatory medication her doctor had recommended and took two of them. She knew she was going to need it later on and it was best to stay on top of the discomfort.

Jenny didn't even look up from the monitor and her fingers were flying across the keyboard. Miss Savannah could hear Tawnie in the back of the house working to complete the list she had been given. She noticed the shelves of already entered books was growing and knew that by the weekend there would be enough to warrant David returning so he could climb the ladder and get them placed in their new home. She pulled a chair up next to Jenny to watch.

"Is there something wrong, Miss Savannah?" Jenny asked. "Are you okay?" Those wonderful bubbles spread into the room when Jenny spoke.

"Nothing that I don't think can be fixed. I have an idea if you want to listen for a few minutes."

Jenny finished entering the data she was in the middle of and folded her hands in her lap. "There now. I hate to quit in the middle of an entry." She smiled and the area around them lit up. "What's up?"

"Well, I've been thinking and I think I have come up with a solution."

Jenny was drawing a blank. "A solution to what?"

"Yesterday when you guys were getting ready to leave Tawnie said something about you staying with them"

"Yes Ma'am, I am."

"I don't mean to get personal or anything but is this by your choice or because you have to?"

"Ma'am. I really don't like to talk about things like that but since you asked, it's because I have to at this time. My husband passed away and shortly after that I lost my job at the corporate office. So finances were real tight. It got to where I couldn't pay my rent so I had to sell my car to make the last couple of rent payments, pay my utilities and finish paying the funeral expenses."

Miss Savannah slowly shook her head. "It's a shame. No. It's a dirty shame that you've lost everything while there are people out there not even trying to work and living off the taxpayer's money."

"I've tried and tried but I can't find a job that would pay much so I've been working at whatever I could find. You know convenience stores and places like that."

"At least you've been working. That's more than can be said about most people in your situation."

"Yes Ma'am, I have."

"Well getting back to why I've interrupted you. I just went out and took a look at the little apartment over the garage. It used to be servant's quarters but it's a nice little apartment and it's partially furnished. I thought..." She paused forming her thoughts because she didn't want to embarrass Jenny. She could tell Jenny was proud and didn't want her thinking that this offer she had planned was a hand-out. "Well, I thought if you wanted to … well, you might want to take a look at it and see if you'd like to move in to it. It's not very big. But I thought if you wanted it, that you could work part of the rent off working for me." Words rushed out of her mouth before she lost her nerve. "If you get another job, I'll understand. It's not going to be a freebie because I don't

73

believe in that. You'd have to pay something even if it's just a minimal amount."

A tear was threatening to spill down onto her cheek. "I can't expect you to do that! You don't even know me."

"Don't underestimate me. I'm a pretty good judge of character and from the minute you stepped into my kitchen I knew you were a special person."

"Besides that, there's no way I could ever afford anything in this area. I use to drive through this neighborhood when I was younger and dream of what it must be like to live in one of these houses. I'd drive the streets and try to catch a peek in windows to see how they lived, especially at Christmas time!"

"Don't say you can't afford it before you know the conditions. Just think about my offer. I don't expect an answer today. That apartment isn't going anywhere."

"Yes Ma'am, I'll be thinking about it."

"And another thing I was thinking about. There's no reason you couldn't take your meals here with me. I hate eating alone and it's so hard to cook for just one person. That's why the freezer is so full."

"The keys are in that little key cabinet inside the butler's pantry just in case you want to take a look before you decide." Miss Savannah scooted her chair back and moved it out of the way.

Jenny nodded.

On their lunch break Miss Savannah noticed that mother and daughter took the keys and headed across the driveway. She watched as they climbed the stairs with their sack lunches in hand and their heads close together in deep conversation. A while later she watched them descend the stairs with smiles on their faces. She couldn't help but notice how much they looked alike, the same flashing eyes, their smiles, even the way they carried themselves. They walked like proud, strong women. She stepped away from the window so they wouldn't think she was spying on them. She hadn't realized it but she had been standing there with her fingers crossed.

When they came in the back door Miss Savannah was slicing a banana to put on her peanut butter sandwich. Without turning around she asked, "Well, what did you think of it?"

Both of them started speaking at the same time talking over each other. Miss Savannah heard, "It's perfect! It's wonderful! It's great! It's just right!"

"But we still haven't discussed how much you want for it." Jenny said.

"That's because I haven't really thought of a price yet." Miss Savannah said as she was slicing her sandwich on half. Thinking a minute before she spoke, she finally said, "As you know I don't need the money for it right now. It would be more of a convenience to me to have you near for the next few weeks until the books are finished"

They stood there looking at her.

"Now what I was thinking is this. "I'll call Quinn and have him draw up some sort of agreement that states you have the first six months free, then you start paying a nominal rent, something you can afford."

"I could never do that! That just wouldn't be fair to you."

"You didn't let me finish. You can help with the household chores around here because I'm sure Tawnie's going to be placed in a position soon and she'll no longer be here to pick up after me and do the things she's been doing in addition to what she's hired to do. Now, Quinn will send you your check each week so you can support yourself and perhaps get caught up on everything. If the right position comes along that you feel you need to take, then at that time we'll just have Quinn write a rental agreement. I'll be fair on the rent. I know he's going to want to ask more but that's what he does." She laughed. "He's strictly business."

Mother and daughter glanced at each other again. Miss Savannah could tell that they were so close nothing had to be spoken. They nodded in agreement.

"Settled?"

They nodded again.

"Now. When do you want to move in?"

75

Jenny spoke. "Maybe Saturday? That is if it's okay with you. So far as we know David doesn't have to work that day and we could borrow his brother's pickup and move my things."

"David's not going to know how to act being able to get the car back in the garage." Tawnie chirped in.

Miss Savannah took a bite of her sandwich and chewed. "So we can consider it a done deal?"

"Oh yes!"

Chapter 14

Saturday arrived and the driveway was busy with David's pickup backed up to the apartment and people carrying boxes up the stairs. Miss Savannah had noticed them when she came down to enjoy her first cup of coffee that morning. She stood at the windows and watched them laughing and enjoying themselves in spite of the moving they were doing. She didn't think she had ever seen an entire family so filled with good nature.

After she dressed she loaded a tray with muffins and slices of different breads, even put a few bagels on it just in case someone didn't want anything sweet to snack on. She had fresh made iced tea brewed too but grabbed a tube of paper cups and paper saucers and piled them on top of the tray. When David saw her making her way across the driveway he hurried over and took the tray from her.

"Where do you want me to set it?"

"I thought you could take it upstairs and it would be handy for everyone when they needed a break. I have iced tea in the kitchen if you want to send someone over after it. I'm headed back to the house. It's too hot for me out here."

He nodded. "Be right over. You don't know how much this is appreciated."

"Well, just enjoy it."

He cleared his throat. "I don't mean just this food, I meant for everything you've done for our family. Thank you."

This surprised her because David had always been a man of few words. "You're so welcome. I'm always happy I could be there for you."

"Ma'am. You're like a God send to us." He ducked his head and said, "Things were beginning to look pretty bleak for me and my family, you know."

"Well, things are definitely looking up now."

"Thanks to you."

"Now if you're not careful, you're going to make this old woman blush." She reached out and patted him on his shoulder. "Now get those goodies up there so all of you can take a break. You've been at it since right after daylight."

"We didn't disturb you did we?"

"No. I didn't even know you guys were here until I came down for coffee. I noticed how much you had done and knew you had gotten an early start."

She turned and headed back across the drive. Calling over her shoulder she said, "Don't forget to send someone over for the iced tea."

A large moving van started backing into the driveway.

Miss Savannah raised her voice and called to David, "Looks like another load is here!"

"That's not for us. This was our last load."

The driver climbed out of the cab with paperwork in his hands. "Is this where Miss Savannah lives?"

"Yes. That's me."

"I have a delivery for you."

"But I'm not expecting anything." A quick thought flashed across her mind. *"I bet Gypsy has bought something at market and had it shipped ahead."*

She reached for the delivery papers. She scanned them and sure enough it was from Gypsy. *"Strange she hadn't called and let me know to be expecting something!"*

The driver flipped to the back of his clipboard and said, "I need to know where the master bedroom is. That's where this goes."

"Master bedroom?"

"That's what it says."

"Well the easiest way to access it is from the front of the house. I'll go through and unlock the door for you."

He got back in the truck and pulled back towards the street a bit so the unloading would be easier. He got back out and handed her an envelope. "Now I have these hand written instructions that I'm to read to you."

"What in the world. I never heard such nonsense."

"Well, that's my instructions. He started reading, "Girlfriend. Go to your herb garden and relax. I have everything under control. The driver will let you know when it's alright for you to come back into the house. Another thing. The driver should have an envelope for you. Don't open it until he comes and gets you. See you in a few days. Caio Bella."

David had been standing there through the entire conversation. He handed the tray to Tawnie and took Miss Savannah by the arm and led her to the herb garden and motioned for Tawnie and Jenny to come over and stay with her. "I'll go see what this is all about. Want to make certain this is on the up and up. Never hurts to make sure."

In a few minutes they heard David laugh. Puzzled, they looked at each other.

A small boy ran over and wrapped his arms around Tawnie's leg. "Mama, when can we have some of those cakes?"

Miss Savannah looked at the child. He was the spitting image of his father. "You hungry?"

He hid his face behind Tawnie's leg. She reached down and pulled him forward. "Don't be bashful now. Can you tell this nice lady your name?"

He shook his head.

"Now don't go being rude. Tell Miss Savannah your name then go get your brothers so all of you can have some."

He stepped forward and said, "My name is Dustin."

Miss Savannah leaned forward and said, "Nice to meet you Dustin. My name is Miss Savannah." She held out her hand and he placed his little hand in it and gave it a firm shake."

Tawnie smiled. "That's a good boy. Run and go get your brothers now."

Jenny had been sitting beside Miss Savannah admiring her grandson. "Wonderful children. I love them to pieces."

"Do you care if I let them set at the little table on the porch? They can make an awful mess if I let them carry their food around and eat it."

"Of course not. Go right ahead."

Jenny was already up and separating the paper plates and putting them on the table.

"There's iced tea in the house unless you want them to have milk. There's a brand new carton in the fridge." Miss Savannah called after her.

"I think milk would be best." She got four cups and went into the house. "I'll be right back." Jenny said.

Tawnie called out, "Dustin. You and your brothers get over here right now. Junior. You stop that and help Dustin. You hear me?"

When the boys made it to their mother's side Miss Savannah's was looking at a stair step of four little boys that looked like they had been stamped from the same mold… carbon copies of their father. "They look exactly alike!" Miss Savannah exclaimed.

Tawnie began starting with the tallest. "This is David. We call him Junior." She placed her hand on the next one's head. "You met Dustin a few minutes ago. This is Daniel and the little guy here is Douglas, however he refuses to answer to that so we call him Doug."

Jenny came out of the house with the paper cups turned upside down over the neck of the milk jug. "It seemed easier to do it this way than for me to try to juggle four cups." She laughed. "I'm not the most graceful person in the world." She laughed again and bubbles of happiness popped in the air. She motioned to the boys and they ran across the little expanse of lawn to the porch. "Now, let's see what Miss Savannah has here for you!" She passed the tray around and let each child point to what he wanted. She poured the milk and told them to set right there until she got back. She went back in the kitchen and placed the milk back in the fridge, returning with three glasses of iced tea. "I saw this setting there so went ahead and poured us some."

Miss Savannah asked, "Did you see what they were taking upstairs ... the movers?"

Jenny shook her head.

The boys settled in to eating and were allowed seconds. Miss Savannah had forgotten how much energy children had. She found that she was enjoying watching them pick at each other's food and argue over who had the largest muffin or who could take the largest bite. They all four had milk mustaches and all four of them ended up wiping those mustaches on their shirt sleeves.

The mover at last came around the corner of the house and headed their way. Miss Savannah had been sitting there with the envelope in her lap. Watching the children she had forgotten about it. She looked up at the driver and picked the envelope up. "Now?" she asked.

He nodded.

Upon opening it the first thing she saw was another envelope inside and a folded note. She unfolded the note and fifty dollars fell into her lap. She began to read. "The money is a tip for the movers since they usually don't work on Saturday's I kind of promised them something a little extra." She handed the note to the driver along with the money. He nodded thanks but didn't leave. She slipped her finger under the flap of the inner envelope and opened it. She pulled out the card. "Happy Birthday, Girlfriend!" Inside was a personal note. "I know you never remember your own birthday and I wanted this one to be special for you. The driver will now take you upstairs so you can start enjoying what has been waiting for you ever since the first time you saw it. Love You! Caio Bella."

"What's the date?" she asked.

"It's the twenty first of June. The first day of summer."

"Well, I'll be darned! It is my birthday! Let's go see what Gypsy has been up to now!"

Jenny and Tawnie were just as curious as she was. Tawnie said, "Mother, you go on ahead with Miss Savannah. I'll stay here with the boys. I can see later."

"Miss Savannah replied, "Nonsense. Bring them along."

"But they're dirty and have food all over them."

"Like that house hasn't had dirt in it before? Now bring them along."

So together they were escorted by the driver to the upstairs. Miss Savannah and the driver took the elevator while the boys raced up the stairs in front of their mother and grandmother.

The elevator door slid open and she looked around waiting for the driver to indicate to which room she should go. He led her to her bedroom and when she stepped in there was the white Italian bedroom suit that Gypsy had purchased on one of their shopping sprees. That had been years ago. "Oh my word! It's still as beautiful as I remembered it being but I know Gypsy loves it even more than I do." She was walking around running her hands across the pieces of furniture and noticed that the bedding was even there and on the bed.

Tawnie and Jenny were holding a child with each hand to keep them from running around the room. The boys didn't know why all this fuss was being made over a place to sleep. Tawnie's and Jenny's eyes were tearing up.

"It's beautiful!" Tawnie said.

Jenny's words were. "It's very special isn't it Miss Savannah?"

"Yes indeed."

Miss Savannah noticed a piece of paper on the dresser. She picked it up and there was a drawing of her bedroom and where each piece of furniture was to be placed. It was initialed by the large flowing G that Gypsy always used. She looked closer at it and it was dated the day Gypsy had to leave. "So this was the errand she had to run! Wait till I get her on the phone!"

"Everything to your liking?" the driver asked.

"Everything! Thank you so much."

"When you talk to your friend would you thank her for us too?" He held up the fifty dollars.

"I sure will! And thanks again."

He turned to leave.

Miss Savannah said, "Just a minute. What did you do with the bed that was in here?"

"Put it in an empty bedroom down the hall."

"Want to make another tip?"

"Sure. What you got in mind."

"Take the bed that was in here and move it to the apartment above the garage."

Jenny gasped. "You can't do that. I was planning on sleeping on the sofa. That's good enough."

"You're going to stand there and tell me you'd rather sleep on a sofa when there's a perfectly good bed just being stored in an empty room here? Besides that, I would have to put a bed in there anyway sooner or later. It just so happens it's going to be sooner."

"But you've already been so generous."

Miss Savannah nodded to the driver and they proceeded as per instructions. And, indeed a very generous tip was tucked in the driver's shirt pocket when they finished. She had convinced him to load up the empty book boxes and take them away too.

The driver smiled to Miss Savannah and said to his helper, "These crazy people. Never know what they're going to do next!" He pulled out of the driveway and headed back to the closed office.

The rest of the afternoon was spent with Jenny and Tawnie getting the apartment in order. Miss Savannah spent hours on the phone with Gypsy and ended her call hearing her friend say "Sleep tight. Caio Bella."

And she did that night. To her the whole house felt like it was relaxed.

Chapter 15

Sunday morning arrived hot and sultry. Over the years she had grown used to it but the humidity still sapped her strength. Before it got too hot she took her coffee out to the herb garden. It had become kind of a ritual to her to go outside in the mornings and enjoy listening to the world wake up. As she had gotten older though, greeting the day at daylight had slowly slipped. Now it seemed like the day greeted her instead of her greeting it. Occasionally she still was able to get up and around so she could watch the sunrise paint the sky with its glow but not as often as when she was young.

Memories of her youth crept into her mind. She reached up and ran her finger across the wrinkles that had etched themselves in her once smooth skin. She'd be kidding herself if she said she honestly liked them but that's how life had chosen to sketch her experiences and adventures. She was sitting there sipping her coffee and reminiscing and was startled when she felt something touch her shoulder. She knew immediately it was Jenny when she felt and heard the tiny sparks of energy surge through her body.

"I didn't mean to startle you." Jenny chimed. "You didn't answer me when I called to you and I wanted to make sure you were okay."

"Oh. I'm just fine. I was just lost in thought."

"Everything's okay then?"

Miss Savannah nodded. "What's that you got there?"

"It's a hummingbird feeder. When I was unpacking I found it and was wondering if you would care if I hung it over here by the herbs. I love to watch them and thought you may enjoy them too while you have your coffee in the morning."

"Well, that's awful thoughtful of you."

Jenny pointed to a low hanging limb she could reach. "Maybe if I hang it here?"

"That'd be fine."

Jenny reached up to loop the hanger over the limb and the sweet red liquid splashed on her tee shirt.

"Here. Let me help you. You're going to get that all over you."

"If you'd steady the bottom I think I can reach up far enough to hang it out of the way."

Between the two of them they got it placed and almost before Miss Savannah could get back to her chair a tiny iridescent bird dropped out of nowhere and poked its long beak into the flower shaped feeding opening. Another swooped down and to her surprise the first one let out a loud chirp of warning and a battle for territorial rights began. It was like watching two kaleidoscopes of color shimmering in the air.

"They're beautiful!" she exclaimed.

Jenny smiled. "I'll leave you now and let you enjoy them."

"You don't have to go. I have coffee made if you want to get a cup and join me."

"Miss Savannah. I don't want to take up your time. You don't have to entertain me, plus I have things I can be doing."

"You almost unpacked?"

"It's getting there. Tawnie did so much for me yesterday that all's that's left is just a few things. When she gets something in her mind there's no stopping her and it seems like she was intent to get me settled in yesterday. She's always been like that though. Even when she was a little girl she had that take charge attitude." She laughed and the world was happier.

She smiled. "I could tell that about her the first day she was here. I took a liking to her right away. You mentioned the other day that you have other children."

"Yes Ma'am. I have six. Tawnie is the third oldest."

"Oh my goodness! You weren't kidding when you said you had a houseful."

"Nope. I'd not kid about something like that!"

The shimmering little hummingbirds were battling over the feeder again. They filled the area with a rainbow spatter of tints and hues.

"Just look at those little guys! They're something else!" Miss Savannah said. "God created such wonderful things for us to appreciate."

Jenny could tell that Miss Savannah was enjoying watching them. "He sure did."

"So do your children all live here?"

"Most of them. They're all grown and have lives of their own so I don't get to see them as often as I like and some need more love than the others."

Miss Savannah glanced over to her and decided not to say anything.

"You know it seems like the ones that are the hardest to love are the ones that need my love the most. Just wish I could do more for them but I can't. Some things you can't do for them. They have to do for themselves."

"Those are very wise words that you just spoke."

"Well. It's taken me a long time to realize it."

Miss Savannah thought it time to switch the subject. "Those boys of Tawnie's and David's are the cutest little children and they seemed so well behaved for them being so close together in age and everything."

"Yes they are. They've done a good job with them."

"You have any other brothers and sisters? I never hear you speak of them."

Jenny paused and thought a moment like she was trying to make a decision. Then she spoke. "Not blood siblings that I know of. You see, I was adopted so I don't know for certain. I've often wondered."

Miss Savannah nodded understanding.

"Miss Savannah, do you have any? Brothers and sisters, I mean?"

"Unfortunately, no. I was an only child back when being an only child wasn't, shall we say, fashionable."

"Really?"

"Yes. My mother always wanted more children but it just never happened so she spent her life taking care of me."

"Bet you were spoiled rotten!"

Miss Savannah shook her head. "Quite the opposite. I think Mother was determined that I not be a spoiled brat, if you know what I mean. We were poor but at that time I didn't realize it because all Mother and Dad's friends and family were in the same boat as us. And as it turned out, maybe it was a good thing that I was the only one. Time and circumstances have a way of making everything right."

Jenny noticed that Miss Savannah's coffee cup was empty and she had set it aside. "Can I get you more coffee? I'd be glad to."

"If you don't mind. I would like just one more cup but I can get it myself."

"Nonsense. I can do it. If I hadn't wanted to I wouldn't have asked. You just set right there and enjoy watching the hummingbirds. I'll be right back."

While Jenny was pouring coffee she looked around at her surroundings and wondered how a child raised poor could have all this. It puzzled her but she knew in time Miss Savannah would tell her if she wanted her to know. She opened the fridge and poured a splash of creamer in the cup as she had watched Miss Savannah do.

"Here you are." She said holding the cup out to Miss Savannah waiting for her to wrap her hands around the cup. "Maybe it'd be better if I just set it back on the table so you can get hold of it the way you want. I sure don't want to spill hot coffee on you. By the way I went ahead and turned the pot off while I was in there. Hope you don't mind."

"Not at all. You are so thoughtful." She pointed to the feeder. "I think that one is a little female. See? Her feathers aren't as bright as the other ones."

"Yep. I bet she has a nest around here somewhere."

"By the way, I have a pot roast laid out and thought you might come over later and have dinner with me. When I go in, I'll stick it in the oven and later put some carrots and potatoes in with it so they can soak up all that good flavor."

"Sounds wonderful but you don't have to do that."

"I know I don't have to, but like I told you I hate to eat alone. It'd be a pleasure for me."

"Did your mother teach you to cook?"

"Oh yes she did! There wasn't a finer cook I know of. You know, since a child, I have memories of everyone gathering at our house for dinners. Be it for one or twenty one, there was always more than enough food to go around, even in the leanest of times. Mother had a way a splitting a penny four ways and saving part of it for rougher times. Her economizing, bartering, preserving foods and "just in case" methods always assured a well set table.

"Unexpected guests could appear at the door and within an hour there was food on the table. She would get everyone set with a glass of iced tea then disappear while guests visited with my father. She would go out back and wring the neck of a chicken and get it on frying, and she always saved the soft under feathers for pillows. Then she'd whip up a batch of homemade biscuits; open a jar of green beans and new potatoes and get them boiling with a seasoning of bacon grease; clean a few green onions and radishes from the garden; and make a pan of her famous cream gravy. A meal fit for a county king was on the table. Plus she would throw together a plain cake as she called it and top it with canned peaches for dessert. Of course there were always several different jellies to go on the hot biscuits too. That woman knew her way around a kitchen and boy, could she cook!" Miss Savannah paused to take a sip of coffee.

Jenny knew Miss Savannah was talking about someone she adored and loved dearly. She nodded and continued listening without interrupting.

"On holidays she knew everyone's favorite dessert and when her guests arrived, the wonderful sweets were already prepared and waiting to be served. She would bake, not for just one, but for everyone. She used the top of her chest freezer to set the finished desserts on and it was always filled with cakes, pies, cookies, and breakfast cinnamon rolls with no room for anything else. My mother spent hours and hours measuring, mixing and creating the delectable desserts, and on arrival, a trip straight through the house to view the desserts was in order. She took so much pride in her cooking and baking. However, she did have little secrets that cut her preparation time. For example, she would prepare a huge pot of plain vanilla flavored custard. Then she would take out enough for one pie, flavor it with chocolate, fill the pie shell, top it with meringue and get it in the oven. Then she would repeat it with coconut, drained pineapple or any variety of flavors and do the same. All her base filling was prepared at once, then it was just a matter of flavoring each, pour it into the prepared shell, top it and pop it in the oven. She could make half dozen pies in the length of time it took me to make one.

"Since she was raised on a farm in southern Oklahoma and was taught, at an early age, to prepare meals "from scratch" for a large family, it was just second nature to cook, and in large amounts. Farm home-style cooking was her forte. This really becomes evident in her canning recipes.

"I grew up enjoying mother's cooking. Be it fresh from the garden, freezer or opening a jar of canned food, it was always a treat to set down at her table. When she was canning she would tease me about whether I was helping her can green beans and new potatoes or new potatoes and green beans. The difference was which vegetable was layered on bottom and which was on top. Many an hour was spent helping string and snap green beans, shelling peas and scraping new potatoes, getting them ready to put in jars and the pressure cooker.

"Searching through the stored canned goods for a jar of Mother's apple butter was something I never minded doing. When Mother made apple butter, the house was filled with the aroma of the bouquet of spices, apples and sugar that set the mouth to watering. The apple butter was so thick from long hours of cooking it down to that consistency, and was so dark from the spices. One of my favorites was to fill a fresh baked jellyroll with this wonderful treat. Store bought could never compare with the apple butter mother made. So far my searches through her recipes have not unearthed that recipe. Somewhere in heaven, the angels are probably smiling down on us because they are eating Mother's apple butter every morning."

Jenny had leaned back against the bench and was enthralled with Miss Savannah talking about her mother.

Miss Savannah wrapped her fingers around the coffee cup as if she was trying to absorb the heat into her hands.

"You know, I realize some of those recipes are not as she prepared them. Her written recipe was only a basis for her cooking. She always cooked by taste. So, even though I have the recipes as they were in her collection, they may not taste just exactly like they did when she prepared them. Then again, they may not taste the same because the little pinch of love, that she always added in all of her cooking, is not there now. That's not an ingredient you can buy. It has to come from the heart.

"There are recipes that are missing from her collection too, recipes that she prepared from memory that she never wrote down. Like her biscuits, bread pudding, apple butter and pancakes. Those, I'm sure, are somewhere in cooking heaven. Maybe somewhere up above she's there whipping up a batch of those heavenly biscuits that opened in the middle without having to cut into them and serving them up with apple butter. Her biscuits were always made in man-sized proportions. Mother didn't believe in tiny, little servings of anything. If you were going to eat at her table, you ate like you had not had anything to eat in a week. No one ever got up from her table hungry. If you did, it was your own fault.

"I use the word 'heaven' as to where she is because, in my mind, there was never a kinder or more considerate person I have ever known. Even when she was so ill and in pain, she never deliberately spoke an unkind word. She was concerned that everyone around her was not getting enough rest or that they were hungry. And yes, in the delirium of drugs to ease her discomfort, she offered her guests something; a piece of pie, a slice of cake or something to eat."

Miss Savannah paused again and was quiet.

Jenny knew Miss Savannah was still mourning, that she always would.

"I'm sorry, Jenny. I didn't mean to bother you with an old woman's reminiscing. It's just that it feels good to talk about Mother sometimes. She was such a special person."

Jenny leaned forward. "Believe me. It wasn't a bother at all. I enjoy hearing about her and I can see where you got your love of cooking. It would have been impossible to not."

Miss Savannah sighed. "I still miss her."

"You always will. Do you look like her?"

"Well, she was short, blue eyed and had blond hair and a kind of warmth filled the room when she walked in. All I can say is that I'm short and female." She laughed. "My father had the dark eyes and olive complexion like me."

Jenny noticed beads of perspiration had formed on Miss Savannah's face. "Think it's getting a bit too hot out here to stay much longer?"

"I suppose it is but I sure enjoy watching those little hummingbirds. I just hate to go inside."

"I'm not certain but I think you can probably watch them from the windows in the kitchen. Want to go check it out? Oh, and I've still got a package of the mix so I can keep the feeder filled for quite few days yet." Jenny reached out to take Miss Savannah's elbow to help her get steady on her feet. "Looks like that hip is bothering you this morning."

"Dang old hip! Sometimes it's a nuisance. It's just getting old like me." She smiled and for some reason reached out and laid her hand against Jenny's cheek.

When they got in the kitchen Jenny went over to the windows and looked out to see if Miss Savannah was going to be able to see the hummingbird feeder. It was visible but the little birds were flitting around so fast you could hardly see them. She turned around to Miss Savannah and said, "Sorry. I thought sure you'd be able to see them from here."

"That's okay. Some things are meant to be pleasurable in their own environment."

Jenny started towards the back door. "I'm going to head back and get a few more things taken care of before it gets too hot."

"Isn't the air conditioner working?"

"It's working just fine. I just hate to use it more than necessary."

"Why?"

"'Because the electric bills can get out of hand in the summer if I don't watch it."

"That's all and well but you need to be comfortable. Hear? And you are going to be here for dinner tonight?"

"Yes Ma'am." Jenny left and pulled the inner door closed behind her.

Miss Savannah went to the sink and pulled the wrapping from the pot roast and started getting spices from the pantry. She reached over and turned the oven on and busied herself getting tonight's dinner to going. It felt so good to know someone was going to be there for dinner. While she was preparing the roast she realized that she did get lonely sometimes.

Chapter 16

With the roast in the oven and nothing planned for the remainder of the day Miss Savannah decided to go up and take a look at what cartons had been taken to the top floor. She had some ideas and wanted to see if they were feasible or if she should just forget them. Over the years she knew that's exactly what she should have done in some instances. On the way up she stopped the elevator on the bedroom level to make up her bed. When she woke up this morning all she could think of was coffee. *"Maybe I should bring the Keurig up to the dressing room."* She thought. Then, immediately dismissed the idea. *"If I do that, I'd never make it downstairs. I'd be spending all my time up here in bed reading and sipping coffee."* She straightened the covers on her bed and smoothed the comforter.

She wandered down the hallway to the cedar lined linen closet and opened it to take a look. There on the shelves were all her mother's hand make quilts. There were a couple of the ones she had made too. It felt good to see them intermingled, hers and her mother's. She ran her hand across the fine stitching her mother was known for. She took the 'Dove in a Window' quilt down and carried it back to her room and spread it out on the bed to admire it. It brought back bittersweet memories. Her mother had made three of them, one for her best friend, one for herself and had given the third one to Miss Savannah. Her mother's had been displayed on an easel by her coffin along with flowers. After all the well-wishers and friends had departed, the quilt had been placed over her mother before the lid was closed. That was the last time she had laid eyes on her mother. It had broken her heart.

She reflected and her mind took on the narrative quality it always did when she was alone, like she was telling a story to someone.

"Some of my very first memories are of spending time with Mother and grandmother while they stitched away the hours to create beautiful quilts. These two special ladies had unintentionally imprinted a lasting impact in my young mind. Being an only child, I was allowed to play in their *scrap boxes* to keep me occupied while they quilted. This was my babysitter and my toys. Oh how I remember sorting the pieces of fabric into little stacks of the same color, tying them around my doll to make her a new dress; if a piece was large enough, I'd tie it around myself for an apron. I would get so frustrated when I would lay pieces side-by-side and try to push them together with my little hands to make them stay like mother and grandmother's fabrics did. Sometimes mother or grandmother would let me play with a quilt block and I would use it for a make-believe tablecloth to serve tea to my doll. I could spend hours occupying myself with these scraps of cloth. I was fascinated by all the patterns and colors of the fabrics. To me it was like I was in the midst of a living kaleidoscope where I could actually touch the colors and feel the different textures. I watched as my mother and grandmother made wonderful designs from the bits and pieces of fabric.

"Finally when I was allowed to help, I remember sitting on a little stool to the back side of my grandmother's treadle sewing machine and clipping the pieces apart as they were sewn together and slipped over the edge of the sewing machine cabinet to where I could reach them. I then placed the sewn sections into a shoebox and when it was filled to the brim, my grandmother would press them open and then join those together. By repeating this over and over she could create the most wonderful pattern I had ever seen. I was absolutely fascinated by this. Watching her feet making the treadle teeter-totter, the belt going round and round and listening to the steady rhythm as she stitched was so peaceful. It was something I have never been able to experience in my adult life even in the best of times. To a youngster just beginning to notice what was going on in the world, it was a totally tranquil and secure experience.

"Quilting also provided an early education. I knew all my colors at a very young age because mother and grandmother were patient enough to tell me what color the scrap of cloth was each time I would bring one to them. This game must have got terribly tiring for them, but I knew when enough was enough. I realized if I ever wanted to make a quilt of my own I would have to know how to count, so I listened and watched and before long I could count to nine. My first block was a Nine Patch. I learned to recognize the words *Print* and *Solid* and that triggered the interest in reading. Under my mother's tutelage, I was reading, spelling and counting long before I started to school. Very basic geometry was also a part of my quilting education. My grandmother had no idea what an angle was or at what degree it was set in, but she taught me the common sense way of making everything fit together correctly. All these subjects came easier for me in school as I had been taught the basics from the time I was a very young child. My classroom had been my mother and grandmother's sewing rooms.

"I felt like I had reached a milestone when at last I was permitted to actually help select the pieces of fabrics for a new quilt top and press them for cutting. Now, you must realize, most of these quilts were not color coordinated, did not have a single piece of *store bought yard goods* in them, or much prior planning as to how they were going to look once they were completed. These quilts were intended for *everyday use*. At that time quilting was not a hobby nor were the quilts and comforters intended to serve as *décor accessories*. They were a vital part of our livelihood. These hand-made quilts were made to provide warmth and were intended to serve a very utility and necessary purpose.

"My grandmother did not own a television until just a few years before her death. She did not have time to *just sit around wasting time with nonsense.* Her time was spent at her treadle sewing machine stitching together all the tiny pieces into quilt blocks and sashing them together for another top. Her companion was her radio. We listened to

Young Doctor Malone, Inner Sanctum, The Lone Ranger, Red Rider, Amos and Andy, Fibber McGee & Molly and other programs long forgotten in my mind. She could listen to the radio and not have to look up from her needlework. We would spend hours carding cotton, laying the smooth white fluff on the lining secured in the frames, placing the completed top over this and basting everything together. I was allowed to help pick the seeds out of the cotton so mother and grandmother could do the carding. Only later in her life did she purchase batting and *yard goods* for her quilts.

"She lived in a one-room house so space was at a minimum. The quilting frames were suspended from the ceiling by cords that were connected to eye hooks in the ceiling then to each corner of the frame. When she was finished quilting for the day, she would wind up the cords, which raised the frame to ceiling height, out of the way.

"Since money was in short supply around her house, her tops and quilts were an excellent means of bartering and proved time and again to get her through another tough time. As my cousins and I were growing up, we anticipated Christmas and birthdays, hoping for one of our grandmother's quilts. She saw to it that each of us received one but only after we were responsible enough to take care of it. The quilt I received, as a wedding present was a hand appliqued blue satin tulip quilt. She appliqued using the blanket stitch method.

"I must add a very interesting item here. My grandmother was illiterate. Being born on the Indian Reservation in southern Oklahoma and not attending any school, she could neither read nor write, with the exception of recognizing her name and making her "X". But she had the gift of being able to look at a pattern and mentally figuring the yardage needed for an entire quilt to within a few inches. She used the measurement "from tip of nose to fingertip" to estimate her yardage. She had the capacity to look at a quilt block then take scissors and cut a pattern from paper that was more accurate than the ones I spend hours over the drafting table scaling. To this day I envy her ability to master this feat in spite of the disadvantage of illiteracy. My grandmother quilted right up to the time she became critically ill and passed away in 1966.

"My mother pieced and quilted, especially during the winter until her death. Also being an avid gardener, the spring and summer each year are involved with planting, nurturing and preserving the produce her garden provides each year. But, even those spring and summer evenings were filled with her handwork. She firmly believed, "if you keep your hands and mind busy, you won't have the time to cause problems". Idleness sows the seeds of dissension. Beside her place in the living room there was always a quilt or two in the making and a few sample blocks of new patterns. Paper and pencil were always close at hand in order to jot down sketches and ideas that had come to mind for future projects and most of the time a quilt is in a nearby frame. Mother was a traditional quilter through and through. Being of Irish descent, she had the perseverance, patience and diligence of very few people I have met in my lifetime. The more intricate patterns and tiny pieces only put her tenacity to the test. Her hands grew arthritic and bothered her, but even the last quilt she quilted she maintained the 12 stitches per inch.

"She always had a supply of emergency quilts on hand. These quilts were usually heavy comforters that were tacked-out. "They may not be beauties, but they are warm and warm doesn't have to be pretty" was her comment. If she could only have realized that the "beauty" was there in the thought. If one of the residents in her small community had a house fire or if there was a new baby born, a quilt was in order for the family.

"During my last visit, there were almost twenty new quilts. These quilts had never been slept under and were folded and put aside for gifts, emergencies and some were very special which she would not part with. Not only did my mother make the traditional pieced quilts; she also appliqued and embroidered. She had marvelous creations and each visit warranted the time to take them all down, unfold them and admire the finest handwork in that area of the state. She had the blue ribbons from the county fair to prove her skills. These she was so very proud of, but her true pride was in her work. "Anything worth doing is worth doing right" was something she lived by when it came to her quilting. Her Irish grandmother was also a devoted quilter. Our visits to her always included a look at her latest endeavors and then the exchange of the latest patterns.

"My wedding gift from my mother was six quilts and a crocheted bedspread."

Tears brimmed in her eyes and threatened to spill onto her cheeks. Miss Savannah reached out and pulled the quilt over herself and lay there for a long time. It was like her mother was wrapping her arms around her and comforting her. After a while she sat up and refolded the quilt and stored it back in the closet. *"What's gotten into you today, old woman? It's not like you to get so sentimental! You best pull yourself together!"*

She didn't make it to the upper floor. She decided to go back down to the kitchen and bake. She didn't know what but she'd pull out the recipe books and find something that sounded yummy and was time consuming. She had all afternoon. She stopped and slid a CD in the player and headed on to the kitchen. Lively reggae music filled the house and she couldn't help moving her body to the rhythm. She made an iced coffee, pulled several books from the bookcase and piled them on the table. She found a recipe in the 'Southern Living Cookbook' and began assembling the ingredients from the pantry. In a short while a torte was in the oven and the house began filling with the wonderful aroma of chocolate. She loved having double ovens!

Jenny popped in later that afternoon to see if she could do anything. When she opened the door she heard the music and began dancing around. Miss Savannah and Jenny bobbed around the kitchen laughing like two children. When the tune finished Miss Savannah plopped into one of the chairs. "Oh Jenny, I can't remember the last time I acted a fool like that!"

"That's not acting a fool. That's just letting things flow. It's good for you!"

"I guess so but it sure did take my breath away. Look at me. I'm panting and sweating like I don't know what."

Jenny saw Miss Savannah was a bit flushed but also knew she was okay. "What smells so good? I could smell chocolate all the way outside."

"Just a little something I decided to cook up. I needed to bake this afternoon."

"Is there anything I can do to help with dinner?"

"Actually I have everything ready except the salad. The roast is resting and when I put it on the platter I'll make a little gravy with the drippings."

Jenny had stepped to the fridge and was removing the makings for the salad. "Where's the salad bowl?" Miss Savannah started to say something but Jenny said, "Never mind. I think I know. Tawnie told me about the dish room." She opened the door. "Ah ha! Just as I thought. Got it!"

Between the smell of chocolate, the reggae music playing and Jenny's effervesce of happiness bubbles bursting in the air Miss Savannah found she was delighting in the mood.

"I have to ask." Miss Savannah said. "Are you always this happy?"

"Not always but most of the time. This is just me being me." She rinsed the lettuce under the running water in the sink and put it aside to drain. "There's so much negativity and stuff out there that I can't see contributing to it. Why do that to yourself? Our higher power didn't intend for it to be that way." She picked up a tomato. "Do you like yours peeled or do you want me to just chop it up like Mother Nature made it?"

"Doesn't matter to me." Miss Savannah cleared the cookbooks from the table and put them away. She opened the dish room door and in a couple of minutes came back with plates and bowls. She pulled back the foil covering the roast and removed the roast and veggies to a platter she had already set out. "I'll just put these drippings in a saucepan and thicken them up and I think we'll be ready to eat. Want to grab the bread board and put that loaf of bread on it? I decided to reheat a loaf of that Rosemary bread I made the other day. Thought it'd go good with dinner."

"There's enough food here to feed an army."

"Yes. I've been told that before but when you love to cook it's hard to not overdo it."

"Miss Savannah, you want iced tea to drink?" Jenny had glasses set down and filled with ice.

"I think just some bottled water."

The food was on the table and they sat down.

Miss Savannah picked up her fork and started to eat when she looked over to Jenny. She was sitting there with her head bowed. Miss Savannah laid her fork down and reached her hand across the table and slowly slipped it into Jenny's.

Chapter 17

The next couple of weeks seemed to fly by. Almost every day Gypsy was calling and telling her that another shipment was on its way and that she'd take care of them when she got there.

More than one time Gypsy had said, "Oh Girlfriend this is just perfect!"

And more than one time Miss Savannah had asked, "Do you need me to transfer funds? This has got to be costing a small fortune."

"Don't worry about it. Got everything under control and it's not costing what you'd think. Sure wish you were here with me."

"Have fun and don't make a pauper out of me." Miss Savannah would reply.

"Gotta run. Trying to get things wrapped up so I can head that way. Love you! Caio Bella."

The day arrived when the shipments started to arrive. Miss Savannah got to where she knew the delivery men by first name. There were always tags on the cartons indicating which room they should be placed. Gypsy was certainly organized and efficient.

Jenny, Tawnie and she were having to weave their way through the rooms around the cartons that were growing in number each and every day.

Once Jenny got the hang of cataloging the books, it seemed like she was flying through boxes every day. And, since the delivery men were there so often, a tip insured that the empty boxes were loaded and hauled away. The shelves began filling and the transformation of the empty room into a library began. David was there each Saturday to place the books on the upper shelves as he said he would. During the week Jenny could fill the lower ones. She always had them in order so all David had to do was move them to where they were going to live. Tawnie was always there to supervise. "David, there's too many on that shelf. Leave some wiggle room. Miss Gypsy might want to set something there when she gets here and you don't want to have to start all over again."

David would nod in agreement and follow her directions.

While Tawnie and David were busy, Jenny captured the time to spend with her grandsons. Miss Savannah could hear her outside talking to them about school and other things young boys liked to talk about. One time she glanced out the kitchen windows and saw Jenny and all four boys down on their hands and knees looking for something under one of the shrubs. A few minutes later she saw the boys looking in Jenny's hands which were cupped around something.

Junior came running into the house. Tawnie had grabbed him by the arm. "You know you're not supposed to run in the house!"

"But Grammy caught us a lizard. Can we take him home? Please!"

Jenny was setting down on the bench with the other three boys around her.

"Please, mama!"

"Do you think the other lizards in the terrarium will like him? We sure don't want anything to happen to him."

"Junior's head bobbed up and down. "He'll be okay. Remember when we put that other one in there?"

"Well, okay but you need for Grammy to find a box or something to put him in."

Junior started to run then slowed down. But, the minute the door closed behind him he was in a full run. Miss Savannah could tell by the reactions of the brothers that mama had said it was okay. They began jumping around and acting like the little boys they were.

The doorbell rang and Miss Savannah was certain it must be another delivery. Opening the door expecting to see the hefty young man that was usually standing there she was surprised to see Melody.

She stepped back and said, "Well, young lady, what brings you to our neighborhood?" Miss Savannah laughed and reached out her hand. When Melody took it, instead of shaking it as she had expected, Miss Savannah took her hand and led her into the house. "Come see. There's been so much progress made since you were here months ago. Don't mind the cartons. My friend has been shipping furnishings from Lord knows where."

Melody's eyes widened when she saw shelf after shelf of books. "I don't think I've ever seen this many books in one place outsides of a public library. I had no idea."

"Beautiful aren't they?"

Melody nodded and as she walked by them she would stop every now and then to run her fingers down a binding. She was saying, "I remember reading this book … My best friend gave me a copy of this one years ago … I didn't even know you could get copies of this anymore." She was astounded.

David nodded to Melody as she passed the ladder he was standing on and Tawnie flashed her one of her big smiles.

"Come on in here to the kitchen. I have fresh baked cinnamon rolls and there's coffee or maybe you'd like something cold. It's a scorcher out there today."

Something nice and cold would be wonderful."

"Iced tea … bottled water?"

"Water would be great!"

Miss Savannah placed a cinnamon roll on a saucer and stuck it in the microwave for a few seconds. "Needs to be warmed up a bit. They're better when they're warm." She opened a drawer and took out a fork.

Setting the food and bottled water on the table she motioned for Melody to take a seat."

"So tell me. What brings you to my door today?"

Melody had taken a bite of the cinnamon roll. She leaned her head back and said, "This has got to be the best cinnamon roll I've ever had! Oh Miss Savannah. Where did you buy them?"

"I didn't buy them. That would be a sin. I make my own."

"You made this?"

"Sure did. I love keeping something baked around here. Lately it seems like I never know when someone's going to need a snack or something."

Melody glanced out the back windows and saw the boys carrying around a box and Jenny setting on the bench. Miss Savannah offered no explanation. There were still some things that she thought was no one's business.

"So?"

"What?"

"So what brings you here today?"

Melody had a blank look on her face for a second then replied, "Oh. Yes. There's going to be a zoning meeting for this area and I thought you might want to attend since you're a resident here."

"Zoning for what?"

"Well, it seems like there's a homeowner down the street that wants to turn their home into a bed and breakfast."

"That's a *wonderful* idea! So what's the problem"

"You really think a bed and breakfast would be befitting this beautiful historical residential area?"

"I don't see why not. Is it someone that's just purchased the home or have they been living here for some time?"

"They've lived here for twenty years or more."

"Then, like I said, what's the problem? Maybe all their children are grown and moved away from home and they just want to have people around for company sometimes."

"Well, I think they should sell and let someone that can appreciate the area move in."

Miss Savannah spoke. "Okay Melody. Listen to this scenario. First off, I didn't know anything about this until you just now told me but listen to this. Second, you're going to set there and tell me that they should sell a home that they've worked hard to pay for … where they most likely raised their children … and now that they're probably retired and want to fulfill a dream … that they should sell? Because it might be a detriment to the neighborhood?"

Melody didn't know how to answer. For one thing Miss Savannah had hit the nail right on the head. She heard Miss Savannah mumble something about snobs … should be run out of the neighborhood themselves … sure going to be there at the meeting. Melody paled.

"Miss Savannah. On second thought I know you're much too busy to attend something like that. You don't need to be concerned about it."

"Not concerned about it! You give me the time and place. I want to be there. This is the most ridiculous thing I've ever heard of."

Melody handed over a flyer that she had laid beside her saucer.

Miss Savannah waited until Melody had finished the cinnamon roll and said, "I see that you took my advice and got some sensible shoes to work in and you look good in a pair of jeans."

She nodded. "I hate to admit it but back in late spring I got my heel caught in a lawn sprinkler and took quite a fall. I broke a couple of bones in my foot so it's going to be awhile before I can wear them again.

"You're actually considering wearing them again?"

"I have spent so much money on them, it kills me to see them on the shoe rack and not be able to wear them."

"Then why don't you donate them, take it as a tax write-off and mark it up to a lesson well learned?"

Melody just looked at her like she had two heads.

"Thanks for the cinnamon rolls. You should be marketing them! Well, I hate to eat and run but I need to visit your neighbors and speak to them too. Everyone needs to be aware of what's going on."

Miss Savannah put her hands on her hips and said, "You just don't get it do you? "

All she got was another deer in the headlight looks.

"I need to run. Nice talking to you again. See you at the zoning meeting?"

"You betcha!" Miss Savannah replied. She knew that was the last thing Melody wanted to hear. "Let me show you to the door."

As she opened the door the delivery man was there getting ready to ring the doorbell. "Another load?"

"Not this time. Just one item that's marked fragile. Where's your sitting room? I think that's the one room I haven't put anything in yet."

Miss Savannah laughed. "Gypsy has kept you busy lately, huh?"

"No problem, Ma'am. The company is loving it."

"Tawnie, will you show this young man where my sitting room is, please?"

It was just one carton but it was a large one. The young man wrestled it up the stairs with David's assistance. When they came back downstairs Miss Savannah motioned him to the kitchen. This had become part of the delivery routine.

"Cinnamon rolls today. Baked them this morning. Coffee?"

He nodded. One bite and he was in heaven. "You should sell these!"

"Funny. You're the second person that's told me that today." She smiled.

Chapter 18

Gypsy called saying she finally had her reservations and she was headed to Tulsa.

"Hey, Girlfriend. I should be there tomorrow afternoon barring any more problems. I tell you it's been a fiasco. I had to make another trip back to the project I left your house for in the first place. I don't think there's any pleasing that lady. If she changes her mind again, too bad! You know, well, I don't know if I told you or not but everything is in black and white and shades of gray. I added minimal colors to make it pop and it was breathtaking. Well, she wanted everything I had put in to be replaced with orange. Can you believe that? It looks like freaking Halloween in there now. This time I made her sign off on it and got a final check right there and then."

"I know this is a crazy thing to ask but, need me to pick you up?"

"Got it covered already. By the way I'm guessing everything arrived in good condition?"

"I don't know. I haven't opened anything. Everything you shipped is still in the cartons in the rooms you designated."

"You mean you didn't even peek?"

"Nope. I haven't opened anything and we only have a path to walk through now. It reminds me of why I bought this house in the first place. I couldn't even walk through my apartment because of all the books stacked everywhere. Now its boxes and boxes of furniture or whatever you shipped."

Gypsy laughed. "I'll take care of it when I get there. No problem. Got it under control. By the way, how have you been disposing of your boxes? There's going to be a truckload by the time everything's unpacked and uncrated. You have been throwing them away this time haven't you? The boxes?"

"Oh yes. After all the years I hoarded moving boxes, saving them for the next move I'm having them taken away as soon as they're empty. I don't want to have to save another box as long as I live. Oh and to answer your question. When the delivery guy brings another load of things you have shipped, I just tip him and he takes away all the empties. So if you haven't sent anything else, I don't have the foggiest idea how we'll dispose of them."

"Okay. No problem. I can make a couple of calls and get it taken care of. However, your driveway may be stacked with empties for a few days until everything is unpacked. Just hope it doesn't rain with them all piled out there. Listen, I'm sitting in a prospective client's driveway waiting for them to show up. I need to let you go so I can scan over my notes."

"See you tomorrow then."

"You got it! Love you. Caio Bella"

Miss Savannah put the phone back in the cradle and sighed. "It looks like we're finally going to get to see what's in all the crates and boxes. Gypsy will be here tomorrow!"

"Anything I can do to help?" Tawnie asked.

"I don't know yet. We'll just have to wait until she gets here. You know I haven't been curious about what's in them until now. Now that I know Gypsy is going to be here and start decorating."

"Sure are a lot of things!" Jenny said.

Miss Savannah looked around and replied, "Yep. Sure is. I know she took lots of pictures and measurements but I'm wondering where everything's going to go. Sure looks like a lot to me, but Gypsy can do miracles with her decorating. I know that for a fact."

Tawnie glanced at her watch. "Hungry? It's past our lunch time and I'm starving."

Miss Savannah looked around once again. "Tell you what. If you'll go pick up, I'll buy."

"Pick up what?"

"Whatever you want just as long as it's hot food. I know you've got to be getting tired of sandwiches every day. As a rule I don't eat fast food but I noticed a little Chinese food restaurant near here the other day. Is that considered fast food too?"

Tawnie and Jenny both laughed.

"Miss Savannah, I don't have the car today. David dropped me off."

"That's no problem. Take the Jag."

"Oh no! I couldn't do that. I'd be scared to death that something would happen to it."

"Then take "Baby" if you're not too embarrassed to drive her."

Jenny spoke up. "Baby" has got to be the coolest things I've seen in years."

"You like her?"

"Sure do."

Miss Savannah had been looking through the phone book while she was talking. She jotted something down on a note pad, tore off the sheet and handed it to Tawnie. "That's the address. I'm not picky what you bring back. I like it all just as long as it has broccoli in it." She reached for her purse and handed them enough money to cover everything. She pitched the keys to "Baby" to Tawnie.

"Is it a standard shift?"

"What?"

"Does "Baby" have a standard transmission? I can't drive one."

"Then let your mother drive." She looked at Jenny. "You've got a license don't you?"

"Yes Ma'am."

"Then it looks like you'll be the driver. Just don't hurt "Baby".

"Oh. I'd never let that happen."

The two headed to the garage and Miss Savannah noticed Jenny was twirling the key chain around her finger. In a few minutes "Baby" backed out the garage with Jenny behind the wheel. Jenny had that wonderful smile on her face and Miss Savannah swore she could see bubbles escaping out the open windows and floating through the air.

After they had eaten their meals, Jenny pulled out three fortune cookies from the pocket of her tee shirt and kind of dropped them on the table. "The one that points in your direction is yours," she said.

They each reached out and took one and began reading them out loud to each other.

Miss Savannah broke the cookie open and picked the little slip of paper from the crumbs, smoothed it out and read, "Amazing things are going to happen." She laughed. "The amazing thing is going to be able to see my floors again when all these boxes are out of here!"

Jenny cocked one eyebrow and smiled. "Well, I need to get back to work. I want to get those boxes I've got stacked over by the computer done before I leave this evening. I'm finally feeling like I'm accomplishing something. When I get those done, I'll be ready to start on the shelves in the next room. WooHoo!"

Tawnie got up and started pushing the office chair back to the computer for her mother.

"I've got to think about getting a larger table and more chairs in here." Miss Savannah said. "I just thought I'd never need anything larger than this little set."

The next day Gypsy arrived as she said she would. In a flurry of hugs and clipboards, stacks of shipping documents, pictures, drawings and her phone she set to opening boxes and checking off items as received.

Miss Savannah knew there was nothing she could do to help so she just left Gypsy to what she was occupied with and kept her supplied with coffee. She had expected Gypsy to maybe relax for the afternoon but probably should have known better. Gypsy was determined to make some progress on unpacking the items and setting them about. She looked each one over to make sure there was no damage before she checked it off.

"Where do you get all that energy?" Miss Savannah asked.

"Gotta keep things under control," was her answer.

"You were telling me something about a prospective client in Dallas?"

"Oh that! Yep! Think I got it all lined out. At least I gave them an estimate for what they want."

"So what does it involve?"

"Well, there's a story behind it. When I was at the Dallas Market I visited a booth and there was a home builder standing there too. You know me. I didn't know that's what he was when I struck up the conversation but we got to talking and ended up having a drink that evening." She pulled her box cutter from her pocket and sliced through a carton. "He was thinking about furnishing the homes he built so people could see what they would look like. You and I both know that's been done for years and years."

"'Sure do."

"I guess he didn't want to invest in furnishings so I explained that the furniture manufacturers allow you to place their items in the home as long as they're mentioned in the brochure. It took quite a while for him to grasp the idea but in the long run he decided to allow me to stage a few homes for him if I would do all the ground work for him." She unwrapped the bases of a couple of lamps and examined them, checking them off on her list. "I guess he's an excellent builder but doesn't know anything about decorating or staging or anything to show off his properties. He even has a few homes setting that have been on the market for some time that he wants me to do."

Miss Savannah could not even imagine trying to carrying on conversation, unpack cartons and check things off all at the same time. "That sounds like a great set-up for you."

"Yep! I think it'll work. I've taken a chance and promised to do the first one for half the price I usually charge just to get my foot in the door, but it's the quantity of work that he has that's going to pay off." She ripped another carton open and stood admiring the contents.

"Sounds exciting!"

"It is!" Gypsy grabbed a drawing and picture and studied it. She nodded her head. "I've done it before for open houses for real estate companies and things like that but this will be my first time in this field."

"I remember some of our conversations about those."

Gypsy nodded again. "All I know is I've got to give it a try and hope it proves profitable. I know I can make more profit off staging instead of nursing egos of homeowners." She shook her head. "This last 'Halloween' lady just about did me in. I think I broke even and that's not why I'm in business, Girlfriend." She picked up her cup of coffee and took a sip.

"I hope it works out for you. You'd be closer to here too. Need me to freshen that coffee for you? Maybe fix an iced coffee for you."

"Oh Girlfriend. Iced coffee would be wonderful."

Miss Savannah brought the iced coffee and set it on a coaster. Gypsy was busy examining the contents of yet another carton.

"I'll be in the kitchen if you need me. I have a couple of things I need to get started for dinner."

Gypsy placed her hand on the side of her face and was scrutinizing whatever was in the box. "Hmmm. Okay. I'll be right here."

Chapter 19

Gypsy had been up for quite a while before Miss Savannah made her way down to the kitchen the next morning. She had her Daytimer open on the table and was absorbed in scanning pages and checking things off. Coffee was made, so Miss Savannah poured herself a cup, and after giving Gypsy a good morning hug, she went outside to enjoy the hummingbirds. Gypsy was juggling the phone while making notes so it was best to just leave her alone.

About half an hour later Gypsy joined her out in the herb garden.

Miss Savannah looked up and smiled. "Got everything under control this morning?"

"Like you're not going to believe!" She sat down and looked around spotting boxes piled on the porch. "Looks like I need to get those things unpacked so they can be used. There's not much seating area out here."

"Yep. I agree."

"I'll get that taken care of today."

"But it's supposed to get awfully hot today.

"Girlfriend, you don't *know* how hot it's going to be around here after while!" She laughed.

"What's so funny?"

Gypsy said, "Oh nothing," and smiled again.

"I think I'm already ready to switch to iced coffee. Want me to fix you a glass while I'm at it?"

"Sure. I need to get started inside so if you don't mind I'll just get it on my way through the kitchen."

"No problem."

"I'll go inside with you. I don't know if you need to be out here or not. It's so humid."

"Maybe I should get dressed for the day. I've gotten into this habit of having my coffee out here and watch the hummingbirds then I go upstairs and get dressed. I kind of enjoy lazing around in my pajamas or nightgown. They're so darn comfortable. It's a luxury I wasn't able to enjoy before I retired."

Gypsy reached out and opened the door. "I can't wait for that time to come for me. I'd love to not have to get dressed and fired up every morning."

"For some reason I don't think that's ever going to happen for you. Oh, you'll retire one of these days but I can't imagine you not hitting the floor running every morning."

Miss Savannah took her iced coffee upstairs with her. As she was stepping into the elevator the doorbell rang."

"I'll get it!" Gypsy yelled. "Go ahead and get dressed."

"It's probably for you anyway." She shouted back. The door slid open and Miss Savannah stepped inside. She took time for a refreshing shower and chose something not quite as casual as she usually wore. She still pulled on a pair of her favorite jeans but slipped on a pull-over and layered it with a button up shirt. She surveyed herself in the mirror. She spoke to herself, *"You still look like and old woman!"* She leaned closer to the mirror and traced the lines in her face then ran a comb through her hair. *"There. That's as good as it's gonna get, old woman."*

When she stepped in the room to say good morning to Jenny, Jenny nodded her head towards the back yard. Miss Savannah followed Jenny's cue and went into the kitchen and looked out the window. Gypsy was out there directing two of the most gorgeous young men she had ever laid her eyes on. Miss Savannah stepped nearer the windows.

Gypsy had them uncrating the outdoor furniture and they were already soaked with sweat and had taken off their shirts. Sweat glistened on their muscled bodies. Their jeans already looked like they were painted on, clinging to their bodies. Gypsy was there with her clip board checking things off and checking out the scenery.

Miss Savannah motioned for Jenny. "Do you believe what that Gypsy has gone and done? Look at those young men!"

"Oh Miss Savannah. How could I *not* look at them! I can say one thing for her. She has excellent taste in beefcake!"

Miss Savannah laughed. "I have to agree with you." They watched as Gypsy said something and motioned to a box. The young man leaned over to make certain there was nothing else in it and Gypsy smiled. She noticed them at the window and gave a thumbs-up. She said something to the young men and came inside.

She took a long drink of her iced coffee and said. "See, Girlfriend. I told you earlier that it was going to be hot out there! Believe me now?"

"Gypsy. How could you?"

"Do what? I needed strong men so that's exactly what I got."

Watching one of them walk around a box twice to find a box knife that was sticking out of his pocket, Jenny said. "It's sure a good thing they're pretty! Know what I mean?"

The three of them burst out laughing.

"Well, ladies enjoy the scenery. They'll be inside in a while to carry empty boxes out back and help uncrate some more things. Today is going to be sweet! Eye Candy Sweet!"

"Tawnie is going to be so upset when I tell her."

"Where is she today?" Gypsy asked.

"Teacher's conference for the boys. Don't know if she's going to be finished in time to come over or not."

"Tell you what. I'll snap a few pictures with my phone so she won't miss out completely."

"That'll do." Jenny laughed. "I gotta get back to work before I go out there and offer to wipe sweat off their bodies! ... With my tongue!"

When she laughed this time the invisible bubbles filled the room and began zipping around.

"You feel that?" Gypsy asked.

"The happiness?" Miss Savannah replied. "That's Jenny."

Gypsy reached over and laid her hand on Jenny's shoulder. "I need to figure out a way to bottle that. We'd make a fortune! Girl, that's something else!"

Jenny headed back to the computer and the stack of book-filled boxes she had set for her goal today. "Maybe if I hurry up I can get one of those hunks to carry out the empties for me."

Gypsy winked. "You got it."

It was a wonderful day for the three women. Gypsy actually got most of the cartons opened and unpacked. Jenny's fingers were flying across the keyboard, entering data, emptying one box after another, and Miss Savannah kept the young men plied with iced tea and bottled spring water.

More than once Gypsy just dropped things on the floor to make the guys bend over and pick them up for her. Of course it was always perfectly timed so Jenny and Miss Savannah could take advantage of the view too.

As they passed Jenny's computer she'd ask, "Are you sure there's nothing in the bottom of those boxes. You know Miss Gypsy will be mighty upset if something's still in there." Invariably they set the box down and leaned over searching the bottom of it.

As the two young men left, Jenny heard them say. "Those have got to be the clumsiest women I've ever been around. Couldn't hold on to a dang thing! And I swear if I have to search the bottom of one more box I'm going to rip it apart."

She just shook her head. "They don't have a clue. Like I said before, it's a darn good thing they're pretty!"

Gypsy mixed a cocktail and swirled the ice around in the glass. "Well ladies. Did you enjoy the Wrangler Watch today?"

Jenny replied, "I know I watched the back of those Wrangler's all day!" Mmm Mmm Mmm! They sure grow them pretty now days, don't they?"

"Gypsy, I thought you were going to run out of things to throw on the floor to make them bend over and pick up." Miss Savannah chuckled.

"Was I that obvious?"

"Only to us." Jenny giggled. "Miss Gypsy, they still don't have a clue. But when the dark haired one went outside and poured that bottle of water over himself to cool off, I just about tackled him right where he stood! They going to be here tomorrow too?"

"Afraid not. I need someone that can think tomorrow. Not that those young men couldn't."

Silence followed her last remark. Then all three of them shook their heads and said at the same time. "They couldn't." Laughter followed.

Gypsy spoke up. "It's time to start assembling everything and getting things in place. Believe it or not practically everything is out of boxes, crates and whatever they were shipped in and ready to start making this house a home. I've tried to be so careful not to mar the floors. Everything's sitting on moving pads so they can be moved around until I get them in the right place. By this time tomorrow this won't look like the same place and those liquid honey colored floors will be seen again. I promise. I think I can have the downstairs completed tomorrow!"

Miss Savannah smiled at the thought of getting to see everything pulled together and decorated.

"I just have one more shipment which should be here tomorrow too. I thought of it this morning and ordered it. They said it would be shipped priority."

"Oh Lord, where's it going to go?"

"Just wait and see."

"Anyone getting hungry?" Miss Savannah asked.

"I know I am," Gypsy said. "Why don't we run down to a seafood place and grab a bite to eat?

"I made a stew today if you'd rather have that. It's already cooked. Maybe it's too hot tonight to have stew."

"Oh yeah! It's been a hot one around here today!" Jenny exclaimed fanning herself with her hands. "You two go ahead. I think I'll head on home."

Miss Savannah caught Gypsy's eye and rubbed her fingers together indicating that Jenny probably didn't have the money to eat at an expensive restaurant.

"Tell you what! My treat! How about it? I promise I'll get you back almost before you could go home and cook a meal for yourself."

"I don't want to intrude."

"If we invite you it means we'd love to have you join us. It's no intrusion at all. I'm going just the way I am. Not going to change clothes or anything. I'm sure they'll take my money. You ladies ready?"

Miss Savannah grabbed her tote and Jenny grabbed her wallet she brought to work with her every day. Miss Savannah had a notion that all the money Jenny had was in that wallet and she kept it near.

They loaded into Gypsy's car and were at the restaurant in a few minutes.

"Look. No waiting to be seated. Perfect!" Miss Savannah remarked.

Gypsy stepped up and told the young lady that they needed a table for three. The young lady grabbed three menus and led them to a table. Before they could be seated Gypsy had ordered a round of wine, the same kind they had drank a few nights ago at the house.

"Give us a few minutes with the menus please. We'll have our orders ready when you bring our drinks."

Much to Jenny's pleasure, they had a combo platter of surf and turf; Steak medium rare and Lobster, her favorite. Gypsy ordered the Shrimp and Lobster and Miss Savannah the Shrimp Remoulade Salad with a small lobster tail on the side. The orders were taken and glasses of wine set before them. Gypsy raised her glass for a toast. "To Wrangler Watching! A hot day on the old home front!" They laughed, clinked their glasses together and settled in to wait for their food, which proved to not be too long.

Miss Savannah looked over to Jenny and asked, "Do you think this is the 'amazing thing that's going to happen?'"

"Don't think so. This was entirely too much fun. You're going to have to wait for amazing."

Gypsy looked at them questioningly.

Jenny explained. "Her Fortune cookie."

"Did you eat it all? It won't come true if you didn't."

"Sure did. Now I wonder just how long I'm going to have to wait for amazing."

"Just be patient and not try to force it. It'll happen when you least expect it." Gypsy added her bit of philosophy.

Their food arrived and it took no time for them to dig in. It sounded more like an orgy than a meal with all the moans and groans going on at their table. They really were hungry.

When they finished Miss Savannah dug into her tote and put the tip on the table. Gypsy picked up the tab. Jenny reached for her wallet. Gypsy reached across the table and put her hand on top of Jenny's. "You just put that away right now. I told you before we left that it's my treat."

"Thank you Miss Gypsy. This is very kind of you. I haven't had steak and lobster in a very long time. I really enjoyed it."

"You're very welcome."

"We all ready to head home?" Miss Savannah asked.

"Don't think we can do any more damage here so might as well head that way." Gypsy picked up her keys and they were at the house in no time at all.

They said goodnight to Jenny at the garage and waited for her to go upstairs and heard her door close and lock. Then they walked across the driveway trying to avoid the mountain of boxes that were piled there. "These will be taken care of in the morning when my shipment arrives."

They rode up the elevator together and went to their rooms. In a short time they were both in bed, Miss Savannah in the big white one and Gypsy down the hall in the guest bedroom.

As Miss Savannah was dozing off she heard children playing and music. Tawnie must be paying her mother a late visit to catch her up on the results of the teacher's conferences.

"Goodnight Girlfriend."

"Goodnight Gypsy."

Chapter 20

Tawnie arrived, Gypsy was pouring coffee and the delivery truck all arrived at the same time the next morning.

Gypsy said to Tawnie, "That's a surprise I ordered and if we time it right we can have it set up by the time Miss Savannah comes down for coffee."

Gypsy went outside and motioned for the driver to unload the carton into the kitchen. She explained the situation and quickly he cut the carton away and helped them set a new table and chairs that matched the Hoosier cabinet. She had paid a bit extra so it would already be assembled. Gypsy handed over a hefty tip and the truck was leaving when Miss Savannah come into the kitchen.

"Oh my word! What's this?" she asked. She ran her hand over the table. "Oh Gypsy, it looks just like the cabinet. How on earth did you ever do it? I love it! Now we can all sit around the table without having to roll office chairs in here and get the little stool out from the cabinet!"

"Well, it was quite evident that you had outgrown the little ice cream parlor set so time has come to replace it with something with a lot more seating room. I thought the little set could be put over in the corner by the windows so you could set there and look out over the herb garden. There's plenty of room. Matter of fact there's room for three or more sets like that. This kitchen is enormous."

Tawnie was busy polishing the new furniture. "She's right, you know, Miss Savannah."

"I know. She always is when it comes to furnishings. I always thought maybe at one time there was a large harvest table in here. You know one for a large family."

"That may very well have been at one time." Gypsy replied. "There's plenty of space for one."

"I know what." Miss Savannah said. "Everyone get a fresh cup of coffee and let's christen it. We all have a place to set now. I have a decadent amaretto cheesecake in the fridge that's just waiting to be cut. There's nothing on this earth as good as cheesecake and coffee!" She laughed.

"Almost sinful!" Jenny replied and giggles escaped and happiness and joy filled the room. With everything ready, Jenny bowed her head and reached out for Miss Savannah's hand. Tawnie reached out and took Gypsy's and a circle of hands was created. A short blessing of thanks was said and they dug in.

Putting a forkful of the cheesecake in her mouth, Jenny rolled her eyes. "This is the most delicious cheesecake I think I've ever tasted in my life!"

Gypsy smiled and nodded. "Ever since I first met her, she's always has been able to bake up the most superb desserts. At one time we actually thought about opening a tea room together. It never happened because of time and circumstances but I still dream of it sometimes."

This was the first time Tawnie and Jenny had witnessed her when she was laid back and not going ninety to nothing.

"What happened?" Jenny asked.

"Well … first it was finances. Then when we had the finances life started taking us in different directions. Then life started dealing hard blows." She tilted her head down.

Miss Savannah cleared her throat and said, "If it had been meant to be it would have happened."

"Well, who knows. It might still come about for you. Life isn't through with you yet." Jenny replied.

Gypsy looked at her. Are you always this positive?"

"I found out that it doesn't pay to be any other way!" She laughed and her laughter broke the solemn atmosphere that had settled upon the four women setting around the table.

"Girlfriend, did you hear children laughing after we went to bed last night?" Gypsy veered the conversation in another direction.

"I sure did and was going to ask Jenny if Tawnie and the boys had visited.

"Nope." Tawnie answered. "I figured since I'd see her this morning, I'd catch Mother up on the news of the teacher conferences when I got here."

Miss Savannah and Gypsy exchanged looks.

"It's a good thing you didn't come over too." Jenny said. "After that wonderful dinner we had last night my tummy was so happy I crawled into bed and read for a while." She looked across to Gypsy. "And, I want to thank you again. I enjoyed it so much!"

"No need to thank me again. You thanked me enough last night." She reached across and patted Jenny's hand.

They heard a vehicle pull into the driveway. "Bet that's my help for the day."

Jenny glanced at her.

"Sorry Sweetie. Today is work day. Real work so I needed an entirely different crew."

Tawnie looked at her mother with questions written all over her face.

"I'll explain later." Jenny said.

Gypsy pushed her phone across the table to Jenny. "I snapped a few photos."

Jenny picked up the phone and held it against her heart. "Of course you did!" and laughed.

Miss Savannah freshened her coffee and went out to the herb garden to watch the hummingbirds for a while. She could hear Tawnie's and Jenny's giggles behind her. She was sure they were already viewing the eye candy pictures from yesterday. Gypsy was already directing the two man crew through the house to the room she wanted to start in that day.

It was a productive day and by that evening all the major pieces of furniture were in place downstairs. Everything had been cleaned and straightened and the paintings that were to be hung the following day were leaned in place against the walls. Lamps, statues, pillows, throws and a myriad of other decorator items were waiting to be placed.

Gypsy motioned to them. "All these small things can wait until the men get everything in place, then we can play like we used to. Remember?"

"How could I ever forget? Those memories are etched in my mind." Miss Savannah gave her a hug sat down and leaned back. "I love this fainting couch and it fits right in with all the other furniture. It's already looking fantastic. You work wonders!"

"I have a special floor lamp that goes with it too."

"You think of everything!"

"Try to."

"You getting hungry? While you were busy in here I made dinner."

"Now why does that surprise me? And, yes I'm starving."

Gypsy uncorked a bottle of wine while Miss Savannah set the table and put the food on it. She carried a glass through for Miss Savannah. After they had begun eating Gypsy said, "About the laughter we heard last night ... It seems like no one else heard anything."

"I know. But you and I both hear it."

Gypsy nodded.

"There's been a few times I've heard things like music and one time the sounds of a dinner party going on. I just never mentioned it before because I thought it might be someone playing loud music in their car or something. That could have explained the music but I've heard it more than one time since I've been here."

Gypsy raised an eyebrow. "Do you think there may be restless spirits in this house?"

"No. Not restless in a bad way. I think they're happy."

"So you do think something is here?"

Miss Savannah nodded. "They don't mean any harm. It's like they're pleased. Like the house is coming back to life. Understand what I'm saying?"

"I think so but I haven't felt anything. Have you?"

"Not a thing." Miss Savannah replied.

"If we hear anything or sense anything we need to talk about it. Okay?"

"Okay. But talking about it isn't going to do anything."

"You remember my friend I used to go to for readings? I might contact her and see if she would drop by. Just to see if she picks up anything. What do you think about that?"

Miss Savannah shrugged. "I can't see that it would hurt anything. But, they just seem so happy … whatever it is I've heard. I don't want them disturbed. Understand?"

"Yep. Sure do Girlfriend."

With dinner finished they straightened the kitchen, loaded the dishwasher and Miss Savannah set up coffee for the morning. They carried their wine glasses through and sat in the library area admiring how it was coming along.

"I'm so glad you left areas on the bookcases for me to set decorator items. It really makes it pop!"

"Actually it was Tawnie's idea."

"She's quite the young woman, isn't she?"

"Sure is. Someone was really looking after me when He put them in my life. They came at a time when I needed someone reliable and honest and that's exactly what they are."

"I must agree your Higher Power is looking after you!"

"He is. Isn't He?"

The two friends sat there taking in the beauty of the home and finishing the last of the wine.

Chapter 21

The next few days were filled with the unpacking of furniture and final placement. More than once Miss Savannah saw Gypsy step back, turn around and walk off then re-enter the room and take another look. She would shake her head and motion for the men to move it back like it was. Perfection was her nature and if it wasn't just impeccable, it wouldn't do.

Miss Savannah was surprised that Gypsy hadn't put her finishing touches on the rooms as she went. She had not arranged the small items, the accessories that Gypsy so loved to work with. But Miss Savannah also knew that she had her reasons and when the time was right she'd pull everything together.

They had been lucky in as much as Gypsy's phone had calmed down and she could concentrate. The Dallas job she had talked about came through and in the late fall she would be temporarily relocating there to get things kicked off. Evidently the Home Builder's Association was going to have a Holiday Parade of Homes and her builder was going to have four ready for Gypsy to do her magic. There had been a flurry of calls to vendors after she had received the good news to insure everything was in order but after that Gypsy relaxed and she proceeded working her magic on Miss Savannah's home.

"Girlfriend, I've been thinking about something." she said at dinner one evening. "I'd like to do a brochure of before and after of your home to use as a hand-out at this upcoming Dallas project. What do you think about it?"

"Do you really think people want to see a historic old home? I thought all the people that attended that sort of thing wanted new, modern homes."

"Not always. Sometimes they want to take a new home and give it the ambiance and warmth of an older one. Let's face it. Not everyone can fall into a deal like you did. The price of these historic homes has skyrocketed and also not everyone can afford to fully refurbish one. That must have cost almost as much as the home."

Miss Savannah nodded. "It did cost a pretty penny, especially when I wanted an elevator too."

"That's what I thought."

"Now if a person could have what you have here, and not have to go through what you did and spend the money you did, don't you think they would?"

"I suppose."

"Wouldn't you? I mean if you could have found a new home…"

Miss Savannah was already shaking her head. "Nope. Not me. I knew I had to find just the right house and this is it. Why, I almost jumped out of Melody's car when I saw it. I knew it was the right one the instant I laid eyes on it! The one for me!"

"Well, not everyone's as eccentric as you!" Gypsy smiled.

"You really think I am? Eccentric?"

"Until they come up with a better word, eccentric is going to have to suffice."

"I never really thought of myself that way. I've lived frugally. Not now but I used to."

"I know. Sometimes I wondered about you and worried a bit too."

"Really?"

"Oh yes. You and your books. It was like you were living through them."

127

Miss Savannah winked. "I still do."

Gypsy picked up her camera that she had left lying on the kitchen cabinet and took a few shots of the Hoosier cabinet and the windows across the back. "Just want to see how they come out in this light. I'll upload them in the morning. May have to get a better camera for professional prints for the brochure ... that is if you're in agreement."

"I've never been able to deny you anything. Go ahead but I want to see them before you put the brochure together. Deal?"

Gypsy smiled. "Deal!"

"Now I need to get this kitchen done before I go up to bed. Kind of tired tonight. I think a nice hot shower and a good book is in order for tonight."

"I have a few things I want to take care of before I go to bed. Need to get them done so they don't haunt me all night. I'll be up later."

They got everything done and Miss Savannah went to the freezer and took out a couple loaves of banana nut bread for morning.

She gave Gypsy a hug and said, "I hate to leave you down here but you know where everything is and if you need me you know where I'll be."

"Got it under control."

Miss Savannah smiled. "You sure do. See you in the morning. Goodnight"

Gypsy heard the purr of the elevator and settled in to making notes and review her Daytimer. She picked up her camera and turned it on to view the picture of the Hoosier cabinet. She ran her finger across the tiny screen. There was something on the picture. She flipped to the next one of the windows and it was clear. Pulling the chip out and going into the computer station Jenny worked at, she inserted it and pulled up the picture. She reached out and touched the monitor screen then set back and stared at it. It looked like orbs. She had read about them before and they were usually a sign that a presence was there... an invisible presence. She tilted her head back and looked up the stairs. She decided to take more pictures and see how they turned out before telling her dear friend about them. She also made a note to call her friend that did her readings.

She removed the chip and slid it back into her camera and shut down the computer.

Chapter 22

The next morning gypsy was on the phone with Alexandra.

"Morning Alex. This is Gypsy."

"Well, I haven't heard from you in a long time. I know you've been busy but thought you might call.

"Oh Alex. I apologize, but I've been so busy you wouldn't believe."

"Oh yes I would. Remember, I told you that once you got everything in order, things were going to be hectic and be prepared for it."

"I do but I never dreamed it'd be like this."

"So when are you going to come and visit?"

"Well, that's what I'm calling about. I'm decorating a friend's house here in Tulsa and there's things happening. There's music in the night and I've heard children's laughter and there's no children living here. Last night I was viewing some photos I took and in a few of them I think I see orbs."

"Hmmm."

"I was wondering if I could get you to come over here and see what you think."

"You mean like a séance?"

"No. Nothing like that. Just walk through the house and see if you pick up anything."

"Can I ask whose house this is?"

"It belongs to a very dear friend of mine. She bought it a few months ago and it's finally to the point that it's ready for me to decorate."

"So it was lived in before she bought it?"

"Oh yes. By what I understand it was constructed sometime prior to the 1920s. It's located in the Historic Maple Ridge District. However, I think it has remained in the same family until now."

"You mean the area over by the museum?"

"Exactly. It's a beautiful home."

"When do you want me to be there? I've always wanted to see inside one of those homes."

"At your convenience."

"How about this afternoon? Maybe after lunch."

"Wow! That was fast. Why don't you plan on joining us for dinner?"

"Your friend won't mind?"

"She'd love it!"

The conversation had ended by the time Miss Savannah made her way to the coffee pot. "You're up and at it early today."

"I had a call I wanted to make early to make sure I was able to contact her."

"Her?"

"Yes. When you get awake good I have something to tell you … and show you too."

"And this has something to do with your early call?"

"Yep. Sure does."

Miss Savannah sliced a piece of the banana nut bread she had laid out the night before and slathered it with butter. "Want some?"

"Think I'll pass. Not too hungry this morning.. Maybe later."

"You okay? Never knew you to turn down banana bread."

"I've just got something on my mind. I may as well talk to you about it now. It's going to make me crazy if I have to wait any longer."

This got Miss Savannah's attention. "So?"

"So. Remember the pictures I took in here after dinner last night?"

"Yes. And?"

"After you went to bed I looked at them and there's something in one of them I think you need to see." Gypsy removed the chip and placed it in the computer as she had done the night before. She pulled up the picture and pointed. "See those?"

"There must be something wrong with your camera!"

"That's what I thought too but those little white spots aren't in any of the others I took. Just this one."

"So what does that mean?"

"Wait a minute. I have some more to show you." She scanned to the kitchen pictures she had viewed last night. She selected the picture of the stove. "See. They're over and around the stove too. Now those pictures were taken weeks and weeks ago. It can't be the camera because all the other pictures are clear."

Miss Savannah stood, looking at the picture.

"Girlfriend, these are orbs."

"No. They can't be!"

"I'm afraid they are. They concerned me, so I called Alex this morning to see if she would come over and see if she feels anything."

"You think this could explain the music and children's laughter?"

"I think it could have something to do with it. Yes."

"But why just in the kitchen?"

"I don't know, Girlfriend but we're going to try to find out."

Miss Savannah sat back down at the table, staring down at her cup of coffee. "Remember our conversation the other day? I told you I don't want whatever it is disturbed."

"I know, but wouldn't you like to know who it is?"

"Some things are best left unknown, you know."

"I know, but if orbs are showing up, maybe whoever it is, is trying to get a message through."

"I don't know about this. Some things are just out of my comfort zone. You say you've already called this Alex lady?"

"And she'll be here this afternoon."

"Oh, Gypsy!"

"She's just going to walk through the house and see if she picks up anything. It's not going to be a séance or anything like that. I know how you feel about that sort of thing."

"Well. Okay, but I'm still not comfortable with it."

"I understand and ordinarily I wouldn't go ahead without your approval, but for some reason I feel like this needs to be addressed."

Miss Savannah glanced up at the clock. "Jenny's late this morning. That's not like her. I think I'll take a walk over and see if anything's wrong."

"I'll go. Those stairs and you just don't get along. Be back in a few minutes." Gypsy walked across the driveway and climbed the stairs. She knocked on the door and in a few minutes Jenny opened the door and peeked out. "Are you okay? Miss Savannah is concerned about you."

"Didn't you find the note I put on the back door? Junior fell out of a tree late yesterday and we spent most of the night in the emergency room with him."

"Oh no! Is he going to be okay?"

Jenny smiled. "He's going to be just fine. He's just a little boy and things like that are going to happen. But I'm all pooped out and need some more sleep, so I thought I'd take the day off. I'm ready to start on the reference books and need some guidance from Miss Savannah anyway. And, with the weekend coming up, it was my thought that she wouldn't mind."

"Okay, Sweetie. You take care of yourself and get some rest. I'll tell her."

"And Tawnie isn't going to be here either. She needs to look after Junior for a day or so."

"I understand and I'm certain Miss Savannah will too."

When Gypsy got back to the house, sure enough there was the note stuck in the door. She hadn't even seen it when she went out. She took it in and laid it on the table. "This is why Jenny isn't here this morning."

Miss Savannah opened and read it. "Is Junior going to be okay?"

"Jenny said he was going to be just fine, but I can tell you, after seeing Jenny, I could tell she needs the rest."

"That's no problem as long as everyone's okay."

"You know what? This is all kind of weird that it's happened the way it has, because now the house will be empty and Alex will be able to really get a feel from the house without any outside influences."

Miss Savannah just looked at her and said, "Whatever."

Right after lunch the doorbell rang and Gypsy hurried to the door. Miss Savannah was in the living room relaxing on her favorite piece of furniture and heard conversation and waited for them to come to her. She wasn't real thrilled about this entire thing, but it was going to take place. She was never deliberately rude to a guest, but at this moment, she wasn't going to greet this Alex person with open arms.

In a few minutes Gypsy entered the room with the most striking woman Miss Savannah had seen in years. Beautiful, she wasn't, but there was something about her. She glowed.

"Girlfriend. This is Alex."

Alex didn't reach out to shake hands. She smiled and said, "It's going to be a pleasure to have met you. I already know that."

Miss Savannah didn't know how to respond.

"Your home is the most beautiful I've ever seen. Just the two rooms I've been in I can tell it's a home not just a house."

"Thank you."

"Do you mind if I just kind of wander through and see everything?"

Gypsy replied, "I can show you through if you want. And, after you see it, I can show you the before pictures."

"I think that would be a wonderful idea." Alex answered. "You don't care do you, Miss Savannah?"

"Not at all. I think I'm just going to stay here and read a while. I'm not intending to be rude, but I'm in the middle of this book and I can't seem to be able to put it down. I've really missed my reading time lately."

Gypsy and Alex disappeared into the house. In a few minutes she heard the elevator hum taking them to the upper floors. Quite a while later, they reappeared and Alex was gushing forth her appreciation of the home and how so many people would have tried to make it look modern inside.

"You've done the home justice." She cooed. "Beautiful. Absolutely beautiful!"

Miss Savannah laid her book aside. "I can't take credit. Gypsy has done all this," she said, motioning to the furnishings."

Alex explained, "The furnishings are beautiful too but I was talking about the house. There's such a good feeling in here."

"Have you felt anything?" asked Gypsy.

"Not anything I can pinpoint at this time. I just feel warmth and happiness."

Miss Savannah stood and started to the kitchen. "How about me fixing us some iced tea while I put dinner on?"

"Iced tea would be so refreshing. These late Indian Summer days can be quite warm."

"I'll bring it to you. I know there're some pictures Gypsy wants you to see."

"Thanks, Girlfriend."

As Miss Savannah filled the glasses with ice and poured the tea, she had second thoughts about her opinion of Alex. She wasn't what she had expected. She really didn't know what she had thought, but certainly not the charming woman in there with Gypsy, looking over photographs. She carried the iced tea through and returned to the kitchen. She busied herself by starting a nice dinner. When everything was baking, simmering and otherwise taking care of itself, she joined Gypsy and Alex. She'd excuse herself occasionally and check on dinner, then rejoin them for a while longer.

Miss Savannah set the table and called out to them that dinner was served. Alex entered the kitchen and something went through her like a streak of lightening! She grabbed the back of a chair and held on.

Gypsy rushed to her side. "Are you okay?"

"I'll be oaky in a minute. Did either one of you feel that?"

Miss Savannah looked from one to the other not knowing what had just happened.

Alex sat down. "Miss Savannah. I'm going to be frank with you. There's a spirit here; a very strong spirit, as strong as I've ever encountered."

Gypsy sat down beside Alex. "Are you able to tell us anything about it?"

"The name George or something like that keeps popping into my mind. But the force I felt just then was definitely female. It was like she was protecting something."

Then all three of them unmistakably heard children laughing. The CD player came on and music from the "Big Chill" CD Miss Savannah had listened to a few days ago began playing. Marvin Gaye was singing "I Heard It Through The Grapevine". They looked at each other.

"Okay. This has never happened to me before." Alex said.

"What's going on?" Miss Savannah asked.

"Well. I'm not exactly positive but I think whoever is here is welcoming us. She wants us to know she's here."

"She certainly did that!" Gypsy exclaimed.

Miss Savannah nodded but smiled at the music playing in the background. "It's definitely not my choice of dinner music but what say we go ahead and eat while it's hot."

"Do you still have the name of the former owner's?" Alex asked.

"All that information is on the closing papers. I have them up in my room."

"Would you mind getting them after dinner? I'd like to take a look at them."

"No problem." And after dinner she immediately retrieved them.

Alex glanced over them then looked at her watch. "It's not too late and I'd like to give this Mr. Billingham a call. How do I put this on speaker phone?"

Miss Savannah showed her and the call was made.

A distinguished voice answered the call.

Alex began. "Mr. Billingham, this is Alex Rodale. I need to ask you some questions about the piece of property you sold recently; the house in Maple Ridge District."

They heard a hesitation.

"Let me explain. It seems that there is a presence in the home. Not a bad one, but it's here none the less. Miss Savannah is here with me. She's the one that purchased the property and another friend is here also. We've all three experienced the presence." She laughed. "As a matter of fact I think she just had dinner with us."

"She?"

"Yes, I definitely know it's a female, but the name George is the one that keeps coming to my mind."

They could hear him sigh. "Somehow I knew she was still there. Her name is Georgina, Miss Georgina. Even us kids called her Miss Georgina, not grandmother or anything like that. Grandpa called her Georgie. He was the love of her life and when he passed, had she not come to live with us, I don't think she would have lived much longer. Oh, how she grieved over that man. The love she had for him was transferred to us. Sometimes I think it was all of us children that kept her going. She was so full of love it had to be given and shared. She loved to hear the laughter and she'd turn on the radio and tune in music. She loved the music. She'd get all of us seated around that big old harvest table in the kitchen and give us cookies while she was cooking. I can still hear her singing along with the songs. Her voice had at one time been strong and pure, but as she grew older it began to have a quaver to it, but we kids didn't care. It was our grandmother singing for us."

He paused.

"Mr. Billingham. This is Miss Savannah. I have a question to ask. Did she like to cook?"

"Did she! From the time her feet hit the floor in the morning her every waking thought was of the kitchen and what wonderful meals she could prepare. Her life had revolved around the kitchen. Many times she had stood in front of the Hoosier cabinet, measured out ingredients and made a batch of bread. That old cook stove was in use every day, cooking and baking her delicious victuals, as she called them. I wonder what ever happened to it, probably been junked years ago."

"Actually that stove is still in the house. When I bought the house it was still there but in sad shape. It's been repaired and still works. I still use it occasionally."

"Really? I would never have imagined it'd still be around."

"The Hoosier cabinet too. It had to have a lot of work but I use it for my computer desk in the kitchen now."

"Is there anything else you can tell us about her?" Gypsy asked.

"I don't know where to start. I can remember her so clearly. She was born right around the turn of the century and I wasn't born until the 40's, but she's as clear as a bell. I can see her now, listening to her radio and keeping a fresh pot of coffee going on the stove. She always wore an apron. Aprons that she sewed herself. You know the kind with a bib. I don't think I can remember her not ever having one on, unless she was going to church or something like that."

The three women continued to listen as he seemed to gather his thoughts.

"She loved that house so much and I can imagine how heartbroken she would have been to see it fall into ruin like it did. She had so many wonderful times watching her grandchildren and great-grandchildren grow up in it. And, like I said, she loved to cook for them. I'm sure some of the best times in her life had been when everyone was gathered around the table and sharing their day.

"I'm very sure of that too, especially after talking to you about her." Alex said.

He added, 'She lived to a nice old age in that house."

"I'm glad she did. Mr. Billingham, I'm not going to keep you any longer. You don't know how much I appreciate you speaking with us. Normally, people don't want to talk to me when they find out who I am and what I do."

"It's been my pleasure ladies. And if I can be of any more help, just call anytime."

"Thank you again. Goodnight."

They sat there staring at each other after the connection was broken.

"Georgina. Huh?" Gypsy said. "Alex, you were so right-on."

Miss Savannah sighed. "What a wonderful heart tugging story. She loved this house as much as I do."

"And, she liked to cook too!" Alex replied. "That's why the orbs are around the stove and Hoosier cabinet. Those are the only pieces of that time in her life she has to cling to."

"It seems like when the family was gone and the great house sat in ruin she roamed it and waited...waited for it to come back to life."

"I think you're right."

They heard the CD player switch and Bonny Raitt began singing "Feels Like Home".

"Oh my goodness!" Gypsy said, as she went to the wine cooler, took out a bottle of wine and opened it. "That's just too eerie."

Miss Savannah said quietly. "Relax Gypsy. Miss Georgina is just letting us know we're welcome in her home."

Gypsy poured and handed the glasses around.

They held up their glasses and toasted. "To Georgina."

Chapter 23

Miss Savannah lay in bed the following morning, thinking about what had happened the day before. At least she now knew who was sharing the house with her and it wasn't something she felt needed to be changed.

Thinking of changes ... Today both David and Tawnie would be here. She realized that the time was drawing near that she wasn't going to need David on Saturday's any longer. And could she justify keeping Tawnie full time? Jenny had almost completed entering the thousands of novels, and they were in place except for this week's entries. David would take care of that today. Jenny was now ready to start on the reference books. It wouldn't take her very long to finish them up at the rate she was going.

Miss Savannah swung her legs over the side of her bed and wriggled her feet into her house slippers then reached for her robe. She changed her mind and went to the closet and pulled jeans and button-up shirt from the rack. She was going to go ahead and dress for the day before heading downstairs.

While dressing, her mind jumped back to her previous thoughts. The arrangements she had made with Jenny were working out great. It benefited both of them, but when Jenny was finished with the books ... well, that was something she'd have to think about when the time came.

She realized that she really loved this little family and was going to hate to see things change. When the boys were running around outside and playing, she always found herself watching them and smiling at their antics. And, Tawnie and Jenny were so good with them and David … well, in his quiet way he was a wonderful daddy to them. She knew they were still struggling to recover from the financial set-back, but they were coming along just fine; she could tell by Tawnie's demeanor. She was more relaxed now and didn't seem so driven. Oh, she still had that take charge attitude but it was somehow different now.

Miss Savannah splashed water on her face and ran a comb through her hair. She looked in the mirror and thought, *"This is as good as it's going to get today, old girl."* Her body was craving that first cup of coffee so she headed downstairs. Stepping out of the elevator, she heard movements and knew David was already shelving books with Tawnie directing him. She glanced out the back windows while she was pouring coffee and saw Jenny with the boys. She always spent this time every Saturday morning with them while Tawnie and David were busy. Everything worked for them with the schedule that had kind of fallen into place over the past months. A twinge of guilt flashed through her mind at the thought of things changing. Was she going to take away from this family a bit of comfort they had grown accustomed to? Well, perhaps not comfort but a sense of well-being.

She heard noises coming from the dining room and peeked in, carrying her coffee. Gypsy was finishing up the final touches in there. Somehow, somewhere Gypsy had located a long buffet that matched the dining room suit perfectly. Gypsy had told her that it wasn't solid Rosewood like the suit but no one would ever know if not told. She had also located a small table for four and matching chairs which she had placed in one of the corners. She said it was a tea table. And the matching tea cart was stationed close to it. All of it was in the rich Rosewood. Miss Savannah remembered having seen almost the exact pieces in San Francisco when they had purchased the dining room suit, but the apartment they had leased just didn't have room to accommodate it. They had always planned to order the pieces when they relocated to a larger house. After all, they relocated about every fifteen months when her husband was assigned to the next project. Those had been the days of new projects, new people in their lives, new challenges and building the life together they had chosen. Miss Savannah shook her head to shoo away memories that if she allowed to take hold, would set her on the path of grieving and reflection that could encompass her for days or weeks. They were wonderful memories of sequin dress, tuxes, furs, theater, fine dining and limos. Those days were in the past and she knew they would only live in her memory, that they could never be duplicated and there was no way to relive again except in her memory.

Gypsy looked up when she entered the room. "Well, what do you think, Girlfriend?"

"It's wonderful. I really didn't know if it would go with the house, it being Oriental and everything, but you have made it look like it was bought for this home. As a matter of fact you have tied everything, I mean everything together with your magic touch."

"Thanks. You have such great things to work with that all I had to do was ... well, what I've done. You do realize that everything is completed now? I was saving this room until the last. I finished up the bedrooms last week. And anything left to do, especially the bookcases, Tawnie or Jenny can do. I already have the decorator items in place. The books are to be shelved around them."

"I didn't realize you were that close to finishing. I've gotten used to you being here."

"I know, Girlfriend, but I got a call from Brandon this morning and the houses are ready for me to stage for the upcoming Holiday Parade of Homes. I'm going to have to head back to Dallas. As a matter of fact, I have already made plans to leave tomorrow morning. It's not that long of a drive so I should be there in a few hours. That way I can be there to start Monday."

Miss Savannah was startled. "I knew that you had contracts already signed but had no idea it was going to be so soon."

"It's not so soon, like you said. I've been here for months enjoying myself and it's time for me to get back to work. Got to keep the dollars coming in!"

"Can't be months!"

"Think about it. I was here before your birthday in June and had to leave for a few weeks. Once I returned from Market I've been right here. That was in early August. The Fourth of July has passed. Labor Day is in the past and the holidays are quickly approaching."

"I guess you're right, but where did the time go? It was like you got here yesterday!"

"I know. I feel like that too, but it's time for me to get back to business."

"Has Quinn been being paying you? I mean, is he up to date on everything? He has a way of putting things aside sometimes."

"All paid up. When I submit this final invoice, everything's paid for including the purchases I made. He's stayed on top of everything."

"And, probably holding his breath every time another bill arrived, afraid to open it. He's so protective of my money. You'd think it was his! I'm glad everything's paid. Makes me feel good."

"Oh. I almost forgot. That Mr. Billingham we spoke to last night … he called and left a message for you to give him a call when you have time. He said he remembered that he has his grandmother's bowl and pitcher set and wants to know if you'd like to have it."

"That's awfully generous of him, especially when we've only talked over the phone one time."

"I know."

"Well, I'll call him back later. Right now I just want to spend all the time I can with you before you take off again. Never know when you'll be back!"

"If you don't care, I'd like to come back for Christmas. I know I'll still be busy for Thanksgiving, but I'd love to be here to help decorate for Christmas."

"Really? Oh Gypsy! That would be perfect! Of course you can!"
She put her arms around her friend and gave her a hug.

The remainder of the day was spent visiting and Miss Savannah sat in the wing back chair in Gypsy's bedroom and watched her pack everything, except for what she was going to need during the next few hours of her stay.

They put the suitcases in the elevator and took them downstairs so they could load them in the back of Gypsy's car.

"I don't remember arriving here with this much stuff!" Gypsy exclaimed. "And I even left a few things in the closet."

David was outside firing up the grill he had brought over for Jenny. When he saw them struggling with the luggage he dropped everything he was doing and headed their way. He didn't say anything, just took them and headed to the garage. Miss Savannah punched in the code and the garage door smoothly opened. In a few minutes he had everything loaded, including the two additional suitcases Gypsy and Miss Savannah had returned to the house and brought out.

When they returned to the house, David shook his head. He couldn't understand why women needed so much. It was just clothes!

As Gypsy had said, the next morning she carried her small over nighter suitcase out and loaded it in with her other luggage. She was getting ready to climb in her car and get on the road when Miss Savannah pulled her into her arms and gave her a hug. Gypsy melted into it realizing it was going to have to last her for a while.

Chapter 24

Late that evening a thunderstorm rolled across Tulsa. It arrived with a vengeance and the winds howled, raindrops the size of half dollars flooded the streets and hail pelted down on the area. Miss Savannah turned on the television in her bedroom to watch the storm channel. On the radar a bright red center surrounded by dark green was moving across Tulsa and the weather man said it was headed towards the northeast corner of the state. Tornado warnings were being issued and viewers were being told to take shelter. She heard what she thought was an explosion, and as she got out of bed to peek out her window everything went dark. She pulled aside the drapery and saw the entire neighborhood was black. Lightning flashed across the sky and in that flash she saw a limb from one of her neighbor's tree come crashing down in the street. Making her way back to her bed she pulled open the top drawer of the nightstand and felt around until her hand located a flashlight. She pushed the button and there was light but not very bright. She shook it and then whacked it against the side of the bed. Her theory had always been, if it didn't work, smack it and see what happened. That applied to almost everything, not just flashlights.

All of a sudden it dawned on her that without power she couldn't use the elevator to go downstairs to get fresh batteries. They were stored in the utility room on the ground floor. She crawled back into bed and turned off the flashlight in case power wasn't restored soon.

She had just gotten comfortable when she heard Jenny's voice coming from downstairs. "Miss Savannah. Are you oaky? It's me. Jenny."

'I'm just fine." She yelled back down. "What are you doing out in weather like this? You could get struck by lightning!"

Jenny stepped into the room. She was drenched, her hair plastered to her face and her clothes were dripping wet. "Mind if I grab a towel so I don't drip on the carpet?"

"Not at all." Miss Savannah replied and started to get out of bed. "Here I'll get one for you."

"You just stay right where you are. I know where they are."

A streak of lightning lit up the sky directly overhead and the clap of thunder immediately followed. "Boy. That was close!" Jenny said. "Isn't it exciting?"

"Exciting? Did you say exciting? Are you nuts?"

"I've always loved watching them. You can see them coming and feel the power as they get near. People think I'm crazy when I stand outside and watch them."

"I think they're right!"

Jenny laughed that wonderful laugh and the room seemed brighter even though it was totally enveloped in darkness. As she was drying off she replied. "I hope you don't mind me using the emergency key to the house you entrusted to me. When the power went off I was worried about you. I didn't know if you were already in bed or what. Need anything from downstairs?"

Miss Savannah thought it amazing that Jenny was checking on her.

"There're robes in the closet if you want to get out of those wet clothes. You can slip one of them on if you want."

"Well, actually I was thinking about going out front and seeing what I can see. I think the portico will shelter me some. It's really blowing out there!"

Miss Savannah scooted up in bed. "Do you think you should be doing that? Going out there when the lightning's so close?"

"Aw, I'll be okay."

"Jenny do you think you could help me downstairs? I just need someone there in case my hip starts to bother me. I think I can make it but …"

"No problem, but why do you want to go down?"

"I think I'd like to have some coffee. It looks like this storm is going to be with us a bit. How about it? Wouldn't you like a cup too?"

"Miss Savannah, we don't have any power."

"I know but we have the old gas cook stove. It works. And, I have a Dripolator coffee pot stored in the dish room, a French press one, too."

"Are you sure you can make it?"

"I'm positive! I know I can if you're there. Sometimes I think it's more me being afraid of falling than anything else."

"Sure wouldn't want that to happen."

Miss Savannah pulled sweats from the chest and slipped in to them. "Ready?"

"Yep. Be careful now! Here, let me get in front of you and you can put your hand on my shoulder. It's very dark but I think our flashlights will be enough light."

A few minutes later they were standing downstairs and Jenny was shining her light for Miss Savannah to make her way through to the kitchen.

"Jenny. Do me a favor. Go look in the utility room and in that plastic shoebox above the washer, there're some batteries. Would you bring it in here so I can replace these? They're getting awfully dim."

"No problem."

Miss Savannah thought a moment and said, "I'm afraid that's exactly what I am this evening."

"What's that?"

"A problem to you."

"Don't be silly. If I hadn't wanted to come over here, I sure as hell wouldn't have. We believe in taking care of each other!"

"And you do. Thank you!"

When the batteries had been replaced and Jenny was sure Miss Savannah had light, she slipped out the front door and stood there on the portico watching the sky. When she could no longer see any activity, she went back inside and Miss Savannah was sitting at the table sipping coffee and breaking pieces of chocolate chip cookies and dunking them. "I guess this is why I held onto that old coffee pot all these years," Miss Savannah said as she broke off another piece of cookie. "Join me?"

Knowing she wasn't going to get much sleep that night anyway, Jenny said, "Sure. Why not?" She poured a cup and together they sat there in the halo of two flashlights dunking cookies and just being together in the midst of a storm.

Chapter 25

Miss Savannah woke up on the sofa in the living room the morning after the storm. She noticed a pile of folded quilts on the one opposite of where she had slept. She couldn't imagine why Gypsy had arranged them like that but now she was glad she had. Jenny had climbed the stairs last night and they had giggled like two school girls as she tossed the quilts over the banister into the entry, then found pillows and done the same thing. It was like they were sneaking around and doing something mischievous. Together they spread the quilts on the sofas and listened to the distant sounds of the storm passing.

She was surprised that Jenny was already awake. She knew it had been way late at night before they finally fell asleep. Making her way through to the kitchen, Jenny wasn't there, but fresh coffee was made. Pouring herself a cup she walked over and looked out the back windows. She shook her head when she saw the condition of her herb garden. The hail had really taken its toll on it. Since she didn't have any plans for the day she decided she could spend it trying to salvage what was left. She set her cup down and saw a note with Gypsy's handwriting. It was the neatly written message she had taken from Mr. Billingham. She picked up the phone to call and there was no dial tone. She pushed the note further back on the counter. Staring at it she tapped the rim of her cup with her fingertip. Thoughts of tossing it crossed her mind but second thoughts made her leave it lying on the counter. *"Old girl, maybe it's time for you to start being a little bit more sociable instead of relying on others. It's not going to hurt you one bit to return that nice man's call."* She tried the phone once again and there was still no dial tone. *"Okay, I promise myself as soon as I have service again, I'll call."*

When she came back in the house with a basket of fresh herbs she had clipped from the torn plants the phone rang. She set the basket on the counter. "Hello".

"Miss Savannah. This is Mr. Billingham. I was wondering if you got my message and also if you got any damage over that way from the storm."

She eyed the note. "I have the message right here. I tried to call earlier but didn't have any phone service. They must have gotten everything repaired while I was outside in the herb garden."

"I saw on the news that your area got some damage."

"Oh, we didn't get damage here but the house next door ... well, it looks like they're going to have to have a tree removed. I don't know if it was from the wind or if lightning hit it but half of it's on the ground and in the street. Shame too. It was such a nice big tree."

"If it's the tree I think it is, it's been there for what seems forever. Big old oak tree?"

"I think that's the one."

He changed the subject after a pause in the conversation. "The reason I called the other day was to see if you wanted my grandmother's antique bowl and pitcher. I found the plate that goes under the bowl too. I guess that's what you call it. Anyway I think there's a matching soap dish packed away somewhere also."

She thought for a second. "I'd love to have them, but only if you're sure you want to part with them. I know how we can become attached to things like that."

"I'm very sure. I know Miss Georgina would love for them to be back in the house."

"Mind if I ask you something?"

"What's that?"

"Well, I often wondered why someone didn't stay in the house. Why it was left to ruin."

"It's a long story but it got tied up in the estate and it seems like no one wanted to live in it, yet they didn't want anyone else to live in it. So it just sat there for years."

"Would you like to come over and see what I've done to it? I don't mean *done to it* but what it looks like now?"

"I wouldn't want to intrude."

"It wouldn't be an imposition at all."

"You sure?"

"I'm certain."

"What time would be convenient for you? I can box up these things and bring them along."

"Anytime you wish. I'll probably still be here in the kitchen salvaging the herbs that storm tried to wipe out." She reached out and picked up a sprig of rosemary from the basket. "I think I have my work cut out for me this afternoon."

"How about around 2:00. Would that be okay?"

"It'd be just fine Mr. Billingham. See you then." She hung up the phone and went to the sink to wash the dirt off her hands. She laid out paper towels and began sorting the herbs. She decided to put them in freezer bags so she got them out, and the shears she would need to harvest the tender little leaves.

She dropped a paper towel on the floor and when she picked it up she noticed that the knees of the sweats she had slept in last night were covered with mud and that she was a mess. She knew for a fact she hadn't even combed her hair yet. She left everything on the counter and went upstairs to shower and put on clean clothes before her guest arrived. She thought to herself. *"A guest! That sounds nice."*

While she was dressing, she was thinking about the bowl and pitcher Mr. Billingham was bringing over. I think the perfect place for it would be in the guest bath downstairs. When she went back down she looked in to check. If it wasn't too terribly large it would fit perfectly. *"I'll just have to wait and see but I'm sure Miss Georgina would like it there."* This was the first time she had actually thought of the house's in-resident invisible guardian as a real person. Then a thought flashed through her mind. *"What if Miss Georgina made herself known while Mr. Billingham was there?"* She looked around and said out loud. "Miss Georgina. You need to be nice. Don't go spooking anyone. You hear?"

Joe Cocker's "Trust In Me" began playing on the sound system.

Miss Savannah smiled. She was already beginning to understand Miss Georgina's way of communication. It's wasn't the words to the songs necessarily. It was the titles. "Okay. I trust that you will behave!"

Promptly at 2:00 the doorbell chimed. Miss Savannah opened the door and there stood a very distinguished gentleman holding a rather large box.

"You have got to be Mr. Billingham. Please come in. Here, you can set that on this bench."

He sat the box down and looked at her. He had the clearest blue eyes. She always had been a sucker for blue eyes.

He held out his hand. "Miss Savannah?" She placed her hand in his and gave it a firm shake.

"Come on in."

He stood there and his eyes took in every detail of the home from where he stood. It was like he was reliving it. "I must say this is drop dead gorgeous! I never thought it could be restored and brought back like this. This is a true work of love. You can't imagine how relieved I am."

Once again she said, "Come on in and see the rest of it."

"Look at all those books! There must be thousands of them. I love to read and to see so many … well it's … it's wonderful."

She guided him into the rooms giving him a tour. When they passed the small guest bath she opened the door and said, "This is where I thought your grandmother's bowl and pitcher set could live." She held her breath hoping Miss Georgina would remember her promise to be good.

"Shall we take it out of the box and see?" he asked.

She could tell he was anxious to place it in the house. "Of course. Why don't you just carry it through and we'll unpack it here?

In a few minutes it was in place and never had there been a more perfect fit. She had him place it because something told her he yearned to do it himself. She stood back and admired it. "It's lovely, absolutely lovely."

He smiled and she knew memories were flashing through his mind.

"You want to see the upstairs? The very top floor isn't finished yet but you're welcome to see it anyway if you want."

He nodded.

Leading him to the elevator, she pushed the button she had grown to love, and the door slid open to welcome them. He was amazed at the elevator, even more amazed at the bedrooms and the cedar lined quilt closet. When they stepped out into the upper floor he smiled.

"You don't know how many times I'd sneak up here and sit by that window right over there and watch the neighborhood. Sometimes I'd bring a book, especially when it was raining and spend all afternoon reading and napping. I thought it was a secret and that no one knew where I was, but that was just the thoughts of a young boy. I know Miss Georgina knew every move I made. As a matter of fact she knew every move any of us kids made." He laughed.

They went back downstairs and he picked up the box they had left setting by the door of the guest bath. He flipped the light switch and took one more look. "It looks great in there. Thank you."

"I should be thanking you."

"It feels like it's back home again where it belongs."

When he said that Miss Savannah hoped Bonnie Raitt wouldn't start singing. She thought, *So far so good Miss Gerogina.*

"How would you like some iced tea or maybe something else?"

"You got coffee?"

She nodded. "Always."

"I drink coffee all day long. Some people can't understand how I can do that and still sleep at night."

In the kitchen he rested his hand on the Hoosier cabinet and when he saw the stove he couldn't believe it. "It looks just like it did when I was a child."

While he was looking around, Miss Savannah sliced a Cream Sherry Wine Cake and arranged the slices neatly on saucers. She sat the cake in the center of the table in case he wanted seconds. He did have seconds and she lost count of the cups of coffee they drank. He told her stories of growing up in the house. He told her stories of his brothers and sisters and the pranks they used to pull on each other. He told her of holidays, of Thanksgivings when there was so much food on the harvest table it threatened to sway in the middle, of huge Christmas trees, of hand-made presents Miss Georgina always had for them. He told her so many things.

He noticed that dusk was settling over the herb garden and looked at his watch. "Oh, I didn't realize I had been here as long as I have." He stood. "I'm sorry for taking up your entire afternoon. I need to be going. I apologize again."

Miss Savannah stood too. "There's no need to apologize for anything. I enjoyed our visit."

"Well, I'll be running along."

"Want some of that cake to take home with you? It's very good with morning coffee."

"I sure would if you don't mind. That has got to be the best cake I've had in years. You made it?"

She was already wrapping slices in plastic wrap. "I did. I usually don't buy any baked good. I love to bake." She handed him the wrapped package of delicious cake.

"You should sell this. I know I'd buy it. Thank you so much."

She nodded. "You're very welcome."

She saw him to the door. "It's been a pleasure meeting you in person Mr. Billingham."

"Nathan. My name's Nathan."

"Well, it was my pleasure Nathan."

"Goodnight, Savannah."

She started to correct him. No one called her Savannah any more but she didn't.

"Goodnight Nathan."

He walked across the portico and to his car. As he was pulling out of the drive he raised his hand and waved. She found herself waving back.

Chapter 26

Miss Savannah was looking over Jenny's shoulder as Jenny's fingers flew over the keyboard Monday morning. She had started on the reference books, and even though they were entered the same as the novels, they were in a separate block on the spreadsheet.

"You see, they're all separated, like at the library. I used the old Dewey Decimal system for the basis for organizing them. That was the only way I could keep up with them."

"What do I do about these old sets of encyclopedias? Do I enter them individually or as an entire set?"

"Since they're complete sets, I always entered them that way. There are still some sets that I need a volume or two to complete, kind of works in progress. I enter them separately." She pointed to an entry she had made. "See. I still need one volume to complete that one."

Jenny nodded.

"You know what? When you get them all entered maybe you could do a search and see if you can locate the missing volumes for me. You don't know how I'd love to have them all complete."

"Oh yeah. It would increase their value a lot!" Jenny responded.

"I wasn't worried about that as much as completing the sets. I hate to have things unfinished."

"I know." She smiled. "I noticed when I was separating them, before I entered them, that there are a lot of books on genealogy. You have an interest in that too?"

"I did at one time. I kind of gave up on it. Kept running into dead ends and up against brick walls. Never did find out what I wanted to."

Jenny paused then spoke. "Are there any books here about locating a birth parent? I've always wanted to know why. Why didn't my birth mother keep me? Why did she give me away?"

"Jenny, I'm sorry but I never had any reason to … to purchase them. Actually I don't think you can do that … you know, find out things like that on your own."

"That's what I was afraid of. I've never had the money to hire someone to do it for me. For years, since I grew up, it's always bothered me. All I know is what's on my birth certificate; where I was born, my birthday and whatever information was on that piece of paper. It seems like that's all I am, a piece of paper."

Miss Savannah didn't know what to say. After a minute she asked, "Have you ever seen the original adoption documents?"

Jenny shook her head. "I wouldn't even know where to begin to find them. Both my adoptive parents died in a horrible car wreck about five years ago."

"I'm so sorry to hear that. I'm sure it was a great loss to you."

"Yes Ma'am it was. The day that happened it was like I not only lost the only parents I had known all my life, I also lost the only link to who I am."

Miss Savannah patted Jenny on her shoulder.

Jenny kept her eyes on the monitor because she knew if she looked at Miss Savannah she would start crying. She had wept so much over the years and knew now that tears never helped. She crammed the thoughts into the back of her mind and straightened up. "Okay. I think I know what you want done with the reference books. I need to get busy so I'm not sitting here at the end of the day just looking at them."

Miss Savannah knew the subject was closed and not to meddle. It's just that her heart went out to Jenny and there was not a thing she could do.

Jenny was already searching to see if the volumes of "Man, Myth and Magic" had been entered. They had and now she was searching the cyber world of the internet to get a fair market price on them.

Miss Savannah said, "I'll be in the kitchen. I have bags and bags of herbs in the refrigerator I need to take care of. I kind of got sidetracked and didn't get them in the freezer yesterday." Later, while she setting at the kitchen table trimming the leaves from the herbs and carefully placing them on paper towels to dry before putting them into freezer bags, a thought came to her. She walked over and picked up the handset of the phone. She scanned through the menu and dialed Quinn's office. She was startled when he answered the phone himself.

"I was expecting your receptionist to answer the phone."

"Oh its lunch time. She'll be back soon. She just ran down to pick up some sandwiches for us. She's always willing to do the running and picking up if I'm willing to pick up the tab. What can I do for you today? You didn't go and buy more furniture, did you?"

She ignored the barb. "That's not the reason I called, Quinn. I have a question for you. I know you're a financial adviser, not an attorney, but I was wondering if you knew a good lawyer that handles cases where someone is looking for their birth mother."

"Well, not right off the top of my head but I think I can probably find someone for you. What are you up to now?"

She ignored his question. It really wasn't any of his business. "When you find someone, just give me a call and let me know. And, make sure he knows his business. I want someone good!"

She hung up the phone before he had a chance to pry.

Mid-afternoon the phone rang and it was Quinn returning her call with the information she requested. "I've already contacted him and told him that you'd be calling." She jotted it down and thanked him. Standing there she hesitated, then took the piece of paper to Jenny.

Jenny looked at it with a question mark written on her face. "What do I need an attorney for?"

Miss Savannah took a deep breath. "You remember what we talked about this morning? Well, if you really and truly want to find out, call this number. Arrangements have already been made. Just give him the information you have and he'll handle it for you." Miss Savannah turned and walked away leaving Jenny staring at the paper.

Chapter 27

Miss Savannah came in from the herb garden and shuddered. "You feel that nip in the air this morning?" she said to Tawnie.

"When David went to work this morning I swear I saw frost."

"I wouldn't doubt it. I need to get one of the gardening books and see if I need to mulch my herbs for the winter. They're doing so good I'd hate to lose them."

"I was noticing that the hummingbirds have all left too, so Mother and I need to get the feeder down and clean it up for the winter."

"Good idea. I sure enjoyed watching them. I'm really going to miss them, but it'll be getting too cold soon for me to go out and watch them."

Tawnie nodded and turned to leave. "I need to get the upstairs done. If you don't mind, I'd like to leave a little early today. There's a sale on winter coats and the boys all need one. I thought that there'd be hand me downs this year but they've worn them out completely. Looks like all new coats this winter."

"You know I don't mind."

Tawnie pivoted and started to leave the room then turned back around. "I have something to ask you. Mother just hasn't been herself lately, like something's on her mind. Has she said anything to you?"

Miss Savannah shook her head. "Hasn't said a word."

"I worry about her, you know. She's had a hard life raising all us kids and I try to help all I can."

"I know that. I've watched you two together." The phone rang and Tawnie grabbed the Windex and Pledge and headed upstairs.

"Hey Girlfriend!"

"Well, if it's not the long lost Gypsy! Where are you?"

"I'm still in Dallas. I've got things just about wrapped up and was wondering if my room is still waiting on me!" She laughed.

"Sure is. Come on home!"

"I can't right now, but as soon as everything's completed, I'll be on my way."

"So you will be here for the holidays?"

"Right after Thanksgiving, which is only a few weeks away."

"Oh my goodness. You're right. Time seems like it just gets away from me now days."

"I know. Me too."

"So how are things going there?"

"So far, it's been a great success. I know I've made a lot of my vendors happy. Their sales have grown significantly. I've spoken with a couple of them. As a matter of fact *they called me*. They're wondering when I'm going to do this again. They said they'd even send representatives from their offices to help set things up if I need them."

"That's wonderful! Sounds like you've hit on the right formula so you don't have to work so hard and put up with finicky clients."

"Exactly! Finally!"

"I can't wait for you to come back!"

"Me either! Listen I've got to run. Got an appointment in about an hour and I need to grab a bite to eat first."

"Okay. Talk to you later. Bye, bye."

"Love you! Caio Bella."

After their call ended, Miss Savannah got down the cookbooks and started leafing through them. *"I need to bake something!"* she said to herself. She got up and selected tract six on Van Morrison's

"Enlightenment" CD and pressed play. The upbeat sound of "Youth of a Thousand Summers" filled the rooms. Her body caught the rhythm and she danced her way back to the kitchen table like she was young again.

In half an hour ingredients were being stirred, blended and folded together. At the last minute, she retrieved a miniature spring form pan not more than six inches across and set it beside the normal- sized one. She poured batter into the pans and carefully slid them onto the shelf of the preheated oven. She set the timer and busied herself cleaning up. Cheesecake took a long time to bake and she wanted to stay near. When the buzzer sounded, she lowered the temperature and set the timer again. Getting all the cookbooks down had been a fruitless effort. She had decided to bake her original "Raspberry Mocha Cheesecake". It had taken months to perfect it but it was something she was proud of. She had never shared the recipe. She placed the cookbooks back on the shelves and tucked her little recipe box beside them.

While the cheesecakes were cooling she made the raspberry topping that would glaze the top of them. She kept feeling the top, and when they felt just right to her, she spooned the beautiful red glaze on top and put them in the refrigerator. They were so pretty and she knew they tasted as good as they looked. Wiping her hands on a dishtowel, she picked up the phone and punched in a number.

Nathan answered. "Hello."

"Nathan, this is Miss … this is Savannah. I've been baking this afternoon and I have something for you. Care if I drop it off in a little while?"

"Care? I'd be delighted! You know you're going to make me fat if you keep sharing all those wonderful things you bake!" He laughed into the receiver. She loved to hear that sound.

Since he had visited her that first time it seemed like each of them needed that special companionship that had kindled. When they had talked he told her that his wife had passed away a few years ago and since then he had never been able to fill that void. She confided she felt the same way. After that, he had insisted that she allow him to escort her to events. She once again attended the theater, concerts, went to the museums, and they enjoyed fine dining together. She had pulled her dress clothes from the back of her closet and they were now frequently being worn. At times they walked the paths of the rose garden nearby and just enjoyed that comfortable feeling of being together.

She told Jenny she'd be back soon and gathered up the little cheesecake and headed out the door. Placing it on the seat of the Jag, she drove the few miles to deliver it. He had been watching for her and opened the door before she rang the bell. She handed him the cheesecake and he carried it to his kitchen.

"It needs to be refrigerated." She told him.

He looked at the pan with a puzzled look on his face. "Here, let me show you how to work it." She flipped the side latch to release it and instructed him how to remove the cake.

"It's beautiful, almost too pretty to cut. But, I assure you I will cut it and probably eat much more than I should. Want some coffee? It won't take much time to make a pot."

"I really don't have time. I just wanted to get this over to you before it started getting dark. You know how I am after dark, strictly indoor person unless someone else is driving."

"I know Savannah. Thank you again for thinking of me when you baked today. I still say you should sell everything you bake. You could make a fortune."

She smiled at him and said goodbye and headed back home.

"When you get home give me a call so I know you made it safely. It is starting to get dark out there."

"Okay, if you insist."

"I do."

He watched her pull out of the driveway. In a few minutes the phone rang and she told him the Jag was in the garage and she was safely inside for the night. Hanging up the phone he began humming "You Make Me Feel So Young." It had been so refreshing to have found someone that appreciated and loved music as much as he did. She didn't get embarrassed when he began singing when they were grocery shopping or when he sang along with the radio in the car. As a matter of fact, she joined in sometimes.

He went into the kitchen and took the cheesecake from the fridge, and following Savannah's instruction, removed and placed it on a plate. Not bothering to slice it, he used his fork and took a big bite. His taste buds went wild. The tang of the raspberries exploded in his mouth and the smoothness of the mocha cake was like silk. He immediately took another bite. "She really should sell these." He thought to himself.

Chapter 28

That night when Miss Savannah went to bed, memories she tried to keep buried emerged and wouldn't let her push them back into the recesses of her mind. They fought to come forward.

She could sense the tiny bundle in her arms and feel the tiny baby snuggling into her. She could tell the baby was searching for sustenance that she was not allowed to give. Her breasts filled and the nourishing Mother's Milk leaked from her breasts and dripped on her gown.

A nun had come in and taken the baby away. She had tried to hang on to the baby for just a few minutes longer but her attempt had failed. It was as if the child had been confiscated like nothing more than chattel.

She knew when she went to the home for unwed mothers what was expected. She would deliver the child and it would be taken to the waiting adoptive parents. She would not be allowed time with the baby because, as they explained, she would bond with the child and it would make it more difficult for her to give it up. She had already signed the papers months ago and it had seemed easy for her to do at the time. But, the months following, she felt the movement of the child inside her body. She had watched as the healthy baby had kicked so hard it made her maternity shirt move. Miss Savannah placed her hands on her stomach.

She rolled over in bed and tried to make the memories stop flooding her mind.

The adoption of the baby had been as hard on her mother as it had been for her. Her mother had always wanted a houseful of children. Not to be able to keep this child broke her heart.

Oh how the world has changed. Now days, more times than not, young women chose to have their babies out of wedlock. They chose to raise them alone. That had not been an option for her. She had not been of legal age so by law she had no control over her own body. She was forced to abide by the laws and decisions made by someone other than herself.

She thought back to when the Vietnam War was just starting and she, along with a lot of her friends, went to the protests. They were peaceful sit-ins and they sang songs of peace and of protests. For most of the time they were peaceful, but at times escalated into violence. That is how the father of her baby had died.

He was such a gifted and brilliant young man. Already in college, he had a career ahead of him in the family law firm. It had been planned for years and preparations for his future were nothing but bright.

He had picked her up and together they headed to the demonstration site. Some overzealous riot control police officer saw them and without asking any questions swung the club and caught Edison on the back of his head. He fell and she screamed for help. Help was slow in arriving, and by the time they got there, he was already in a coma. Edison was put in the ambulance and taken away. She rushed to the hospital and tried to get in to see him but only family members could visit. She had sat in the waiting room for hours trying to get any information on his condition. His family ignored her.

He had just turned twenty one two days before. Her birthday present to him had been her virginity. They had grand plans. As soon as he finished law school they would be married. She should have her degree about the same time. That night he gave her his initial ring to wear on a chain around her neck.

Two days after the incident at the demonstration Edison had died.

She missed her first monthly flow and thought nothing of it because she was grieving so hard. But when it didn't come the next month either, she had to tell her parents that she was pregnant.

Arrangements were quickly made and she spent the next seven plus months in the Catholic Home for Unwed Mothers.

She had gone in with a child growing inside her and had left with an empty body, empty arms and a empty heart. It had taken her a long time to get over having to give her baby away but over the years she had found a place in the back of her mind to tuck it away.

Miss Savannah knew what had triggered these thought pouring out tonight. Her heart went out to Jenny. She couldn't imagine being an adult adopted child and not knowing from where you came.

She just hoped and prayed Jenny found what she was searching for. She wished her happiness. Maybe by helping Jenny, in a way, she might undo what she herself had done.

She shook her head and began surrounding herself with the bed full of pillows trying to get her nest made. She grabbed the remote and turned the television on and found an old classic movie channel and tried to settle in. That didn't work so she picked up her book from the nightstand. It took some concentration but before long she was lost in the swamp fighting off mosquitoes. She could see the moss hanging from the cypress trees and almost smell the fetid odor of the swamp water. She let Miranda take her with her on the trip. It took almost all night for her to get to a place she could finally close her eyes. The last thing she remembered was helplessly drifting in a boat. The book slid aside and "Miranda" shared her bed with her that night.

Chapter 29

She heard the doorbell chime and fought her way out from under the mountain of pillows. She hurriedly grabbed her robe and then realized that Jenny would be downstairs and take care of it. She felt all disoriented. Lying back on her pillows she gathered her wits together then slowly got out of bed and began dressing. *"Wonder what that was all about?"* she thought to herself. *"Old Girl, you just need coffee!"* She realized that her world seemed to be centered around coffee, of all things. But she did love a good cup! She also realized she had forgotten to put out something for Jenny to have with their coffee this morning. *"There I go with the coffee thing again."*

The foyer was stacked with boxes. "What's all this?" she asked Jenny who was standing there holding a clip board.

"I have no idea but they're from Miss Gypsy."

"Again?"

"Sure seems like it."

"Jon … Jonathan is out there bringing more in."

"Oh. I see you're on first name basis now, huh?"

"How could we not be after all the times he's been here!"

The door opened and Jonathan backed into the foyer with another hand truck loaded to the hilt. He could barely see over the pile of boxes. "Jen, don't let me bump into anything."

Miss Savannah raised an eyebrow and quietly whispered, "Jen"?

"You're clear. Just come straight back with it and you'll be okay."

"Thanks."

He let the hand truck down and started unloading it. Then he noticed Miss Savannah standing there. "Sure looks like your friend has been at it again! Where do you want me to put them this time?"

"I guess I need to open one of them and see what's inside before I'll know. Got a box opener handy?"

"Always." He started to hand it over then said, "Which one do you want to start on? I'll do the honors."

"May as well start with the one on top."

He slid the sharp blade along the shipping tape and pulled back the flaps of the box and stepped back out of the way.

Miss Savannah pulled aside the bubble wrap and there was box after box of Christmas ornaments. "Well, it looks like Gypsy is going to be here for the holidays after all!"

"Looks like she's already sending it ahead!" Jenny replied.

Miss Savannah put her hands on her hips and looked the situation over. "Okay. There's no place to store them down here or in the bedrooms so it looks like it's going to be the top floor for now."

Jonathan looked up the stairs.

"I don't expect you to carry them up. Since I know there's not anything heavy, use the elevator. Jenny can go with you to show you where to stack them." She looked at Jenny, "Any of the empty rooms up there will do. Just don't try to take them up all at once. Don't want anything to happen to my elevator. Hear?"

"Yes Ma'am," they both said at the same time. Jenny laughed and it was the first time in days Miss Savannah had felt the happiness bubbles popping and spreading through the room

"It's good to hear you laugh again." Miss Savannah said to Jenny while Jonathan was loading things into the elevator. "I sure have missed it. Well, it looks like you have everything under control so I'm going to get my coffee. Is it cold outside this morning? I sure would like to go out and do some things in the herb garden."

"It's a bit nippy but I think if you throw on a sweat shirt, you'll be just fine."

"I'm not going to go back up to get one so I think I'll just putter around in the kitchen."

"I left my hoodie on the back of my chair if you want to slip it on."

"You sure? I might get it dirty out there messing around with the plants."

"No problem. It's washable."

Jonathan motioned that the first load was ready to go up. "Just a minute, I'm gonna get Miss Savannah my hoodie to slip on and I'll be right there."

Miss Savannah waved her off. "I can get it myself. You go show "Jon" where to put all those boxes. For Christ sakes, it's beginning to look like it did when I first moved in." She headed to the kitchen. In a little while she was outside adding mulch to her herbs and trying to figure out a way to cover them for the winter without killing them.

She stood up and stretched her back. She spotted the old barbeque pit and made her way to it. She looked it over to see if it was sound and it seemed to be. An idea began forming in her mind. *"I wonder if this can be converted into an outside fire pit? It would be so cozy to set out here and relax with a fire going, especially at night. Oh, I can just see it glowing and putting out warmth and all of us setting around it sipping hot chocolate laced with a little Peppermint Schnapps."*

She scooted her feet around and discovered that a brick surround was already in place, not very large but big enough to put some chairs and maybe a table. She looked up and there didn't seem to be any overhanging branches or anything that would have to cut away.

Jenny came out back expecting to find her at the herb garden. She quickly scanned the area and saw her back by the old barbeque pit. "What on earth are you doing way back there? You need to be careful back there. There're a lots of big tree roots you might trip over."

"I was careful. Come see. I have an idea and need your input."

Jenny made it to where Miss Savannah was standing with her hand resting on the pit.

"I know this doesn't look like much but I have an idea."

"Oh, Miss Savannah, when you say that I start to worry."

"Now listen to what I have in mind before you say anything."

Jenny nodded and said, "Okay."

Miss Savannah explained what she had in mind while she walked around checking out the where the brick surround ended. "So what do you think?"

"I've always loved to set around a fire. When the kids were little I used to have them help me and we'd gather fallen limbs and anything we could find and build us a big bon fire. Oh, how I loved that."

"So you think it might work?"

"I don't know." Jenny lifted one of the rusted out grates and peered down inside. Looks like the brick are all sound. At least I don't see any light peeking through." She leaned down and checked the ash bin. She grabbed a sturdy stick and began scraping years and years of ashes away. "This looks okay too. Of course it's all damp up in there but it would be."

"Do you think it would take much work to get it functioning again?"

"I really don't know but I can have David take a look at it when they come over next time."

"He just amazes me. He can do just about anything."

"Yep. He sure can. If there's any problem he'll be able to spot it."

Jenny brushed her hands together get to the dirt off.

"Well, I think I'm just going to spend some time out here clearing away some of these weeds and things that have grown up around it."

"You don't need to be out here by yourself doing something like that. Let me go shut down what I was working on and I'll help you."

"You don't have anything pending you need to take care of?"

"As Miss Gypsy would say, I got it under control!" She laughed and the day was brighter. "Hand me your cup and I'll refill it while I'm in there. Want me to bring something out for you to snack on?"

"Just coffee would be perfect." She put her hand on her hip and replied, "I've got to watch this girlish figure!" and struck a pose.

"Oh, I wish I had my camera right now!"

"Better be glad you don't!" She laughed.

When Jenny got back Miss Savannah already had a little pile of dead weeds pulled and piled up.

Jenny jumped in and began to pull to. In an hour they stood back and admired their handiwork. "What do you think about burning some of those weeds in the pit? Think it would hurt anything?"

"I don't know. I grabbed some heavy duty trash bags to put them in while I was inside."

"Let's just put a little pile in and see what happens."

"Okay. But just a little pile like you said. Got any matches?"

Miss Savannah shook her head.

"I'll be right back." She returned with a box of wooden matches and a newspaper. "I think we can get them started with this."

"We can always grab a steak out of the freezer in case anyone calls the fire department on us. After all it is a barbeque pit!" Miss Savannah quipped.

"Amen!"

Jenny removed what was left of the old rusted grates and set them aside. In a few minutes she had crumpled up some of the newspapers and piled a few twigs on them. "She struck a match and said, "Well, here goes."

In a few minutes the twigs had caught fire and Jenny piled on some small limbs.

Jenny pulled over a couple of chairs so they could have a place to sit.

With the fire going they put small handful of weeds on top and in no time at all they had everything burned and what was left was a warm glowing bed of coals.

Miss Savannah looked at Jenny. "Seems to have worked just fine."

"It sure does need to be cleaned out though. There's no telling how deep those ashes are in the bottom."

They heard a car drive up and looked around. Nathan hurriedly got out of his car and headed for the back door.

Jenny threw up her arm and waved to him. "We're over here, Mr. Nathan."

Miss Savannah said, "What in the world are you doing over here? I thought you told me you were going grocery shopping today."

Jenny started pulling another chair over but he motioned her away and moved it himself.

"I called several times and there was no answer so I got concerned something was wrong. No, to be perfectly honest it scared me when you didn't answer." He looked around. "What have you been doing? That old pit hasn't been used in years."

"We could tell," Jenny said.

"It's a wonder you didn't burn everything down and you along with it!"

Miss Savannah looked at Jenny. They had been sufficiently scolded.

Miss Savannah began explaining how it had all come about and he sat listening. When she was through he got up and walked over to the pit and looked it over. Jenny followed him and showed him the grates she had removed.

"These are going to have to be replaced, but that's about the only thing I could find wrong with it except that it needs to be cleaned out." He nodded in agreement.

"There used to be a tool shed in the back of the garage. Is it still there?"

"There's some sort of storage there. I've never looked in it." Miss Savannah said.

He walked over and went in the side door. In a few minutes he returned with a shovel. "I think this should do the job."

"What are you going to do? You have dress clothes on!" Miss Savannah exclaimed.

"That's what they make dry cleaners for." He scooted the shovel in the ash bin and pulled out what looked like grey mud. He took the point of the shovel and pushed it down to the bottom and listened. "Sounds solid to me."

He leaned the shovel against a tree. "I can't remove it today because of the embers in it but maybe tomorrow I'll come over if it's alright and I'll clean it out and see what you have."

"You don't have to do that. I can get David to do it."

"No since in bothering that young man. I've noticed he has a pretty full platter all ready. No reason at all to add to it. Plus I love to do things outside, especially this time of year."

Nathan brushed off his hands. "Well, now that I know everything's okay here, I'm going to go on and get my shopping done. Need anything from the store?"

"Not that I can think of. Jenny you need anything?" Miss Savannah asked.

"Thank you. I do but I need to go do big grocery shopping. I was going to ask later if you cared if I took "Baby" out for a spin and do my shopping."

"You know you can and it does "Baby" good to go for a run every once in a while. Keeps her going. You know where the keys are."

Nathan turned to leave. In a gentle voice he said, "Savannah, you be careful out here. You know I do worry about you."

"I promise. And thanks."

He turned back around and picked up the grates Jenny had removed. He wrapped them in the left over newspaper they hadn't burned. "I'm just going to put these in my trunk. I think I know where I can get some new ones."

"You don't have to do that."

"I know. I want to. You wouldn't deny me that would you?"

Miss Savannah smiled. "Of course not."

They watched as Nathan placed the grates in the trunk of his car and backed out of the drive.

"He's a very nice man, Miss Savannah."

"I'm beginning to realize just how nice he really is." She sat up in her chair. "By the way, speaking of nice men what about Jon? I saw the way you two looked at each other this morning."

Jenny was caught unaware. "Jon?"

"Yep. I always thought his name was Jonathan but I heard the way you said his name when he was here. Do I hear a little interest?"

"Oh Miss Savannah. He's such a hunk. Haven't you noticed?"

"Not really but now that you mentioned it, he is pretty muscled up."

"He has to be handling all those deliveries day after day."

"You two been talking?"

"Of course we talk. He's here several times a week."

"You know what I mean. Exchanged numbers yet?"

For the first time Miss Savannah thought she saw Jenny blush.

"There's nothing serious. We're just good friends. We have some things in common and we talk."

"Well, that's a start!" Miss Savannah laughed. She knew Jenny was uncomfortable talking about her personal life so she changed the subject. "Think we can burn some more things? I see some weeds that still need pulling and I saw some dead limbs on the ground back behind the pit."

"Why don't we just concentrate on the weeds around here? We don't need to be   messing around back there. Might be some creepy crawler things and I sure don't like them!"

"Never thought of that. I agree. I'm not particularly fond of them myself." She shuddered.

By the time they stopped for lunch they had cleared about three feet away from the surround. Miss Savannah sat down and took a look at their progress. "Now doesn't that look nice? I love it out here. Maybe if Nathan can get the grates we'll have him over for hot chocolate and enjoy this little bit of heaven! I was so afraid when the hummingbirds went away and now that the herb garden doesn't need me to look after it, that I'd not have anything to do out here. I do so love it out here!"

"I know and I do too. I'm so glad you decided to unearth this old pit! What on earth possessed you to do it today?"

Miss Savannah paused and thought for a minute. "You know Jenny, we have to listen to our inner voice. It will always lead us to our passions and our passions lead us to our purpose. I read that somewhere and never truer words were written. It stuck in my mind and it's kind of how I live."

"It seems to me that it's exactly how you live."

They sat for a few minutes watching the last of the embers of the fire die down.

"Do you think it will be safe to leave it now? I sure don't want anything to catch fire from it." Miss Savannah asked.

"I think it'll be just fine. There's no breeze or anything to stir up sparks. I think whatever is left in there will burn itself out in just a little while. We didn't have anything big, just twigs and weeds."

"Getting hungry?"

"Beginning to."

"Then why don't I go in and put us a lunch together."

"I have a better idea. Why don't I run and get my grocery shopping done and I'll stop back by that little Chinese restaurant and pick us up a lunch to-go?"

"That sounds wonderful! I'll just grab a slice of pumpkin spice bread and that'll hold me until you get back."

They returned to the house and Jenny got the keys to "Baby". "I'll be back in a little while. I don't have to get too many things. Buying groceries for one doesn't take too long."

"How well I know."

Chapter 30

Jenny woke up to the sound of trucks in the driveway in front of the apartment. She peeked out the window and there were men unloading brick and bags of stuff. She threw on her sweats and stepped out on the landing.

"Hey! Are you sure you have the right address? I don't think Miss Savannah has ordered anything like that. As a matter of fact, I'm certain."

Nathan stepped out from behind the delivery truck and waved. "I'm here, Jenny. It's okay."

Jenny looked the situation over and went back inside to grab her shower and get dressed. She heard the truck leave. When she went back outside, Miss Savannah was fussing over a crew of men and serving them coffee and something from a platter she had set on one of the tables in the area of the herb garden.

Jenny walked over to her and asked, "What's going on?"

"It's Nathan. He showed up early ringing my doorbell telling me that a work crew was going to be here today. I was just as puzzled as you are."

"And what are they going to do?"

Miss Savannah walked over to a drawing on the table that was weighted down with a couple of bricks. "I'm not exactly certain, but by what I can tell after Nathan left here yesterday morning, he drew up these plans and went somewhere, I don't know where, and told them that this is what he wanted done."

Jenny's eyes scanned the drawing. "This is going to be beautiful!"

"My goodness, there's so many workers they look like a bunch of ants. People everywhere! They better not damage my herb garden."

"I'm sure Nathan would never allow them to do that."

"You never know!"

Jenny could see that a foundation of sand and gravel had already been spread and tamped down in the area around the pit and the weeds had been cleared back even more than she and Miss Savannah had done the day before. "Wow!" was all she could say.

Nathan walked over and said good morning. "Sorry if I startled you this morning. I wanted to get on this early so they could complete it today. There's a lot to do but there's plenty of men here to get it done."

"But this is so big." Miss Savannah exclaimed.

"Look. It shows walkways and little low wall planters. And the surround looks like it's going to be big enough for a dance floor."

"It's not going to be that big but you do need room to put chairs and a couple of tables out here. Any smaller and you'd have to step off the surround to get around a table. I was afraid a chair might fall off and someone might get hurt. That's why I designed that little wall. I don't want anyone getting hurt!"

"I just can't allow you to spend that kind of money on this place!" Miss Savannah exclaimed.

"It's not costing a thing."

"What do you mean not costing anything? It's got to be costing a small fortune."

"Well normally I guess it would but I've called in a favor. For the past two years I've been wondering just how and when I'd be able to call it in. Yesterday when I saw you and Jenny out here, I knew how I'd finally get my return!"

"But you had to have put out some kind of money a few years ago!"

He gently put a hand on each side of Savannah's face to get her attention. "I want to do this! I think I'll probably be spending time over here too. No. I know I'll be spending time over here! Now listen to me. I don't make it habit of doing things I don't want to. Understand?"

"But …"

He laid a finger across her lips. "But nothing!

He pulled his hands back. "You sure you understand?"

She nodded.

Even with the shortened daylight hours, when darkness crept across Tulsa, everything was completed and the crews were doing final clean up and loading their tools.

"You won't be able to walk on it for a couple of days, but doesn't that look better than it did?"

"It just wonderful!" Miss Savannah said in awe.

"The pit is all cleaned out and minor repairs done to it too. There was nothing major at all. Now I can sleep soundly knowing that you're not out here messing around with a possible fire hazard or anything like that. And I know you'll be able to walk safely from the house out here."

Jenny was walking around and surveying everything at a distance. "Look Miss Savannah, there's even fire wood!" Sure enough fire wood was piled on the backside of the pit.

"There's a small platform under the wood so it doesn't get wet on the ground." He held her hand and led her around so she could see.

"Isn't there anything that you haven't thought of?"

He snapped his fingers and went to his car. The trunk flew open and he reached in and took out new grates. He carefully stepped over the new brickwork and placed the grates on the pit. "There now! I think it's complete!" He smiled.

"So when did you say it could be used?"

"In a couple of days, I'd think, but I'll keep checking on it for you and let you now. Okay?"

"Now that it's all done I can't even seem to remember what it looked like yesterday! I never dreamed it could be so beautiful."

"Oh. One more thing. See those wires sticking up from the planters? When the mortar all gets set, some electricians are going to be here to install lighting for the area. And before you say anything, that was in the deal too. I didn't think you'd want bright lights out here so they're small garden lights. They'll show you where they put the switch. I told them to hook it up remotely so you can turn the lights on before you get out her."

"Oh, Nathan. How can I ever thank you."

"Just continue being yourself, Savannah. Just be yourself!"

Jenny watched this wonderful couple in the autumn if their lives enjoying life and each other so much.

Mr. Nathan had insisted Jenny join them for dinner. Steak and seafood seemed to be what everyone was craving so that's what they had. After he had them safely home and inside, he headed to his own home. Jenny had remained in the house with Miss Savannah until she was certain the house was closed and everything locked. This had become part of her routine every evening. Miss Savannah had said it wasn't necessary, but Jenny thought differently. With Miss Savannah upstairs and their goodnights said, Jenny paused at the stereo on her way out and put on Bonnie Raitt's "Love Has no Pride." She turned it low so it wouldn't disturb Miss Savannah, locked the door and sat on the steps listening to it in peace, unaware that it was piped into Miss Savannah's room.

Miss Savannah lay in her bed listening to the song. A tear fell from Miss Savannah's eye, ran down her cheek and dampened a small spot on her pillow. She knew Jenny was not aware the she was listening too. She so connected with Jenny on a heart level and in her mind too! She could feel Jenny's pain because she had been there herself.

Jenny poked her head in the backdoor called out to Miss Savannah. "Come see!"

"It's already dark. What are you doing out there?

"Just come and see."

Miss Savannah went to the backdoor and four little goblins yelled "Trick or Treat!" and held out their goodie bags.

She began laughing. "Well, you wait right there and I'll get you a treat. Sure don't need any tricks!"

She had bought several bags of candy on her trip to the market. She reached in and pulled out a handful for each one and dropped it into their bags. "Thank you, Miss Savannah." They reached in to get a piece.

"No, no, no. Remember what I told you? Not until we get home!"

They pulled their little hands back and grasped the handles on their Trick or Treat bag.

Jenny spoke up. "We're going to walk them around the block. Wanna go with us?"

"Thanks for the invitation but I think I best stay here so I can give out all this candy."

"Okay. We'll be back later." Jenny took two little hands and Tawnie the other two.

Miss Savannah found she was overwhelmed with little ghosts and goblins for the next two hours. She was glad she had taken Nathan's advice and purchased way more than she was going to.

Jenny and Tawnie returned with the boys in tow. Their bags were bulging with goodies. She heard the boys asking. "Can we have some now? You said when got home we could. Please!"

"Okay. Come over here." Tawnie took each bag. Get two pieces and that's all. I sure don't need the four of you bouncing off the walls tonight." After each got their candy, she rolled the tops down and pulled a marker out of her pocket. She printed each of their names on their bags.

"Lesson from last year," she said recapping the marker. She stuck it back in her pocket.

"They were fighting for a week over which bag was whose. I thought they were going to drive me crazy!"

Miss Savannah started out the backdoor then reached and pushed the button on the remote lighting. I thought I might build a fire tonight. Want to join me?"

"I'd love to," Tawnie replied, "but I need to get these monsters home. They actually have school tomorrow. I'd hate to be one of their teachers. Can you imagine all those kids on sugar highs?" She shook her head. Before long she had all of them strapped into car seats and belted in. "Junior looked over to Miss Savannah and said. "I can wear a seat belt now. I'm a big boy not like the babies."

A chorus of voices yelled back, "I'm not a baby! You're a bully!"

"That's enough of that. Stop it right now!" Tawnie scolded. Shaking her head again she closed the car door and started around to the driver's side. "We go through this every time!"

She hugged Jenny and gave her a kiss. "I love you. Talk to you tomorrow. Oh, and thanks a lot for helping me with them tonight."

"No problem. I love you too. Please be careful out there. It's a crazy night"

Tawnie nodded her head. "I know."

Jenny stepped back and waved as Tawnie and the boys headed home.

"Well, Jenny. You don't have to go to school tomorrow. Want to join me for a little fire?"

Jenny laughed. "Sure. Why not?"

Miss Savannah said, "I'll be right there." She stepped just inside the kitchen and grabbed a thermos and a couple of mugs."

Jenny held out her hand and said, "Here. Let me help you with that."

Miss Savannah surrendered the mugs to her. After a few minutes they had a nice cozy fire going, not too big because they both knew they weren't going to be out too terribly long. Miss Savannah said, "Hand me those mugs please." She uncapped the thermos and the unmistakable aroma of hot chocolate and peppermint filled the air.

Jenny accepted hers and replied, "Woman after my heart!"

"I think you love this as much as I do. I mean the pit and getting to set out and drink Schnapps laced hot chocolate."

Jenny cupped her hands around the mug and nodded. "It's nice out here. Very nice."

They watched the fire burn down to embers and then watched the embers turn grey and flicker out the last lick of flame.

"Tawnie and you are so good with those boys."

"Thanks. I try to help her with them when I can."

"I've noticed. Sometimes I wish …" then she caught herself and let the unfinished sentence hang.

Jenny didn't say anything. She tilted her mug to her lips and drained the last of her chocolate. "I think the neighborhood has calmed down enough and I can call it a night. I don't think I ever saw so many cars on that street."

Miss Savannah just nodded this time.

"People bring their children here because they know it's safe. There's so many crazy people out there. Can you imagine deliberately putting something in that candy that would harm, even kill a child?"

"I can't, but I know what you said happens every year. I hear it on the news."

Jenny shook her head. "Crazy. Just crazy."

Miss Savannah finished her chocolate, stood and started down the walkway towards the house. "I guess we better be getting inside."

Walking along beside Miss Savannah Jenny said, "Yep." Jenny supported Miss Savannah by her elbow when she stepped off the walkway.

Safely inside Miss Savannah clicked off the lighting and placed the remote back on the cabinet.

"I enjoyed that. Thanks for joining me. It's always so much nicer when you're out there with me."

"My pleasure." She rinsed out the mugs and put them in the dishwasher.

"Jenny, there's something I've been wanting to talk to you about. You got a minute?"

"Sure. I don't think I have a hot date tonight." She giggled.

"Why don't we go to the living room? It's more comfortable in there."

Miss Savannah sat in her favorite chair and Jenny sat near. She gathered her thoughts. "Jenny, I was wondering if you'd be interested in becoming a broker? You know a rare book broker. I've been doing a bit of investigating and there's not too many in this area."

Jenny didn't know what to say. Miss Savannah took her hesitation as a negative reaction.

"I don't know what all is involved, but we can find out if you are interested. By what I understand they make pretty good money. And after getting all these books in order the way you did … well, I know it wouldn't take a lot for you to be handling matters like that, you know appraising and brokering."

"Miss Savannah, that's exactly what I've been researching too but I just don't know how much it costs. There doesn't seem to be a lot of information available about it. I've learned so much here in your home the last few months … I've realized that is what I'd like to do. Strange that we both thought of it."

"I don't think it strange at all. I've watched you grow and become more confident. I've seen you looking over your spreadsheet and go pull a book from the shelf and research it again. I can say one thing about you, you know books!"

"I like to think I do."

"There's no question in my mind that you're ready to go forward. Do you think you can find out the information needed … maybe make some calls or something?"

"I'll give it my best effort. It may take a few days, though, for me to even start finding out what is needed and where I go from here."

"There's no hurry. When you find out all the information come and talk to me. Okay?"

"Okay!"

Miss Savannah rose from the chair. "I think this old girl is ready for bed." She ran her fingers over the binding of a few books then selected one to read. "I must have read this half a dozen times but I enjoy it so much. Goodnight." She tucked the book under her arm and in a few minutes Jenny heard the elevator hum.

Jenny sat back down in the chair. She was in shock. She couldn't believe Miss Savannah had just offered her what she had been dreaming of. She sat there awhile, letting her eyes scan the thousands of volumes. If she had to, she could pull a book from the shelf and automatically know its present value and what it had been a few years ago. She was so familiar with them. Standing, she turned off the lamps and checked once again to make sure everything was locked up and secure. She locked the backdoor behind her and headed to the apartment.

She said to herself, "Dreams do come true after all."

That night when she went to bed her prayers were prayers of thanks for putting this special person in her life

Chapter 32

When the day dawned over Tulsa, it was cold and overcast with dark clouds hovering over the city with a threat of snow. While having her usual first cup of coffee, Miss Savannah felt an uneasiness inside. She had not had that feeling in a long time. She thought things over and couldn't pin-point what was causing it. It bothered her, because sometimes it was a precursor to bad news and she worried. She dialed Nathan's number. When he answered the phone she asked, "Is everything alright over there?"

"Everything's just fine. I was getting ready to call you in a few minutes. I got a call last night and I'm going to have to be gone for a few days."

He caught the pause in her voice.

"It's nothing. I just need to fly out to Seattle and take care of some business. Seems like I have to handle some things personally this time."

"I didn't know you had ever been in Seattle. I love that city."

"I lived there for a few years and while I was there I did some investing in, let's just say, the fishing industry. The call I got last night informed me that there was something going on that I need to attend to. It was so strange when the man that called and wouldn't identify himself, but the information he gave me warrants me flying out to make certain things are as they should be. I haven't let anyone know I'll be there this afternoon. Kind of want to surprise them. Anyway, I'm flying out in a couple of hours. I was finishing up packing when you called."

"Oh no. I hope everything's going to be okay."

"Well, I may have to fire a couple of my supposedly financial people but they can be replaced. Seems like they've been lining their pockets with corporate money and I don't need to be called on the carpet by the IRS or anything like that. Proving that I didn't know anything about it would be hard to explain. It seems like there's always something like that going on in this industry. Someone gets greedy and the next thing you know the entire business is in big trouble."

"I can see how that can happen. I'll not keep you because I know you're busy. Just wanted to make sure that you're okay."

"I'm just fine, Savannah. Thank you for calling. I know you're going to worry so I'll give you a call tonight. Okay?"

She nodded her head and said, "Okay. Be safe."

"I will."

She hung up the phone.

She heard Jenny in the library raising cane about something. "Dang internet's down again! Darn you! How am I supposed to get this done when nothing works?" She was working herself into a tizzy.

"It'll be back up sometime today. Don't let it bother you like that!"

"I have things I need to get done!"

"I'm sure everything you need to do will still be there when they get the internet fixed."

"I've already called the service. I think everyone else in this area has problems too. I had a heck of a time getting through. That busy signal drives me crazy!"

Miss Savannah knew things were just going to escalate if she wasn't able to divert Jenny's attention.

"It's just *so* frustrating." Jenny picked up her cup. "Guess I have time to warm this up. How about you? You need me to freshen yours too while I'm at it."

"Sure. I'll go with you. I need to put something in my stomach too. Listen, I have an idea. Instead of me cooking why don't we run down to the pancake house and get pancakes?"

"Oooo. I haven't had pancakes in ages. That sounds so good, especially on a day like this. It looks like it could start pouring down out there at any minute."

"It looks like it's going to snow to me."

"Don't even think that! I'm not ready for snow yet. It's not even Thanksgiving."

"But that's just around the corner, too. It'll be here before you know it. By the way, what if we have Thanksgiving here? There's plenty of room for everyone."

"That sounds okay to me. In the past we've always gotten together where I lived but the apartment is kind of small for everyone to fit this year. Let me talk to Tawnie and see what she thinks. I really don't know if any of my other kids will be here or not this year. Seems like they have so many things going on in their own lives."

"I thought I'd ask Nathan if he wanted to come over. He mentioned the other day that we'd go out and eat but to me, Thanksgiving should be at home."

"Yep."

"Listen to me standing here running my mouth about Thanksgiving. I need some pancakes!"

Miss Savannah grabbed the keys to the Jag and they headed across the driveway. She pitched the keys to Jenny. "Why don't you drive?"

"Really? The Jag?"

"We'll give "Baby" a rest today. That is if you don't mind."

Jenny smiled and they got in and headed to the pancake house.

Miss Savannah reached over and pushed the button on the sound system and the unmistakable sound of Johnny Lang began. The base was heavy the way Miss Savannah loved it.

"Why Miss Savannah, you like Johnny Lang too?"

She was nodding her head to the rhythm of the blues. "Love him." She looked over at Jenny and smiled.

"He's one of my favorites! Mind if I turn it up a little?"

"Not at all."

They drove across town with Jenny glancing at Miss Savannah nodding her head to the rhythm. Miss Savannah closed her eyes and let the music take her over. A glow of youth flushed briefly over Miss Savannah's face. Jenny drove in silence appreciating Johnny and in awe at Miss Savannah being so totally immersed in the music. *I bet she really was something in her youth,"* Jenny thought to herself.

"Wow!" was all Jenny could say. "She drives like a dream! I love your choice of traveling music!" She laughed and pulled into the restaurant parking lot and found a parking place away from the other cars. "Sure don't want someone opening their door and putting a scratch on this little lady!"

When they were seated Miss Savannah told the waitress, "I don't need a menu. I'll have the buttermilk pancakes with bacon. Coffee please."

"Make it two." Jenny replied.

In a few minutes, the waitress appeared with plates of hot pancakes with a mound of butter melting on top of them. She placed a small pitcher of warm syrup in the center of the table. "Can I get you ladies anything else?"

"Not right now. Thank you." Miss Savannah replied.

They bowed their heads and in a minute they were both digging into the stacks of pancakes like they hadn't eaten in days. A little later Jenny pushed her plate back. "I can't eat another bite. That was so good!"

"It did hit the spot didn't it? You ready?" Miss Savannah asked. She left a tip on the table and they stepped outside. On the way to the car Miss Savannah asked, "Have you ever been to that little bookstore over in 15th Street?"

Jenny shook her head. "Don't think so. They call it Cherry Street now."

"I keep forgetting. I guess I'll always call it 15ᵗʰ. Anyway, I'd like to go over and see what they have. It's been quite a while since I've been there."

Jenny turned the key and the Jag came to life ready to go.

"It's somewhere between the fairgrounds and downtown area. I'll know it when I see it." In a few minutes Miss Savannah pointed and said, "There it is." Jenny pulled in and parked.

An hour later they were back in the Jag headed home. Miss Savannah had purchased a couple of books that would almost complete one of the sets in the library. Jenny had looked them over and made certain the publisher and everything was the same before agreeing that they were indeed what were needed.

"Did you have a chance to talk with the owner?" Miss Savannah asked when they got back in the car. She reached over and turned off the music so they could talk.

"Sure did."

"What did you find out?"

"Well, for one thing I found out that there seems to be no certifications required to become a broker of rare books."

Miss Savannah nodded. "And?"

"And he even offered me a job after we visited for a while." Jenny laughed. "Of course I politely turned it down. I know I need to do some more research when we get back to the house, that is, if the internet is back up."

A fine mist of sprinkles began to fall. Jenny turned on the windshield wipers and slowed down. The Jag was so powerful she didn't want to overdrive the street conditions. Just as Jenny had cleared the intersection after making a left turn they heard tires screaming and the unmistakable sound of metal crashing into metal. Jenny looked in the rearview mirror and immediately pulled over, put the gearshift in park, put on the emergency flashers, jumped out of the car and went running back. "Stay in the car!" she yelled at Miss Savannah. Jenny was dialing 911 as she ran back to the accident because she could tell someone was seriously injured.

Other cars had stopped and people were running to the two vehicles that had collided. Jenny was yelling directions to people and in a few seconds she had someone diverting traffic around the accident clearing the way for the emergency vehicles. Miss Savannah heard the scream of sirens nearing. Once the ambulance and police arrived Jenny got back in the car and made her way out of the traffic jam that had been created by the accident.

"That was close." Miss Savannah said when they were clear of the traffic. "If you hadn't already cleared the intersection when you did, that could have been us back there."

Jenny nodded. Miss Savannah noticed Jenny was wet and shivering. "We need to get you home and into some dry clothes! You're shaking!"

"I'm not cold. I think it's just the adrenalin still pumping. Things like that scare to me death but it seems like I never take time to think, just do what needs to be done, then after it's over my body reacts."

"I think you need a good hot shower and something hot to drink."

They rode in silence the rest of the way back home each of them thinking what a close call they had just had.

Miss Savannah carried her purchases into the house while Jenny went to the apartment to shower and change. She laid the books on Jenny's desk and made hot chocolate. Something had been nagging in the back of her mind all afternoon. She picked up the phone and dialed Quinn's number. When she was put through she explained why she was calling. "Quinn, remember when I called a few weeks ago and asked you to locate that adoption attorney for me?"

"Sure do. I have his number right here."

"Oh, I don't need his number. I was going to ask you if you'd contact him and see if Jenny ever called him."

"I'll give him a call and get right back to you."

"Thanks."

Miss Savannah busied herself fussing over the hot chocolate and when Jenny came over she poured a generous amount of Schnapps into Jenny's cup of hot chocolate and handed it to her.

It wasn't long before Jenny's phone rang. It was Tawnie. "Oh my God. I was just watching the news and they were reporting an accident and warning people to pay attention to road conditions. I saw you and Miss Savannah's Jag? Are you okay?"

"Yep."

"Are you crazy? What were you trying to do, get yourself run over or something?"

"Just did what had to be done. I'm okay and Miss Savannah too."

Tawnie's voice relaxed. "Well, the police are trying to locate you. They need to talk to you. It's all over the TV. You need to get in touch with them."

"What are they looking for me for?"

"Just call them. If you turn on the TV I'm sure you'll be able to catch it. I'm going to let you go because I have dinner on and the boys are hungry."

"Love ya!"

"Love you too."

Jenny went into her office area and turned on the TV. Miss Savannah followed her. The report was being replayed and they sat there watching it. A telephone number flashed across the screen. Jenny jotted it down.

Needing refills on their hot chocolate Miss Savannah picked up the cups and headed to the kitchen. She heard Jenny dialing. As she was about to take the cups back in, her phone rang.

"Miss Savannah, Quinn here. I caught him just as he was leaving the office but he said that he couldn't give out that kind of information "However, he did say, that it would be a breach of attorney client privilege. So, I'm assuming she did contact him based on his reply otherwise he wouldn't have referred to her as a client. "

"Thanks, Quinn. I appreciate it."

"No problem."

Miss Savannah carried the cups through and Jenny was just ending her conversation.

"Well?" Miss Savannah asked, setting Jenny's cup down on the desk.

"It's nothing. They wanted to know if we saw what happened and I honestly didn't. I was watching the traffic ahead of us. I only heard it."

"That's all?"

"Not exactly. It seems like one of the families wants to thank me for what I did but I didn't do anything more than any other person would have done."

"Oh, yes you did. You got the area cleared for the emergency vehicles and everything. What you did might well have saved one of their lives.

"It wasn't me. God was watching over them."

"That so true."

Miss Savannah cleared her throat and spoke. "And they took your information down … the police?"

"Yes. All they needed was my phone number and an address where I can be reached. So I gave it to them."

Jenny picked up the books Miss Savannah had purchased that afternoon from her desk to divert the attention away from the conversation. "I need to get these entered and get them on the shelf."

Miss Savannah walked over to Jenny and put her arm around her shoulder and gave her a hug. "I'm headed to the kitchen. I need to bake."

Later that evening Nathan called. He had arrived safely and was ensconced in a hotel near the office. He intended to be at the office early the next morning, waiting when everyone arrived for work.

"I don't think it's going to take me long to get to the bottom of this whole thing. One of two things is happening. Either someone is trying to climb the corporate ladder by stepping on their superiors or there really is something going on. Whichever it is I intend to get it taken care of quickly. When something like this comes up the faster its settled the better it is for everyone."

"I agree."

"So what did you do today?"

She told him about hers and Jenny's day and about the accident.

"You all right?"

"We're just fine but we were so lucky to have been clear of the intersection before the accident. Had I been driving I don't know what would have happened. Jenny is such a good driver and you should have seen her jump out of the car and take charge! I see where Tawnie gets it from."

"They're a couple of strong women!"

"Yes they are."

"Well, I need to get some rest. It's been a long day and I plan on a very early morning and don't know yet what the day will bring. I should be back in Tulsa in a day or two. Maybe we can go out to dinner?"

"It's a date."

"Well, I'm going to say goodnight Savannah. You be careful."

"Goodnight."

Miss Savannah checked the bread pudding she had baked to see if it was cooled enough to refrigerate. The berry sauce to top it with was already chilling. Satisfied that it was cool enough she placed it on a shelf in the fridge and busied herself setting up morning coffee.

Jenny came in the kitchen as Miss Savannah was getting ready to turn out the light.

"If you don't care, I'm going to call it a day." She picked up her jacket that was on the back of one of the chairs and slipped her arms into it. "I think it's this crazy weather that's getting to me. I'm going to go crawl in bed and read a while."

"Of course it's okay. I'm headed to bed soon myself."

Jenny turned to leave.

"Thank you, Jenny." Miss Savannah said softly. "You did a good thing today. I'm sure there are people out there tonight that are thanking you too."

Jenny smiled and said, "It was a God thing. They should be thanking Him."

Jenny opened the door. "Goodnight. See you in the morning." She pulled it closed and made certain it was locked.

Miss Savannah stopped and put on soft music to fall asleep by and went upstairs. Snuggling into the mass of pillows on her bed with her book in hand, she sighed deeply and began to read.

Chapter 33

Nathan returned from Seattle the first of the following week, taking a few more days than he had originally anticipated. He called Savannah to see if she wanted to go out to dinner. Of, course there was no hesitation in her accepting the invitation.

"So, where shall we go for dinner?"

"Where ever you like. But I'm sure you're not going to want seafood. Right?"

"Right!"

He selected a small bistro where he knew the two of them could have a conversation, a glass of wine and enjoy just being together.

Savannah waited for Nathan to bring up the subject of his trip to Seattle.

"Things were worse that I thought when I got there. I'm so thankful I got that call. It really saved me lots of time and money. Had it gone on much longer, I would have had no choice but to bankrupt. I looked over the books and they were a sham. A second grader could see what they've been doing."

"That bad?"

He nodded. "I tried to talk to them but they wouldn't listen. You know, that business has always been just an investment to me. That's all it ever was or ever was going to be."

Savannah took a sip of wine and continued to listen. She knew he needed someone to talk it out with.

"I can make more money by putting that money into securities or in an interest bearing account and letting it ride. I refuse to allow them to keep their pockets lined with my dollars."

"So what did you end up doing?"

"I paid a visit to my attorney and had him freeze all assets at the close of business Friday evening. All permits are put on hold until further notice. And, I engaged a broker to liquidate my holdings in the corporation, hopped on a plane and flew home."

She swirled the wine in her glass and set it down. "It had come to that point, huh?"

"Oh yes. They're going to have quite a surprise when they get there Monday morning and there's a security guard at the door refusing entry to any and all. I told my attorney to order a full investigation"

"Well, sometimes we have to cut our losses and get on with life."

"There's actually no losses yet, but another month or two at the rate the funds were being tampered with and there would have been. I'll still come out ahead."

"That's a shame they'd do that to you."

"All I can say is in the business world, you get one shot at me and that's all. I just don't think they thought I'd lock the proverbial doors and walk away."

"But, don't you have any regrets at all?"

"Only thing I regret is allowing them to take me away from you for even a few days. I did miss you, Savannah."

"Nathan, that is so sweet!"

He reached across the table and covered her hand with his. "I mean it. Just being with you makes everything better."

After dinner they decided to take an evening drive. Tulsa was already taking on the look of the holidays. He saw her to the door but declined her offer of coffee and dessert. "I'm still tired and need to get home and lay this old body down. Maybe I'll take you up on your offer tomorrow sometime."

197

"Perfectly understandable. Goodnight Nathan and thanks for dinner."

"My pleasure. I'll give you a call tomorrow. Night Savannah."

She closed the door and the only thing she did before going to bed was set up morning coffee. She fell asleep, swept up in the building of a great cathedral in the twelfth century. "Pillars of the Earth" rested beside her until late in the night, when she awoke long enough to put the book on the nightstand and turn the lamp off.

The cool snap tried to hold on for all its life but the sun finally won out and warm, late fall weather put everyone in the mood to rake leaves and pick up pecans that had burst forth from their hulls and tumbled to the ground; to build tiny little fires in their backyards so kids could roast marshmallows and quickly put them on a graham cracker with a luscious slice of chocolate on it. Chrysanthemums exploded into full bloom and silently nodded their heads in the gentle breezes that caresses the area before winter.

Days turned into weeks, and Tulsa overflowed with shoppers getting ready for Thanksgiving. Miss Savannah and Nathan talked it over and decided to cook like they had never cooked before. Even though there was just going to be a small gathering of friends and family, they were going to eat good! They spent hours making their menu, marking out things and adding others. Eventually, they had it done to their satisfaction and proceeded to try to buy out the markets. They were running out of space in the pantry, refrigerator and every other available storage space.

Tawnie had been thrilled at the invitation to celebrate Thanksgiving in Miss Savannah's house. It wasn't to be a large gathering of people, just a few friends in addition to Tawnie's family, Jenny, and of course Nathan too. Invitations had gone out to Jenny's other children but Miss Savannah didn't know how many would show up. It didn't matter. There was going to be enough food to feed an army.

A few days before Thanksgiving, Miss Savannah and Nathan began baking breads, cakes, cookies and anything else that would hold for a couple of days. Miss Savannah loved the two refrigerators and double ovens, plus the old gas range. The two of them put on their favorite music, looked up recipes, got out ingredients and baked. They baked an array of desserts that would rival even the best of shops in the Tulsa area. They knew they were baking way too many things, but a tradition at Thanksgiving at anyone's house was to have plenty of food for everyone to take some home with them. They had even thought of that too. A quick shopping trip to a hobby store and they were carrying in baskets lined with pretty checkered napkins.

"These will be perfect." Miss Savannah said when they got all of them unloaded and lined up in the butler pantry. "Plus, it will be kind of a little keepsake for them to remember this Thanksgiving with."

Nathan just smiled at Savannah fussing over the baskets. To him a few paper sacks would have sufficed.

Jenny joined them Thanksgiving Eve. She always had made the cornbread stuffing for her family and they had requested it again. She baked the breads, chopped onions and celery and set everything to rest for the night. The next morning she would put it all together and pop it in the oven. Of course, as she explained, she had to keep a bowl of the raw stuffing for one of her children. When Jenny had everything ready, she excused herself and headed back to her apartment. Evidently there was a family tradition that everyone would gather at her house and play cards and games Thanksgiving Eve. By what she said, it had been that way since her children were very young and had stayed in place all these years. Before long, Nathan and Miss Savannah saw cars parking in the drive and people going up the steps to the apartment. They didn't know where all of them were going to sit, but Jenny had seemed so happy when she left. Later some of the cars left but a couple remained in the drive overnight. Miss Savannah smiled at the thought of Jenny hovering over them and joining in the games with her family.

Nathan opened one of the refrigerators and checked the progress of the turkey defrosting. Miss Savannah was butterflying the pork loin and carefully wrapping it in plastic wrap so all she had to do the next day was stuff it and get it in the oven. They had bought a spiral sliced ham so all it was going to need was warming through.

A beautiful Thanksgiving morning dawned with the glow of the promise of warmth. The chrysanthemums along the walk created a brilliant aisle leading to a expectation of wonderful food and family getting together. Tawnie began setting the table with the dishes Miss Savannah selected for the holiday and carried the desserts through and set up the dessert table.

Jenny jumped in and started peeling potatoes and helping get everything going in the kitchen. The house started filling around two o'clock. The laughter of children and voices of adults enjoying themselves floated through to the kitchen and Miss Savannah found that she couldn't wipe the smile from her face. It seemed permanently glued on. Nathan took it upon himself to keep plates of snacks filled and glasses topped off.

By four o'clock, food was on the table and everyone began taking their seats. Tawnie looked over to Junior and cleared her throat. The room quieted. Junior began speaking low in an embarrassed tone. Tawnie touched him on his shoulder. He began again in a strong voice. "God is good. God is great. Let us thank him for this food. Amen." A chorus of voices followed with "Amen". Miss Savannah was astir over the food. "There's ginger corn soup in the tureen and over there is a wonderful cranberry compote Nathan made. Here, let me put a few more potatoes on your plate. Don't look like you got enough. How about some of these candied yams? Just look how the marshmallows puffed up and browned!" All plates were filled and they had began eating when the doorbell chimed.

"Now wonder who that can be?" Miss Savannah asked to no one in particular.

"I'll get it." Jenny said and pushed her chair back from the table.

Before Jenny could make it to the door, it opened and Gypsy entered. "Happy Thanksgiving, Girlfriend!" she called out. She crossed the dining room and hugged Miss Savannah.

"Well, what on earth are you doing here? I thought you were going to be too busy to join us. Grab a plate and find a place to sit!" Then Miss Savannah noticed Gypsy had a guest with her.

"Now, who is this handsome young man you have with you?"

"Girlfriend, this is Brandon. Brandon, this is Miss Savannah."

"Nice to meet you Ma'am." he replied. "I've sure heard a lot about you. Feel like I know you already!"

"Well, now just listen to that Texas drawl." she exclaimed. "Come on in and get some food before it gets cold. We've just started so you haven't missed out on anything."

Introductions were made and chairs pulled up and Thanksgiving dinner was relished. People were rubbing their stomachs in happy pain and the only ones that wanted dessert right away were the children.

"So, Gypsy, how did you and Brandon end up on my doorstep on Thanksgiving?" Miss Savannah asked, when they had all scooted their chairs back and were relaxing before tackling the dessert table.

She smiled and said, "Road trip, with a promise of dinner."

Brandon looked down at his boots and smiled.

"Actually, it all started out quite innocently this morning. Brandon called last night and asked if I'd like to take a drive, then we'd stop and have a nice dinner someplace."

Miss Savannah cut her eyes from Gypsy to Brandon.

Gypsy continued. "Do you know how hard it is to find a decent place to eat on Thanksgiving Day? Brandon just kept driving and well ... we ended up in your driveway."

"You had to leave at practically daylight this morning!"

"Almost."

The boys came running into the dining room. "You gotta come out and see what they have in their pickup truck! Come see!" They were jumping around. "Come on, see!" They were grabbing anyone's hand that was available and pulling them to the front door.

Everyone followed to see what all the excitement was about.

"Oh my goodness!" Miss Savannah exclaimed. "What in the world have you gone and done now?" She started laughing.

Brandon simply replied. "Ma'am, I was always taught that you don't go to someone's house empty handed. It's just good manners."

Nathan laid his hand on Savannah's shoulder and whispered in her ear, "Lad's got manners. You got to say that for him."

"But where are we going to put it?" Miss Savannah replied.

"I got it under control, Girlfriend." Gypsy replied. She took charge and between all the men and little boys, furniture was moved aside and the twenty foot tall Christmas tree was removed from the bed of the pickup truck and brought inside. Jenny put on music and dessert plates were filled, emptied and filled again and the coffee urn was replenished more than once while the tree was being set up and supported. Gypsy stood back with her hands on her hips and surveyed the tree.

Brandon was putting tools away and the boys were helping him carry them back to the truck.

"How did you know it would fit and how in the world did you think we'd ever get it set up without it falling over?"

Gypsy smiles and said, "Brandon's a builder. He can do marvelous things."

Jenny lowered her voice and said, "I just bet he can!"

Everyone laughed.

"Now come on. I didn't mean it that way." She started laughing too. "I suppose it did sound kinda like that though." She changed the subject. "Anyway, since we don't have to be back until Monday, I thought tomorrow would be a perfect day to decorate the tree. Are the things I sent upstairs?"

"A whole roomful," Tawnie said.

"I have a few boxes of ornaments I've saved over the years too and I can dig them out." Miss Savannah said. "That's a wonderful idea."

That evening everyone departed with their napkin lined baskets packed full of food. "Those of you that want to are more than welcome to come back tomorrow and help." Miss Savannah told them while holding Nathan's hand. "We can't promise another feast like today but there'll still be plenty of leftovers and maybe I'll throw together a nice turkey vegetable soup."

Jenny and Tawnie had summoned the other women to the kitchen while the men had been setting up the tree. They had all pitched in, and the food was stored and all the dishes and pots and pans were washed and stored away.

Savannah and Jenny were saying goodbye to everyone and noticed that Nathan disappeared. Gypsy and Brandon were in the library enjoying a cup of coffee and a snifter of brandy. Miss Savannah and Jenny made their way to the kitchen and started tending to the little things that were left to do when Nathan came in through the back door.

"Ladies, why don't you put on your sweaters and join me out back? Where's Gypsy and Brandon?"

"Oh, they're in the library. That was quite a trip they made today!" Miss Savannah said.

He located them and in a few minutes everyone had warm clothing on and had settled around the fire pit.

"Girlfriend. This is beautiful! You didn't tell me anything about it."

"It was a gift from Nathan. He drew up all the plans and oversaw the entire project."

"Really!" Brandon said.

The men started talking about the fire pit, how it had been converted and the thought that went into it to make it safe for Miss Savannah. The women gathered together and did what women do ... enjoy being pampered.

Jenny told of how she had caught Miss Savannah out there pulling weeds and together they started clearing the area; and told about Nathan pulling up in the driveway scared to death that something had happened because he couldn't reach Miss Savannah by phone that morning. She told the entire story and Gypsy sat listening to the warmth in her voice.

Miss Savannah sighed and looked over at Nathan. "What a perfect way to wind up a wonderful Thanksgiving."

"It is, isn't it?" Gypsy purred.

Jenny nodded. "I think I'm headed to bed. All that good food and the energy of the boys just about has me wiped out." She laughed. "See you tomorrow. Nice to have met you, Brandon." She made her way across the drive to the apartment.

"Goodnight, Jenny." Miss Savannah called to her.

"Goodnight." she replied and began climbing the stairs.

Nathan poked the fire which had settled to glowing coals. "I think when these burn down a little more, I'm going to head home. It was a fantastic day Savannah."

"Thank you for being here." She glanced around. "Thank all of you for being here!"

Brandon spoke up. "I think I'll follow you to the main street, Nathan. Then I can find my way."

"Where are you going?" asked Miss Savannah.

"I have a room reserved over on the expressway." He glanced down at this watch. "If I hurry, I can make my check-in time."

"There's plenty of room here for you to stay." she objected.

"I know. But I think you two have a little catching up to do. There's no telling when you'll make it to bed."

The men stood and headed to their vehicles. Gypsy walked Brandon to his truck. Miss Savannah and Nathan said their goodnight at the fire pit. A few minutes later, Nathan's car hummed to life and Brandon's truck roared its presence. Gypsy stepped back and waved as they pulled out into the street.

A while later Gypsy and Miss Savannah sat looking at the great tree. "It's going to be beautiful, Girlfriend."

"It already is. The beauty is in the thought. Thank you so much and thank you especially for showing up and surprising us the way you did."

They made their way upstairs to their bedrooms and after a short while lamps were turned off. Happy thoughts of the day peacefully lulled each of them to sleep.

Chapter 34

The remainder of the weekend was a flurry of opening boxes, unpacking and getting the decorations to Gypsy so she could work her magic. By early Sunday afternoon, almost all of it was completed. Even as Gypsy and Brandon were pulling out of the driveway, she was calling out instructions as what to do with the things she hadn't had time to mess with.

"Mr. Billingham, don't forget to take care of the tree so it won't drop its needles. Remember to feed it with that little packet of food I left on the Hoosier cabinet."

He nodded.

"Girlfriend, I put the candles in the refrigerator so they would burn nice and slow when you're ready to use them. They're in the bottom right drawer."

Brandon put the pickup in reverse and started backing out of the driveway. Gypsy was still calling out instruction but they were drowned out from the sound of the powerful motor.

Miss Savannah and Nathan stood on the portico smiling, waving good-bye and nodding.

"See you at Christmas!" Miss Savannah called back and threw a kiss.

"Caio Bella." Gypsy called and rolled up the window.

When Gypsy and Brandon were out of sight, Nathan and Miss Savannah went inside and poured themselves a cup of coffee and just sat looking at each other.

"Gypsy has got to have more energy than anyone I've ever met!" Nathan said.

"She always has had, at least ever since I've known her and that's been a long time."

They heard a roar in the driveway.

"Wonder what they forgot?" Miss Savannah replied.

"There's no telling."

Miss Savannah looked out the kitchen window and saw a motorcycle. "Look. a young man's getting off it and heading up the stairs to Jenny's apartment." She motioned to Nathan. "Come see. Do you recognize who that is?"

Nathan shook his head.

"It's Jonathan, the delivery man that works for the moving company. He's the one that's been delivering all the furniture and things Gypsy ordered."

"You know I think you're right."

The next thing they saw was Jenny and Jonathan come back down the stairs. He handed her a helmet. Jenny put it on. They both climbed on the cycle and left.

"Well, what do you know?" Nathan said.

A worried look flashed across Miss Savannah 's face just for an instant. "I do hope they're careful."

"I'm sure they will be. Don't worry about it."

"Oh, what makes you think I'm worried."

"Just don't worry, Savannah. That Jonathan has always seemed like a mighty responsible man to me. And, he's not that young as you refer to him."

"Well, he seems young to me!"

Nathan smiled. "Savannah, at our age everyone seems young. Come on and sit back down and rest."

She freshened their coffee and sat down. In a few minutes she was up and plating pumpkin spice bread for them to snack on. A few minutes after that she was emptying coffee grounds from the coffee pot. Nathan was taking all of this in. He could tell she was still worried about Jenny.

"Tell you what. Why don't you grab a sweater and let's go for a walk in the rose garden and get some fresh air?"

"Oh, I don't know. I'm awfully tired."

"It'll do the both of us good. We can sit on one of the benches and people watch if you don't feel like walking. Are your hips bothering you?"

"Not really. I suppose you're right. Maybe some fresh air would be good."

After their stroll through the rose garden, he drove to a little out-of-the -way restaurant and ordered a plate of appetizers and a nice glass of wine for Savannah. "I know you're going to say that there's plenty of food at the house but you've been cooking for days now. You need a bit of a break."

She knew he was right. "Thank you for being so thoughtful."

He glanced at his watch, just smiled at her and nodded. When they had finished eating it was almost dark and Nathan drove in a zig zag back across Tulsa so they could see Christmas lights. As they pulled in the driveway, Jonathan was pulling out on the big black Harley. He waved at them and roared down the street.

"It sounds like he going awfully fast for this neighborhood." Miss Savannah remarked as Nathan opened the car door for her.

"It just sounds that way. It looks like to me he's handling that machine just fine. He glanced at his watch again. How about I build us a little fire?"

"I think that would be perfect. You're so thoughtful. You waiting on a call or something?"

"No. Why?"

"I've noticed you looking at your watch. That's not like you."

"I just can't believe how early its getting dark now."

"I know. Isn't it? I'm just going in the house for a minute and I'll be right back out. Okay?"

"I'll probably have the fire going by the time you get back."

She came back out carrying a thermos and poured Schnapps laced hot chocolate in mugs and sat them on the little table between the chairs. She took a seat and watched Nathan fuss over the fire. He sat beside her when he had gotten it just the way he liked it and picked up the mug and glanced at his watch yet again.

Savannah ignored it this time and settled in to watch the fire and enjoy its warmth. Nathan reached over and rested his hand on hers. All of a sudden a blanket of tiny lights lit the trees surrounding the fire pit and smooth jazz played softly in the background.

"What in the world?" Savannah exclaimed and sat up in her chair. She looked around. "This is like a winter wonderland!"

"You like it?"

"I love it but ... but when ... and how ... why ..."

"When was when you were busy helping Gypsy decorate the house. How is Brandon's expertise in things like this. And I think you know why. It comes from the heart and we all love you."

"You mean to tell me everyone knew about this?" she said motioning to the delight before her.

"It was originally Gypsy and Jenny's idea."

"Jenny too?"

"How do you think we kept you away from out here while it was being done?"

"And music too!"

"Brandon said it was easy to do with remote speakers. I took him at this word and it seems to be working."

Savannah smiled the biggest smile he had ever seen. Her face was aglow.

Jenny had been watching from her window. When the lights came on she came out with Nag Champa incense and placed the lit sticks around the area. She gave Miss Savannah a hug and declined the offer to join them.

208

Miles away in Dallas, Gypsy and Brandon smiled at each other knowing what was taking place in Tulsa. Brandon winked at her and they lifted their wine glasses to toast Miss Savannah.

"No more questions now." Nathan said. "Just sit back and enjoy it."

"But I do have one more."

"Okay. Just one more."

"How did you know that I loved this music?"

"Well. We all thought of Christmas music but somehow it just didn't fit the mood we were trying to set. Jenny had heard you listening to this CD so she suggested it. It seemed perfect. We'll have plenty of time to listen to holiday music later."

"It is perfect! Thank you."

"It wasn't just me. Everyone did this!"

"I'll have to call Gypsy in the morning and thank Jenny when I see her tomorrow."

"Savannah. Relax and enjoy the moment. You know I remember a quote that fits this perfectly."

She looked over to him.

"Life is not measured by how many breaths you take. It is measured by the times it takes your breath away. I hope you remember this moment the rest of your life."

Through tears threatening to run down her cheeks she said, "I assure you I will."

Jenny stood watching them from her window for awhile and felt like she was intruding on a very special moment between two very special people. She picked "Daughter of Smoke and Bone" and crawled into bed. Opening it to where she had left off she began to read. She flipped to the next page and there was a paragraph that she read over and over until she fell asleep. "She craved a presence beside her, solid. Fingertips light at the nape of her neck and a voice meeting hers in the dark. Someone who would wait with an umbrella to walk her home in the rain, and smile like sunshine when he saw her coming. Who would dance with her on her balcony, keep promises and know secrets, and make a tiny world wherever he was, with just her and his arms and his whisper and her trust."

Chapter 35

True to his word, over the next few weeks leading up to Christmas, Nathan tended the tree everyday. Miss Savannah, Jenny and Tawnie finished up the last minute decorating, just as Gypsy had instructed. Nathan brought over his camera and they recorded a movie of the interior. Savannah insisted they wait until after dark and capture the back area as well. It was something he knew Savannah would want to view time and time again.

Time was ticking down to Christmas and preparations were being made for the number of guests that were expected. At almost the last minute it was decided to have an open house and invite neighbors, business associates and friends that were not going to be able to be there for the actual Christmas dinner. Invitations were issued and a head count was taken. It surprised Nathan and Savannah how many accepted. They thought it was more out of curiosity to see the house than anything. Nathan insisted that the open house be catered. He told Savannah that it was just going to be too much to host an open house then turn right around and prepare Christmas dinner, even with help from Jenny and Tawnie. Actually, he gave her a choice. She could choose either the open house or Christmas for catering. She swallowed her pride and made the choice. So the open house it would be.

They had decided the best and most convenient date would be the nineteenth which would still free up everyone's time for their own Christmas celebration. The day arrived and the house was filled with a bustle of activity. Catering vans were in the drive. Extra help had been engaged for serving and Nathan had even insisted on a bartender. Miss Savannah was overseeing everything and seemed to be in her element.

Jenny was taking care of last minute business with the rare book brokerage she was setting up, contacting clients, emailing appraisals to other clients and making certain hard copies were in the mail. When the postman rang the doorbell, she went to the door and there was a registered letter for her. Not thinking anything of it, she signed the acceptance receipt, thanked him and carried the stack of correspondence to her desk. She started to leave the mail until after the open house but something kept nagging at her to take care of business. She slid a letter opener under the flap of the registered letter and pulled out the document. When she saw the letterhead she hesitated to unfold the document and read it. This is what she had dreamed of all her adult life; to know her true birth mother. At first she laid it aside trying to make the decision if she really wanted to know or not. Her adoptive parents had been so good to her and she knew they loved her with all their heart as she had loved them. It was almost a feeling of infidelity in the pit of her stomach. It felt like a betrayal to them. But in her mind, the answer to the unanswered question lay at the tip of her fingers and all she had to do was unfold it and read. She went to the kitchen, poured herself a cup of hot spiced cider Miss Savannah had prepared and returned to her desk.

Taking a deep breath, she unfolded it and let her eyes travel down the document to that all important name. Then she saw her true birth date. It was today. She calmly folded it back and replaced it in the envelope and put it in the top drawer of her desk. At last she finally knew.

The house began filling around six o'clock and was in a constant buzz of activity until after nine. Between Nathan and Tawnie they kept Christmas music playing in the background. Guests came, guests departed and more guests arrived. Everyone was so impressed with the house and what Miss Savannah had done with it. So many ran their fingers over the backs of the books and more than once Miss Savannah heard, "I remember this. I read it when I was a child or I read it when I took literature in college. This was my mother's favorite book. She read it over and over. I think there's a copy of everything he ever wrote."

Jenny was questioned more than she cared to think about how many volumes were in the library or, if in fact the the collection of a certain author was complete and if they were first editions. She was able to answer all inquiries without once having to consult her catalog in the computer.

Neighbors commented that they had never seen such a fine Christmas tree and with Miss Savannah's permission, stood back to snap pictures of it with their phones."I've got to show this to my kids! It's absolutely beautiful!"

All in all it was a wonderful evening and when the last of the guests left, the caters had packed up and departed and the front door was locked, Nathan brought out a bottle of champagne and filled the flutes he had set out. He held up his glass and everyone awaited his toast.

He put his arm around Savannah's shoulders and said. "Here's to the special people that have come into my life this year."

"Here. Here." was replied to his toast.

Tawnie and Jenny started picking up the area and clearing away things.

Nathan motioned to them and said. "Just leave everything. I arranged for the caterer to send out someone tomorrow morning to take care of that. It won't hurt anything at all for it to be like this tonight. We've all had a long day and now its time to relax."

"Nathan, how you do spoil me!" Miss Savannah replied.

Shortly, everyone left after giving hugs and headed to their homes. Jenny went to her desk and removed the letter. She knew Nathan would be the last to leave tonight so she didn't stay to lock up. Climbing the stairs to the apartment she touched the document in her pocket.

Chapter 36

Gypsy arrived in the mist of a whirlwind of activity. She walked into the house, with hug after hug from everyone. Nathan took her coat and hung it in the entry closet and began carrying in all the packages from her vehicle while searching for places to put them under the tree.

There was cooking, baking, decisions of which china to use, additional seating being planned for everyone that was going to be there and the number of packages under the tree constantly grew. The house smelled so good and everyone was in a holiday mood. Music was playing and the little boys were playing in the backyard with David keeping an eye on them. The little guys were so excited about the new snow that had covered the ground and because they knew they not only had presents at home but they had presents to open at Miss Savannah's the next day. David oversaw snowball fights and their attempt at building a snow man. He'd help them up when they slid down and brush them off. Their little faces were all red from the cold but they refused to come inside so he had started a fire in the pit so they could warm their little hands.

Christmas Eve was to be spent with their immediate families but Christmas Day everyone was to be at Miss Savannah's. She had insisted that there was to be no one at her house after early afternoon that day, saying that they needed time to prepare for their own Christmas Eve's and to make certain they all got home before the streets iced over. So anything and everything that they were going to help with had to be wrapped up early.

By mid-afternoon the frantic activity that had filled the house had subsided to a comfortable hum.

"So who all's going to be here tomorrow?" Gypsy asked.

"Well. I think all of Jenny's children and grandchildren are going to be here. Quinn and his wife, Jenny's friend Jonathan, and several other friends. By the way is Brandon going to make it?"

"He's going to be at his parent's house tonight but he said he's going to head this way early in the morning. Should be here in plenty of time for dinner."

"That's a good thing! I sure like him."

"Yep! He's a good man."

"I've been meaning to ask. Anything serious going on there?"

"He's just a good friend."

"How good?"

"Oh Girlfriend!" They laughed.

Nathan came in from outside. "I think I'm going to go home for a while and let you two chat."

Miss Savannah looked up at him. "You okay?"

"Just fine, Savannah. Just got a few things to take care of."

"So you'll be back over later?"

"You betcha'." He put his arms around her and gave her a hug. "See you after while. Need anything from the store? They'll be closing soon. I don't want you driving out there in the snow. I thought it was going to go away but its still coming down out there. What's it been now, two or three days?"

She nodded. "Yes, three days now. And, I don't think I need anything from the store. At least not that I can think of right now."

"Well, if you do think of something, just give me a call." He pulled the door to and carefully pulled out of the drive and headed home.

"I love the cold weather." Gypsy said. "It reminds me of growing up on Long Island. It didn't get bad until after I crossed I-40 headed this way but its beginning to pile up."

"I just pray everyone takes it easy out there. Sure don't want anyone to get hurt.

Gypsy and Miss Savannah spent the remainder of the afternoon in the kitchen. They put together a lasagne for dinner and Gypsy checked the wine to make certain there was the right one to go with it.

Conversation flowed from one subject to another; anything from how surprised Miss Savannah had been with the lights and music out at the fire pit to what projects Gypsy had planned in the near future.

"How long are you going to be able to stay this time before heading back to Dallas?"

"If you think you can put up with me, I was thinking until right after New Years."

"Put up with you! I'd love it!"

"Brandon has shut everything down until that time so he's going to be here in Tulsa too. He promised to remove the tree for you New Years Day or the day after. It's going to depend on how much we celebrate."

"He can stay in the guest bedroom."

"He's already made arrangements. I haven't told you this before but he has an ex that's just looking for an excuse to take him back to court for more alimony. Even though they've been divorced for some time now, he takes absolutely no chances of doing anything, I mean anything that would give her reason to question his credibility or morals."

"Do they have children?"

"No. But she stills holds interest in the business and could cause problems there too."

"I see. That's the reason he stays elsewhere."

"Exactly. And he always keeps receipts." She laughed.

Jenny was in her apartment in deep thought and looking out at the snow while sipping coffee.

She set her cup down, went over to her little desk and began to write.

David had said he would be over to pick her up so she could be there at their house and watch the boys open their presents. She wanted to be ready when he got there so she changed clothes and set the plate of cookies and homemade fudge on the cabinet. Tearing off a length of plastic wrap she covered the treats. A few minutes later there was a knock at there door. David helped her gather up what she was taking and together they carefully made their way down the steps.'

"As they were going down the steps she said, "Remember, I need to be back home tonight. After the boys open their presents I'll need you to bring me back."

As David was backing up to turn around Jenny noticed Gypsy and Miss Savannah at the kitchen window. She smiled and waved at them.

"I was beginning to get worried about Jenny. She just hasn't been acting like herself these past few days." Miss Savannah said.

"She seemed fine to me."

"For a couple of days after the open house, I was afraid she was getting sick or something. Then she kind of shook it off and has been her old self again only more bubbly, if that's possible."

"I know. You almost had to stick your finger in the air and burst those bubbles that surrounded her. Never have I been around someone that's such a joy to be around."

"She's a good person, Gypsy. Good through and through."

"Yep."

That comfortable silence between friends settled in for a time as they tended to things in the kitchen.

Gypsy was just setting the lasagne out of the oven onto a cooling rack when Nathan returned. He had three packages in his hands. He laid them on the cabinet and took off his coat shaking the snow off it at the door.

"It's really getting treacherous out there and it looks like its not going to let up. I was watching the news and weather and they say it's with us for a couple more days at least.

"So, everyone is going to have that white Christmas they all wish for?" Miss Savannah asked.

"Sure enough." Nathan answered while hanging his coat on the rack by the door.

Gypsy smiled and clapped her hands. "Love it! Love it! Love it! My best girlfriend in the world, one of the best men I've ever met in my life and a white Christmas too. What else could a girl ask for on Christmas Eve?"

Miss Savannah sliced thick slices of French bread and buttered them. Adding a sprinkling of garlic powder, some crushed basil and a generous sprinkling of Parmesan cheese, she slid the pan under the broiler and stood watching it until it was just right. Quickly removing it and setting it on the stove top to cool she took the salad ingredients from the fridge and began breaking lettuce in small pieces.

Gypsy had already gotten the tomatoes and other vegetables and was busy preparing them.

Nathan opened the bottle of wine and got out glasses.

All of them working together, they had the food on the table and were ready to eat in no time. Miss Savannah reached over and took Nathan's hand and he took Gypsy's. Gypsy took her friends hand to make the circle complete. They bowed their heads for a minute to let the Lord know they were thankful.

After dinner they gathered in the library and began bringing their presents in and laying them on the table between the two sofas.

Miss Savannah had brought in coffee and set a bottle of brandy on the table too. "This is a very old bottle I've been saving for a long time just waiting for the right time to open it. Nathan, if you'll do the honors."

Nathan picked it up and reading the label he gave her a smile and proceeded to open it very carefully. Taking one of the snifters Gypsy had retrieved from the bar he poured. "Don't want to waste a drop of this. I've been waiting years to taste this. Do you know how rare it is now days?"

Savannah nodded and smiled back at him.

They clinked the the rims of their glasses together and each took a sip of the wonderful liquor and felt it warm their throats.

"Oh my! It's as wonderful as I've heard!" Nathan exclaimed.

They all looked at the presents. "So who's going to be Santa Clause?" Gypsy asked.

"Why don't we each just give them to the person we brought them for?" Miss Savannah said.

Before long wrappings were piled on the floor and they were oohing and ahhing over their gifts. They were special little gifts that adults can give without the thought of the cost. Sentimental things take priority over monetary value as you get older.

Gypsy had given Savannah her copy of the "Girlfriends" book they had purchased when they were shopping together years before. Savannah laughed when Gypsy opened her gift and it was the same thing.

"I just hope you kept yours updated over the years too!" Gypsy said laughing.

Savannah was leafing through Gypsy's. "I'm afraid not as well as you did."

Nathan had gifted Gypsy with a bottle of her favorite perfume. "I recognized the fragrance the first time I met you. Kind of filed it away at that time for future reference."

Nathan had two gifts for Savannah. The little soap dish that matched the bowl and pitcher set that belonged to his grandmother. "Had it not been for that set I don't know if we would have ever met face to face. Its what brought us together for the first time."

Savannah got up and placed it beside the set in the guest powder room. She stood back and admired them.

The second gift Nathan handed her was an envelope. When she opened it she saw it was season tickets to every theater performance for the upcoming year. Tucked behind them was a brochure with all the ones scheduled so far.

"I thought I might be insured a date for them if I gave these to you. You know how I love the theater and a pretty lady on my arm to escort!"

"Just listen to you. Pretty lady indeed!"

"You are to me and that's all that matters!"

"You haven't opened my gift to you yet. I'm afraid I only got you one."

Nathan pulled back the wrapping and it was a matching bottle of brandy to the one he had just opened. "You mean to tell me you had two of these tucked back all these years?"

She smiled. "That's only two bottles out of the case I have."

Gypsy laughed and Nathan just shook his head. "Are there more surprises in this house I don't know about?" He hugged her.

"Never can tell now, can you?" A mischievous sparkle lit in Savannah's eyes.

They enjoyed their brandy and coffee and good conversation throughout the evening. Nathan looked out the window and when he turned around he said, "It's not getting any better out there. As much as I hate to leave the company, I do need to head home. I'll be back in the morning to help."

"I'm sure I'll have lots of help so don't take any chances on those icy streets too early."

"Don't worry so much. I'll be just fine."

"I know. I wouldn't worry if I didn't care."

"That's one of the best Christmas gifts you could ever give me ... is that you truly care."

Savannah nodded. She couldn't answer him at the moment.

Gypsy and Savannah walked him to the backdoor and with his brandy tucked under his arm he made his way to his car.

The two friends cleaned up the kitchen together. When Miss Savannah was setting up coffee she noticed Gypsy yawn.

"Why don't you go on up to bed? I hadn't even thought about the long drive you had. You've got to be tired."

"I am Girlfriend. I'm going to take you up on that and head upstairs."

"I'm just going to finish up down here and I'll be headed to bed soon myself. Got a busy, busy day before us tomorrow."

Gypsy left the kitchen and in a few minutes she heard the elevator purr. Miss Savannah caught the reflection of lights in the kitchen window of a vehicle in her driveway. She peeked out and it was David's vehicle. Jenny got out and went up the steps waving to David to not get out and to head on back home.

Miss Savannah returned to setting up coffee and was startled when there was a tapping on the door and Jenny stepped in. She took off her coat and shook the snow off as Nathan had done earlier.

"What are you doing out in this weather tonight?" Miss Savannah asked.

"I brought something. Your gift."

Miss Savannah put her hands on her hips. "I thought we agreed that ..."

Before she could finish the sentence Jenny pulled and envelope from her pocket. "Can we go into the library?"

"Of course we can."

Jenny turned on the reading lamp and handed the envelope to Miss Savannah. "I think you're going to need the lamp to read this."

Miss Savannah seated herself and Jenny handed the envelope over.

Miss Savannah slowly opened it and pulled out a letter and began to read.

Dear Mother,

I have often wondered about who you were. During my younger years, I imagined you coming to my door and whisking me off to live a life of complete and absolute bliss; doing the things I saw my friends enjoying with their mothers. Now, don't get me wrong. My adoptive parents were very loving and kind to me, but there was always something missing. Deep in my soul, I always felt like an outsider, never quite "fitting" in. I liked to refer to it as being "unique".

After having daughters of my own, I cherished the friendships we have developed as they grew to adulthood. I would often hold my grandchildren on my lap, wishing I could share them with you. Seeing that unconditional love in their eyes from the moment of birth. Most people are blessed to have these relationships, and it seems the natural order of life.

But we have developed a very special relationship. You have encouraged me to follow a passion that I really never realized I had; the unconditional love that comes from a book, a simple thing, made of paper and ink, but holding all of life's mysteries between it's covers. It reminds me of when you speak of your Mother's quilts, that total envelopment of love and peace that you seem to get from them.

I have seen your utter love of life, and the people in your life; always encouraging and never forceful. I knew that somewhere in my bloodline, there was a very strong woman who was there watching over me during the low points; guiding me to reach the highest goal, always.

In the short period of time I have known you, I have been very lucky to call you my friend, but now I find myself blessed to call you "Mother".

Jenny had watched her mother's face as she read the letter. Then she turned away and watched out the window as the falling snow was cleansing the earth once more.

Miss Savannah reached in the envelope and pulled out another sheet of paper. It was a copy of the document from the attorney. A tear ran down her cheek.

Jenny turned around, put her arms around Miss Savannah and said, "Merry Christmas, Mother."

Chapter 37

Jenny and Miss Savannah stayed up until early morning hours. Tears were shed. They laughed together. They held on to each each other, held on as if now that they were together, nothing was going to ever separated them again.

Miss Savannah told Jenny about her father and what had happened so many years ago, about how he had died not even knowing that she was going to have his child. She told her of the situation of not being of legal age and the decision had not been hers to make as to whether she had an option to the adoption.

She told Jenny of the years of sleepless nights wondering about that tiny baby girl she had only been allowed to hold for a brief few minutes before she was taken away. She told about the loves in her life and her travels around the world. She told her about things she had done that were done in rebellion and things she had done with love.

Jenny shared her first memories, of her school years, of her failed marriages and the death of the one man she loved with all her heart. But her eyes shined when she talked about her children. "You'll get to meet them all tomorrow. No. Today you'll get to meet them." Miss Savannah looked at the mantel clock and it was after two.

Their lives had been so similar to some extent. It's just that Miss Savannah had so many more years to experience, to feel, to love.

Miss Savannah had held on to the two pieces of paper that had been sealed in the envelope. Jenny offered to put them in the desk but Miss Savannah just shook her head. "I need to hold on to them. This is a dream I've been waiting for all my adult life. These papers confirm that dream."

"Thank you Jenny. Thank you for being the wonderful person I always thought and envisioned my daughter to be."

Jenny said. "None of this would ever have happened if not for you. You're the one that put me in touch with the attorney. I could have never afforded it."

"But I had no idea that it was going to turn out like this when I did that. I just wanted happiness for you."

"And you got what you paid for." Jenny spun around and laughed and bubbles of true happiness filled the room. "I'd better go home so you can get some rest. You're going to need it to put up with all your grandchildren and great grandchildren."

"I suppose you're right. But there's just so much we need to catch up on."

"We have a lifetime to do that. Now, you get upstairs and get some sleep. I'll let myself out and lock up."

Christmas morning did dawn early. When Miss Savannah came downstairs Gypsy, Jenny, Tawnie and Nathan were already sitting around the table having coffee and they were enjoying slices of the cream sherry wine cake. She saw the hams on the cabinet ready to go in the oven.

"Thought we'd go ahead and get them up to room temp before putting them in. Sure glad we decided not to have turkey. That's strictly Thanksgiving fare," Tawnie said.

Jenny replied, "The prime rib doesn't need to go in for some time yet. Sure don't want it to overcook. Want it to still be a bit rare in the center. That reminds me. I need to stir up my horseradish sauce and get it to chilling. The longer it sets the better the flavors meld together."

"The roads are starting to clear so I think everyone will make it for dinner. Nathan said. "I have some guys coming over to clear the drive in a little while. I hope you don't mind if I promised them a plate of the finest food in Tulsa!"

"Not at all." Miss Savannah patted him on the shoulder. "You think of everything!"

"Not everything."

"Nathan I have something I need to talk to you about. Can we finish up our coffee in the library?"

A while later they returned to the kitchen. When opportunity arrived, he put his arm around Jenny's shoulder and gave her a hug. Jenny glanced over to Savannah and she nodded confirming she had told Nathan.

Jenny smiled and hugged back.

What seemed like tradition that had been in place for years began. Desserts were placed on the buffet, foods that would hold at room temperature were placed on the side table and places made for the last minute refrigerated items. Little stones that went in the bottom of the bread baskets were put in the oven to heat.

It did truly seem like tradition even though less than a year had passed since any of the people in the room knew the other existed with the exception of Gypsy and Miss Savannah.

The doorbell started chiming and family began arriving. Jenny took time to introduce Miss Savannah to each of them as they arrived. "This is my oldest son, my youngest daughter, my son that lives in Arizona. When all six of Jenny's children were there Miss Savannah saw that she did have quite a family. A family that she didn't know existed until last night.

Most of Jenny's children jumped right in and started helping in the kitchen and dining room. Some didn't but that didn't matter to Miss Savannah. She was enjoying getting to watch their different personalities and the way they all loved their mother.

Brandon arrived a lot earlier than they had expected Gypsy met him at the door and gave him a Merry Christmas hug.

"Did you even get any sleep after leaving your parent's home?" Miss Savannah asked when she saw him. She gave him a hug. "Merry Christmas!"

"Not much Ma'am but enough to make sure I could drive safely. I just didn't want to miss any of this." He leaned over and gave her a little kiss on the cheek. "Merry Christmas to you too." He reached over and shook hands with Nathan. "Sir."

"Welcome back, Brandon. Come on in and make yourself at home."

The boys came running over to him. "It's the Christmas tree man! We sure do like your truck."

He squatted down to their level. "I'm kinda fond of that truck myself."

"Wanna come see what all Santa left here for us?"

Jenny saw that the boys had latched on to Brandon and came to the rescue. "You can help yourself to the bar if you want something. We've got coffee and cider and I don't know what all in the kitchen."

Gypsy slipped up and put her arm around his waist. She guided him through to the dining room and they took charge of arranging seating, then rearranging for more guests.

Tawnie still took command. She was the born leader, not that the others weren't but it always seemed there was one in every family, one born to lead. The tables were laden with food and Nathan had ordered a magnificent centerpiece for the dining table. They took their seats and Junior blessed the food as he had at Thanksgiving.

Unexpectedly Jenny stood and cleared her throat. "I have something very special to say today. God has given me a gift I have waited a lifetime for."

Looks of disbelief were exchanged around the tables.

Jenny picked up a document that she had laid at her place at the table. She began to read, then laid it aside. "What I want to tell you is that I finally know who my birth mother is. I just found out a few days ago and I want to share it with all of you at this time." She walked over and stood behind Miss Savannah. "This great lady we have come to love as a friend, Miss Savannah, is my birth mother!"

Gypsy's head whipped around and caught her friend's eyes. Miss Savannah nodded it was true. She gripped Brandon's hand and whispered. "I had no idea and I can tell by the look on her face, she hasn't known about it too long either."

Tawnie jumped up from her chair and hurried to her mother's side and embraced both of them. "I knew from the first day that there was something special about you! But how did you find out and when? I have so many questions."

"I know all of you do." Jenny said. "Right now why don't we enjoy all this good food God has graced us with and we'll answer any and all questions later." She put her arms around her mother and gave her a hug then sat back down. She noticed that Nathan had been holding her mother's hand for reassurance.

Jenny looked around the table. "Are you just going to sit there and let all this food get cold? Mother has been cooking for days to prepare this feast."

Nathan stood and began carving the ham. He handed a carving knife to David. "How about you start carving on that prime rib?" David turned red and sat there holding the knife for a moment not really knowing what to do.

"Just cut that darn piece of meat! I'm hungry!" Tawnie said.

Everyone at the tables began laughing and shaking their heads at her brashness. Side by side Nathan and David began carving and filling the plates that were passed over to them. Any tension that was in the air relaxed as everyone's plates were filled and seconds were taken.

There was a constant buzz of conversation during and for hours after the meal. When all questions were answered and they realized that Miss Savannah had just found out too they were amazed.

More than once Tawnie hugged her grandmother. "I just can't believe it. It's like a miracle."

"It is, isn't it?" Jenny replied.

As the day was growing to a close Tawnie's brothers and sisters each got to get acquainted with Miss Savannah better. She had a chance to speak to each of them without interruption. Jenny had made certain that the library area was off limits to the children and their toys so her mother could have the chance to visit with her grandchildren for the first time in her life.

Nathan never left Savannah's side. If she needed anything he saw it was taken care of.

Jenny sat with them for most of the afternoon. Her true laughter filled the house with joy as she told little tales about each of her children when they were growing up. It truly was laughter straight from God, one of happiness and delight.

While Miss Savannah was visiting with her grandchildren the tables were being cleared and desserts served. It was pretty much help yourself to the dessert table. Formality had been set aside. Happy tummies were rubbed and the little boys napped on a pallet in front of the television. Quiet conversation replaced the earlier excitement of the day.

In the kitchen, napkin lined baskets were being filled. Jenny had reminded those that had baskets at Thanksgiving to bring them but Nathan had gone back to the craft store and purchased more anyway.

One by one the guests began their departures for their treks home in the ever deepening snow. Hugs were given at the front door with promises that they would drive careful and call as soon as they got home.

Brandon suggested that he and Gypsy go for a ride and see all the lights. So they left for a few hours too. Miss Savannah always remembered how much Gypsy loved the snow and she was certain they would be safe with those big tires on Brandon's four wheel drive truck.

Tawnie, David and the boys were getting ready to leave and they were all standing at the back windows looking out at the snow. While David went out to start the car so it would be warm for his little family, Tawnie made one more trip back through the house to make sure all the toys were in their vehicle and nothing was left behind. The boys were hanging onto Jenny's and Miss Savannah's hands. All of sudden the lights came on lighting the trees and the patchwork of the herb garden.

Nathan stepped behind Savannah and put his arm around her shoulder and they watched the large snow flakes blanketing the earth with white.

Jenny spoke gently. "The way the snow covers everything out there in a sort of patchwork, it reminds me of my grandmother's quilts upstairs. Those patchwork quilts were made with love to cover her family and keep them warm. I so wish I could have met her."

Nathan reached over and put his other arm around Jenny's shoulder and her mother took her hand.

"God is great." Jenny whispered.

"Amen."

Epilogue

Jenny was nervous as she prepared for the evening. This was the first time she was going "out" in many years. After the death of the love of her life, she had taken time to get to know herself again. Raising six children had taken that special time a person needs to just realize who you are, aside from "Mom" or the "wife." Not that she would change those roles for anything in the world; she loved her family, they were her whole reason for waking up everyday.

After spending an hour on hair and make-up, she donned the pretty little black dress that Tawnie said was essential to every woman's wardrobe. Standing back from the mirror and examining herself, a smile crossed her lips. She ran her hands over the soft material that clung slightly to her hips, twisting around a little to get a view of the back. She liked what she saw; not the figure of the models that graced every magazine in the stores, but a nice curvy figure. She liked to call it being "fluffy." This was the body of a woman, one that had birthed and suckled six children and had worked hard in her life. The body of a Grandmother, that was just soft enough to make the babies comfortable, and oh how they loved to nestle on their Grammy's lap!

As she adjusted her necklace, she saw just a glimpse of the tattoo resting over her heart. Funny how she and her mother were so alike, even though they had been separated for years. They both bore a tattoo as expressions of love. She wondered if Jon would approve since he had only seen her in casual wear, mostly jeans and t-shirts, which were the acceptable attire around Miss Savannah's home. "Oh well," she thought, "it will give us something to talk about." Little did she know, that at that same moment, in her room her mother was listening to Bonnie Raitt sing that same song... "Something To Talk About".

Satisfied with her appearance she slipped on her coat and left the little apartment and carefully made her way to the house and let herself in. For some reason she wasn't surprised when she heard what music her mother had selected. She smiled and shook her head. Not seeing her mother, she settled in to wait for her to make her appearance. For some reason she felt a bit restless and walked over to the windows and thoughts began to flood her mind. She allowed them to develop knowing once they had said their say, they would nestle back from where they came and she would be at ease again.

"I'm standing here looking out at Mother's herb garden and it's just starting to emerge from the cover of snow that blanketed Tulsa for over a week. Nathan invited Jon and I to join them for dinner this evening. I can't think of a finer way to spend this evening than with my mother. She's getting dressed and will be down in a few minutes and

Nathan will be prompt as he always is. Jon should be here any minute also.

"It's New Year's Eve and I think back over the past year of my life. So many, many blessings have been bestowed on me. I have so much to be thankful for.

"Christmas has come and gone and each of my children have reacted to my news differently. Some of them so readily accepted Mother and others still have reservations about it. They'll each handle it in their own way. I wish them happiness but it will be up to them.

"Me? I've thanked God every day for putting her in my life. So many questions have been answered. So much of her I find in myself more and more every day. It's just been a few days since I received those papers telling me that she's my birth mother, but it seems like I have known her a lifetime.

"I don't know what lies out there in my future. It looks like what I've chosen to do is going to succeed but only if I apply myself. No one can do it but me. Mother has guided me but always the final decision was one of my own. As she once told me, 'listen to your inner voice ... it will lead you to your passion and your passion leads you to your purpose'. That's kind of become my mantra. A lot of strength comes with those words when you accept them and repeat them over and over.

"I always dreamed of a real family and that dream has at last been fulfilled. I guess what they say about all good things are worth waiting for is true after all. And God has shown me that real love can actually start as friendship and grow when its nourished. Along with it comes respect and as long as you earn and maintain that respect anything can happen. Anything can come from it.

"I'm standing here in Mother's house as proof of that. I know things are going to be changing this year. It really is a New Year, a new start with a whole family for the first time.

"Mother says I'm good clear through to the bone. I would like to think that's true, but I know she's looking at me through a mother's eyes. I know her love for me has carried her through many years. Years that when she, herself wanted to give up at times. I don't hold resentments towards her for what she did. When I first found out I was so angry, then anger turned into gratefulness, then love. I love Mother with all my heart and I know that love is returned as deeply and sincerely as mine.

"Well, I hear a car pulling in the drive. It's one or the other of our dates for the night ... Mother's and mine. I never thought in a million years that I'd be double dating with my mother on New Year's Eve. My real birth mother. I love to just say that word."

Then she spoke it out loud. "Mother."

Seasons of Life

They say that life has "seasons". When you are young you are in the "Spring" season. Everything is new, fresh and exciting. These are the years you choose a career, start a family and start to put down roots.

The next season is what some consider to be the "Summer" of your life. You are working hot and heavy to raise a family, develop your career, and really start to "water" your trusted relationships. You can see your goals and have started on the journey to achieve them.

The third "season" of life is the "Fall of Life". We have gotten our children raised, most married and if we are blessed, we have a few grandchildren. We have well established roots, started a career and have a plan for retirement. We are ready to rest. Autumn is a time of restfulness, enjoyment and those cherished "cold snaps" that precede the long, cold weeks of Winter. Those "cold snaps" seem to energize us, wake us up again, make us open our eyes wide and really look around at the changes.

Those times between the "cold snaps" can become very comfortable and we can become complacent. But if we have determined early on that we are determined to live life to its fullest, we embrace those "cold snaps" and allow them to push us just a little further.

The final "season" of our lives we call the "Winter" of our lives. The time of enjoying the fruits of our labor, time that our memories become cherished treasures. It's a time of reacquainting with ourselves, of building even stronger bonds with our loved ones and of enjoying the freedom that fewer and fewer people seem to realize they have. After spending the largest part of life as we know it up to this point, working and raising kids, we have finally achieved the freedom to do as we please, when we please! We have earned the right to spend all day on the couch reading a good book, eat cake for breakfast and travel the world at our leisure. But we see people who have let the complacency of the "Fall" of their lives carry over into the "Winter" season.

How blessed are those that still strive to achieve excellency and have learned to live life today like it was their last.

Jenenna (Nena) Elise Yochum

Miss Savannah's Recipes

Miss Savannah's Chocolate Chip Cookies

2	Cups	Brown sugar
1	Cup	White sugar
1	tsp.	Vanilla
3	Large	Eggs, beaten
½	tsp.	Karo syrup
2	tsp.	Baking soda
1½	Cups	Peanut butter
½	Cup	Butter
1	Cup	Chocolate chips
1	Cup	M&M's
4½	Cups	Oats (Quick cooking)
1	Cup	Pecans, chopped

Beat until fluffy sugars, vanilla, eggs, syrup, soda, peanut butter and butter. Stir in chocolate chips, M&M's, oats and pecans. Drop by spoonfuls onto cookie sheet. Bake at 325 degrees F. for about 8 minutes.

Miss Savannah's Banana Nut Bread

2	Cups	Flour
1	tsp.	Baking soda
½	tsp.	Salt
½	Cup	Butter
1	Cup	Sugar
2		Eggs
1	tsp.	Vanilla
1	Cup	Mashed banana – (about 3)
1/3	Cup	Milk or Buttermilk
1	Cup	Nuts chopped (optional)

Cream together butter and sugar. Add banana, eggs, and vanilla. Sift together dry ingredients. Add alternately with milk. Blend well. Stir in nuts, and pour into a greased and floured loaf pan.

Bake at 325 degrees for 1¼ hours until bread is done. When a toothpick inserted into the top of the bread comes out clean it is done. Put on baking racks to cool for 10 minutes. Remove loaves from pans and allow to finish cooling on the racks.

Miss Savannah's Breakfast Muffins

4	Cups	Flour
2½	Cups	Sugar
4	tsp.	Baking soda
4	tsp.	Cinnamon
1	tsp.	Salt
4	Cups	Apple, grated
1	Cup	Raisins
1	Cup	Pecans or slivered almonds
1	Cup	Coconut
1	Cup	Carrots, shredded
6	Large	Eggs
2	Cups	Vegetable oil
4	tsp.	Vanilla

Mix dry ingredients. Add apples, raisins, pecans, coconut and carrots. Mix eggs, oil and vanilla. Add to mixture and mix well. Place muffin liner cups in tins and fill half-way. Using an ice cream scoop if the perfect way to do this. Bake at 350 degrees for 35 minutes. Makes 36 regular sized or approximately 30 jumbo sized muffins.

Miss Savannah's Cream Sherry Wine Cake

1	Pkg.	Yellow cake mix
4	Large	Eggs
¾	Cup	Cream sherry wine
1	tsp.	Nutmeg
¾	Cup	Oil
1	Pkg.	Instant pudding mix (Vanilla)

Preheat oven to 350 degrees F.

Add all of the ingredients to cake mix and prepare as directed on package. Pour into a prepared bundt pan. Bake as per package directions. While still warm, sprinkle with powdered sugar.

Miss Savannah's Raspberry Mocha Cheesecake

For the crust:

1½	Cups	Graham cracker crumbs (10 crackers)
1	Tbsp.	Sugar
6	Tbsp.	Unsalted butter, melted (¾ stick)

For the filling:

2½	Lbs.	Cream cheese, at room temperature
1½	Cups	Sugar
5		Whole extra-large eggs, at room temperature
2		Extra-large egg yolks, at room temperature
¼	Cup	Sour cream
¼	Cup	Dutch Chocolate (Powdered cocoa)
1	Tbsp.	Instant Espresso
1½	tsp.	Pure vanilla extract

For the topping:

1	Cup	Raspberry jelly
3	Half-pts.	Fresh raspberries

Preheat the oven to 350 degrees F.

To make the crust, combine the graham crackers, sugar, and melted butter until moistened. Pour into a 9-inch springform pan. With your hands, press the crumbs into the bottom of the pan and about 1-inch up the sides. Bake for 8 minutes. Cool to room temperature.

Raise the oven temperature to 450 degrees F.

To make the filling, cream the cream cheese and sugar in the bowl of an electric mixer fitted with a paddle attachment on medium-high speed until light and fluffy, about 5 minutes. Reduce the speed of the mixer to medium and add the eggs and egg yolks, 2 at a time, mixing well. Scrape down the bowl and beater, as necessary. With the mixer on low, add the sour cream, Dutch Chocolate, and vanilla. Mix thoroughly and pour into the cooled crust.

Bake for 15 minutes. Turn the oven temperature down to 225 degrees F and bake for another 1 hour and 15 minutes. Turn the oven off and open the door wide. The cake will not be completely set in the center. Allow the cake to sit in the oven with the door open for 30 minutes. Take the cake out of the oven and allow it to sit at room temperature for another 2 to 3 hours, until completely cooled. Wrap and refrigerate overnight.

Remove the cake from the springform pan by carefully running a hot knife around the outside of the cake. Leave the cake on the bottom of the springform pan for serving.

To make the topping, melt the jelly in a small pan over low heat. In a bowl, toss the raspberries and the warm jelly gently until well mixed. Spread the berries on top of the cake and it will make the glaze. Refrigerate until ready to serve.

Note: Measure your springform pan. The bottom of mine measures 9 inches, but it says 9½. I put the springform pan on a sheet pan before putting it in the oven to catch any leaks.

Chocolate Brownies with Mascarpone

1	Cup	Unsalted butter
3	Oz.	Semi-sweet chocolate, chopped
1	Cup	Granulated white sugar
½	Cup	Unsweetened cocoa powder
½	Cup	Mascarpone cheese, at room temperature
3	Large	At room temperature eggs
2	tsp.	Vanilla extract
½	Cup	All-purpose flour
¼	tsp.	Salt

Ganache:

6	Oz.	Semi-sweet chocolate, finely chopped
6	Tbsp.	Whipping cream
3	Tbsp.	Unsalted butter

Preheat oven to 325°F. Butter an 8-inch square pyrex pan.

Place chopped chocolate in a mixing bowl; set aside. In a small glass bowl, melt butter in microwave, just until melted- don't let it cook and bubble. Pour butter over the chocolate and let stand for 30 seconds. Stir until chocolate is completely melted and butter is well incorporated. Sift in sugar and cocoa powder.

With a wooden spoon, beat in mascarpone, eggs and vanilla, mixing until smooth. Gently fold in flour and salt.

Pour batter into prepared pan and spread evenly. Place into preheated oven and bake 45 to 50 minutes, or until a tester comes out clean.

Place pan on cooling rack and let brownies cool 10 to 15 minutes while you make the ganache.

Place chopped chocolate in a mixing bowl. In a small saucepan, bring the cream and butter to just below boiling point, over medium heat. Pour this hot mixture over the chocolate and let stand for 30 seconds, then stir until smooth. Pour ganache over brownies while still warm, and spread to cover evenly.

Let ganache firm up before cutting. It's best to refrigerate them until quite firm. Once the ganache is firm and the brownies have been cut, they do not need to be kept in the refrigerator.

Miss Savannah's Bread Pudding

1	Stick	Margarine
1 ½	Cups	Sugar
1	tsp.	Cinnamon
3	Large	Eggs
1	Can	Evaporated Milk (15 ounce)
1 ½	Cups	Water
1	Loaf	French Bread, cubed (16 ounces)
1	Tbsp.	Vanilla

Melt margarine, add sugar and cinnamon. Mix well. Add eggs one at a time mixing after each. Add milk and water and mix well. Add vanilla. Add cubed French bread and punch down in liquid.

Pour into a 9"x13" baking dish. Sprinkle over top a mixture of 2 Tbsp. Sugar, 1 tsp. Cinnamon and 1 tsp. Nutmeg. Bake at 350 degrees for 25 to 30 minutes or until set.

Miss Savannah's Amaretto Cheesecake

Crust:

1	Cup	Graham Cracker Crumbs
¼	Cup	Sugar
¼	Cup	Butter, melted

Topping:

¼	Cup	Sliced Almonds, crushed
½	Tbsp.	Melted Butter
1	tsp.	Sugar

Filling:

1	Lb.	Regular Cream Cheese, softened
1/3	Cup	Sugar
2	Large	Eggs
1 1/3	Cups	Sour Cream
1	Tbsp.	Melted Butter
1	tsp.	Vanilla Extract
1	tsp.	Almond Extract
3	Tbsp.	Amaretto di Saronno Liquer
¼	Cup	Butter, melted

Prepare the crust:

Preheat the oven to 325 degrees and position the rack in the lower portion. Combine the graham cracker crumbs, sugar and melted butter in a small bowl until well mixed. Transfer to a 9-inch springform pan and press firmly into an ever layer in the bottom. Set aside.

Prepare the topping:

Place the sliced almonds between two sheets of waxed paper and crush into small bits with a rolling pin. In a small bowl, toss the crushed almonds with the melted butter and sugar. Spread on a baking sheet lined with aluminum foil and place in the oven to toast lightly while you prepare the filling, about 7 or 8 minutes. Set aside

Prepare the filling:

In a large mixing bowl, beat the cream cheese, sugar and eggs until smooth. Add the sour cream, melted butter, vanilla extract, almond extract and Amaretto and blend until thoroughly mixed and smooth. Pour into the springform pan, place on a baking sheet and bake 45 minutes. The cake should appear set but still wiggle in the center if gently shaken from side to side.

When the cheesecake is done, shut off the oven, open the door completely an leave the cake in the oven for about 30 minutes. Gradual temperature changes help prevent the top from cracking. Remove from the oven, sprinkle the topping evenly over the cake and place on a cooling rack for another 30 minutes. Transfer to the refrigerator for a minimum of 4 hours.

About the Author

Druecella divides her time between her homes in Sallisaw, Oklahoma and the small community of Ethel, Louisiana. Now retired, she has the time to do what she enjoys most; writing. Her stories have been patiently waiting to be introduced to readers. She is a freelance writer, poet and has written novels and numerous essays. Her latest novels are "Miranda", "Genevieve", "Giggles, Grins & Things to Ponder", and a soon to be released collection of her Mother's recipes "My Mother's Apron".

Made in the USA
Charleston, SC
07 January 2014